HEATHCLIFF
FRIENDS
AND ENEMIES
by Geo Gately

TOR

A TOM DOHERTY ASSOCIATES BOOK
NEW YORK

This is a work of fiction. All the characters and events portrayed in this book are fictitious, and any resemblance to real people or events is purely coincidental.

HEATHCLIFF: FRIENDS AND ENEMIES

A TOR Book

Published by Tom Doherty Associates, Inc.
49 West 24 Street
New York, NY 10010

ISBN: 0-812-51084-4

First printing: January 1991

Printed in the United States of America

0 9 8 7 6 5 4 3 2 1

ACKNOWLEDGMENTS

Future Shock — *Angelo DeCesare, writer, Howard Post, penciler, Jacqueline Roettcher, inker*

Lost in T.V. Land — *Angelo DeCesare, writer, Warren Kremer, penciler, Jacqueline Roettcher, inker*

No Parking—*Angelo DeCesare, writer/penciler, Ruth Leon, inker*

You Snooze, You Lose—*Michael Gallagher, writer, Howard Post, penciler, Ruth Leon, inker*

Father and Sun—*Angelo DeCesare, writer, Warren Kremer, penciler, Roberta Edelman, inker*

All Washed Up — *Esposito, writer, Manak, penciler, Roettcher, inker*

Mummy's Boy—*Michael Gallagher, writer, Warren Kremer, penciler, Jacqueline Roettcher, inker*

The Runaway Car — *Dave Manak, writer, Warren Kremer, penciler, Jon D'Agostino, inker*

Heathcliff & Iggy's Movie — *Angelo DeCesare, writer, Warren Kremer, penciler, Jacqueline Roettcher, inker*

Slap-Happy Birthday — *Angelo DeCesare, writer, Howard Post, penciler, Roberta Edelman, inker*

Claws and Effect — *Butler, writer and penciler, Roettcher, inker*

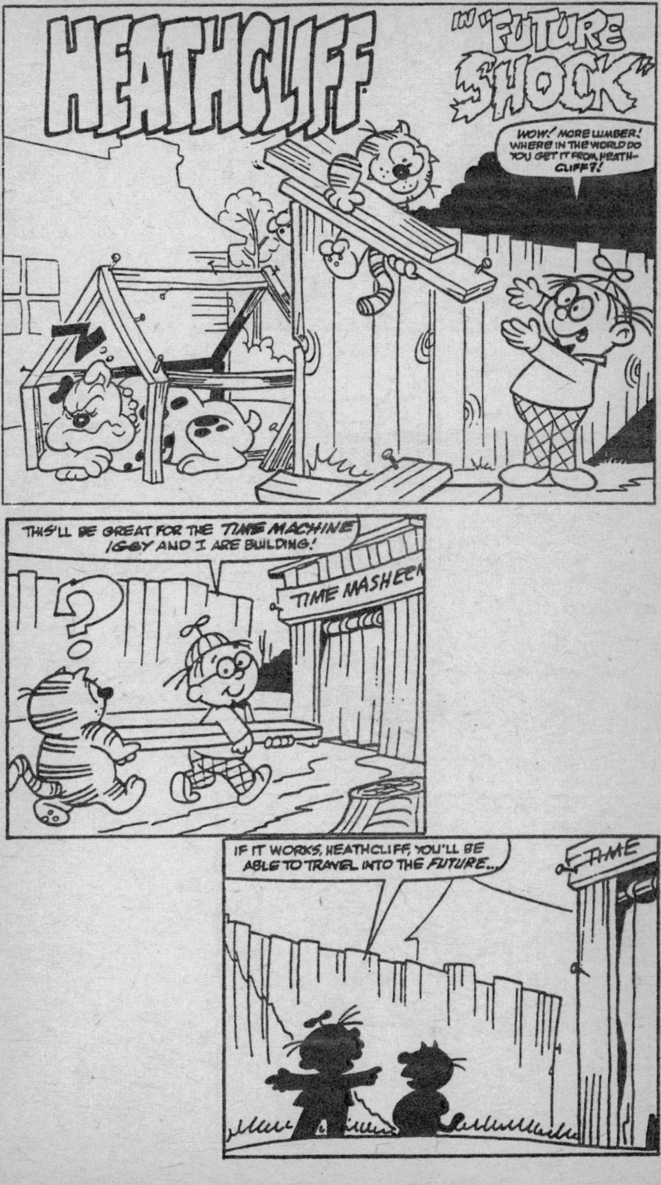
HEATHCLIFF
in "FUTURE SHOCK"
WOW! MORE LUMBER! WHERE IN THE WORLD DO YOU GET IT FROM, HEATH-CLIFF?!
THIS'LL BE GREAT FOR THE TIME MACHINE IGGY AND I ARE BUILDING!
TIME MASHEE
?
IF IT WORKS, HEATHCLIFF, YOU'LL BE ABLE TO TRAVEL INTO THE FUTURE..
TIME

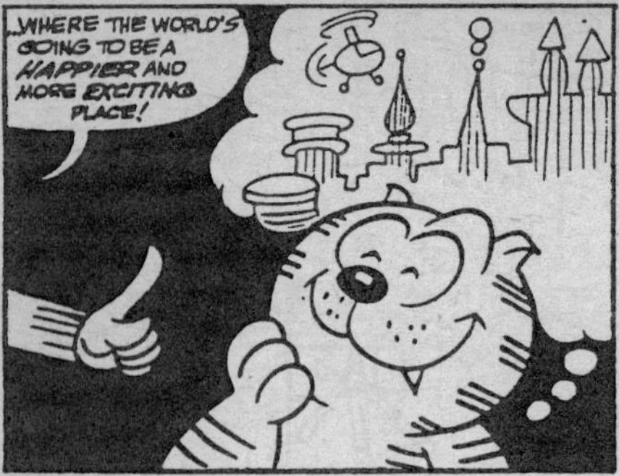
...WHERE THE WORLD'S GOING TO BE A HAPPIER AND MORE EXCITING PLACE!

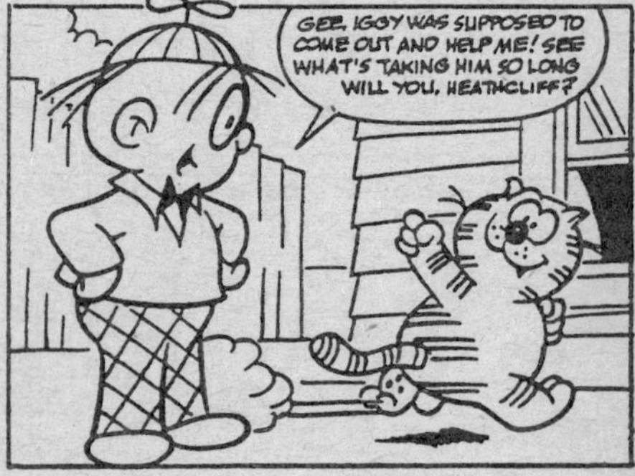
GEE, IGGY WAS SUPPOSED TO COME OUT AND HELP ME! SEE WHAT'S TAKING HIM SO LONG WILL YOU, HEATHCLIFF?

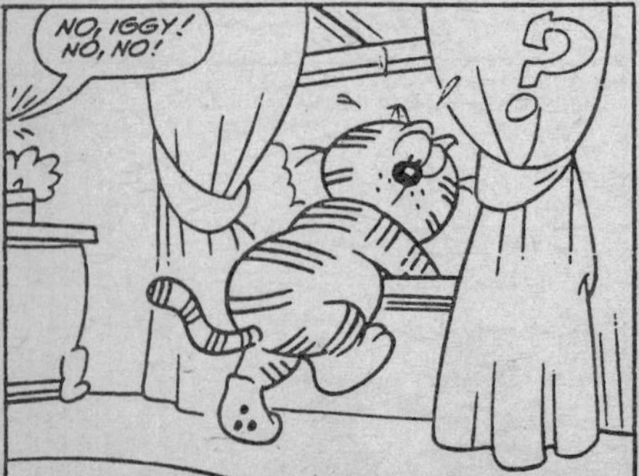
NO, IGGY! NO, NO!
?

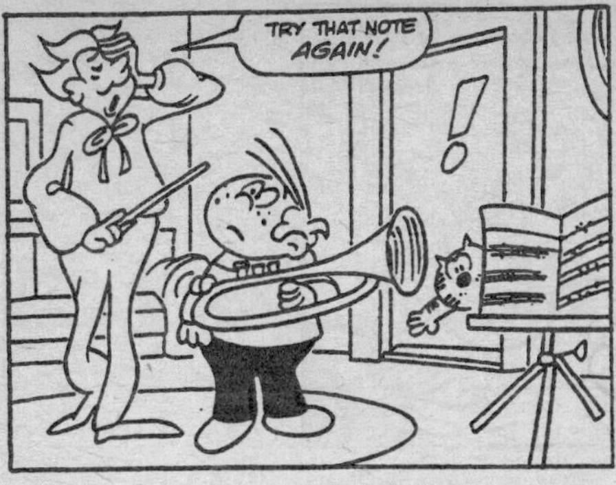
TRY THAT NOTE AGAIN!
!

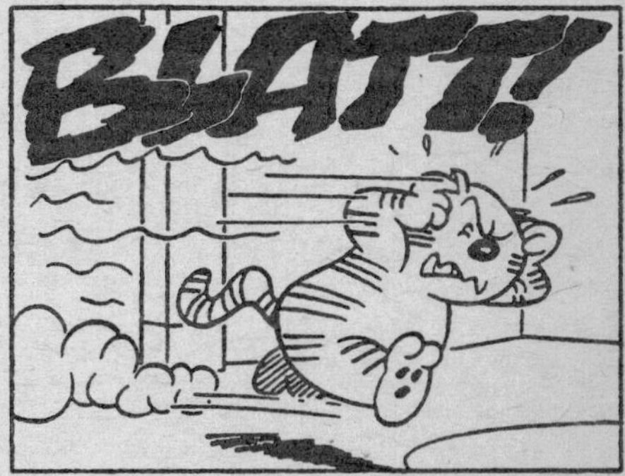
BLATT!

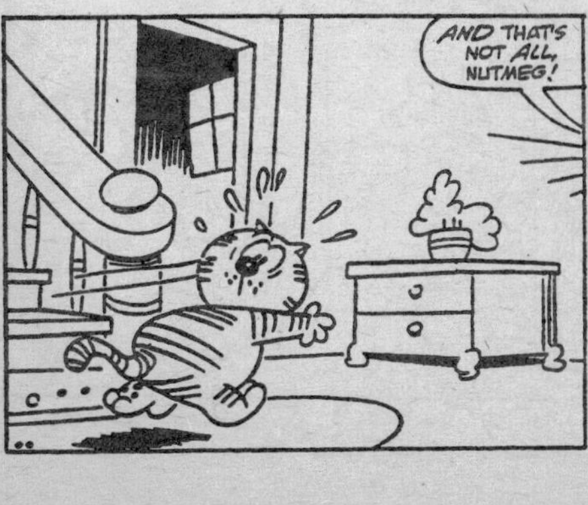
AND THAT'S NOT ALL, NUTMEG!

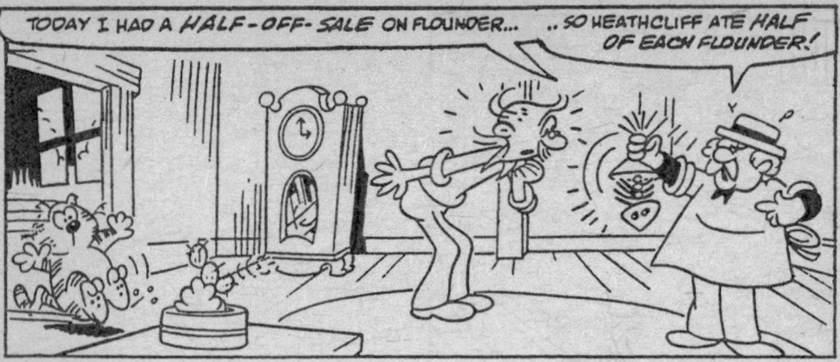
TODAY I HAD A HALF-OFF-SALE ON FLOUNDER...
..SO HEATHCLIFF ATE HALF OF EACH FLOUNDER!

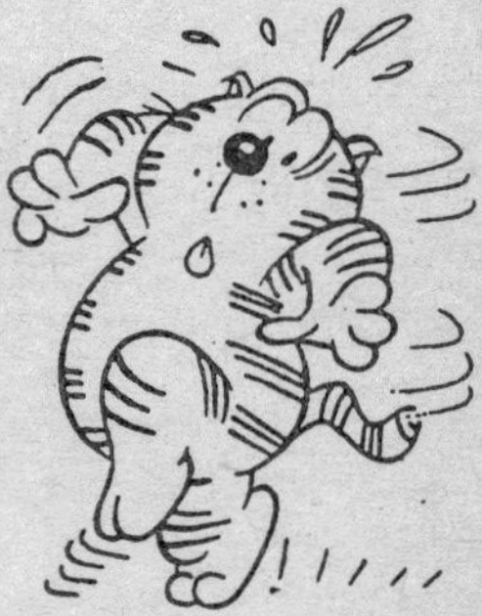

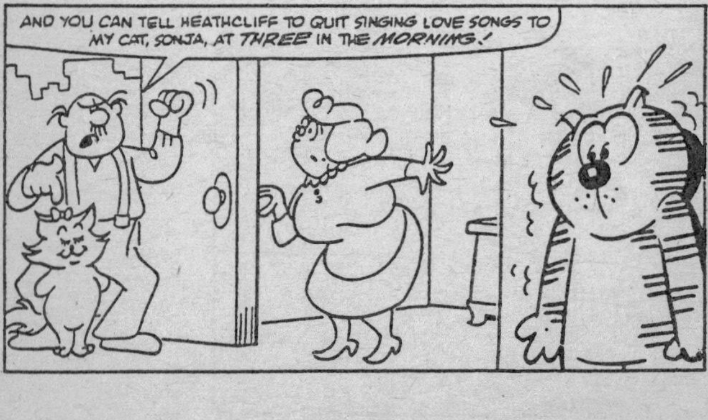
AND YOU CAN TELL HEATHCLIFF TO QUIT SINGING LOVE SONGS TO MY CAT, SONJA, AT THREE IN THE MORNING!

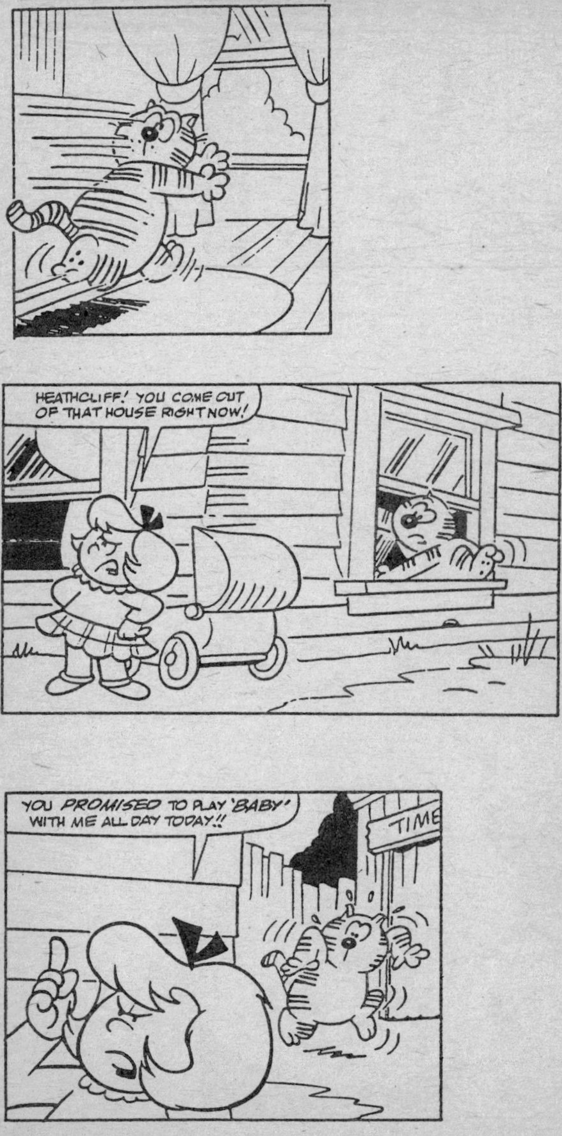
HEATHCLIFF! YOU COME OUT OF THAT HOUSE RIGHT NOW!
YOU *PROMISED* TO PLAY 'BABY' WITH ME ALL DAY TODAY!!
TIME

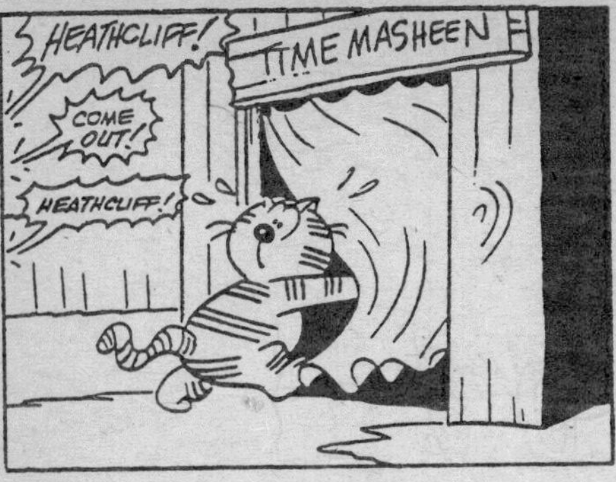
HEATHCLIFF!
COME OUT!
HEATHCLIFF!
TIME MASHEEN

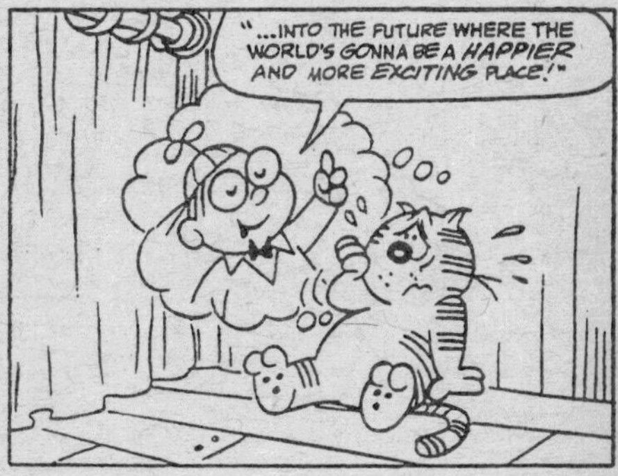
"...INTO THE FUTURE WHERE THE WORLD'S GONNA BE A HAPPIER AND MORE EXCITING PLACE!"

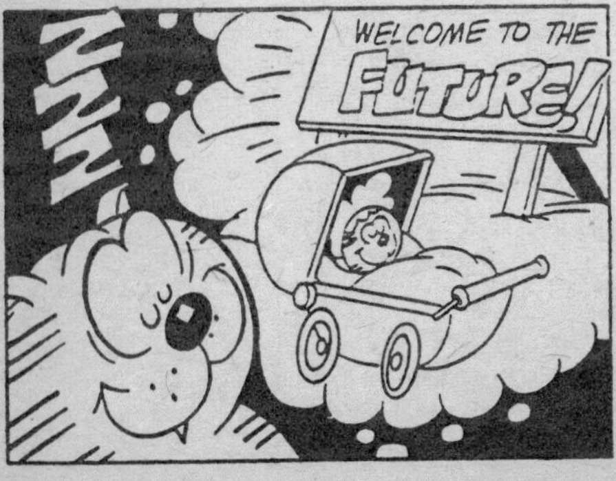
WELCOME TO THE FUTURE!

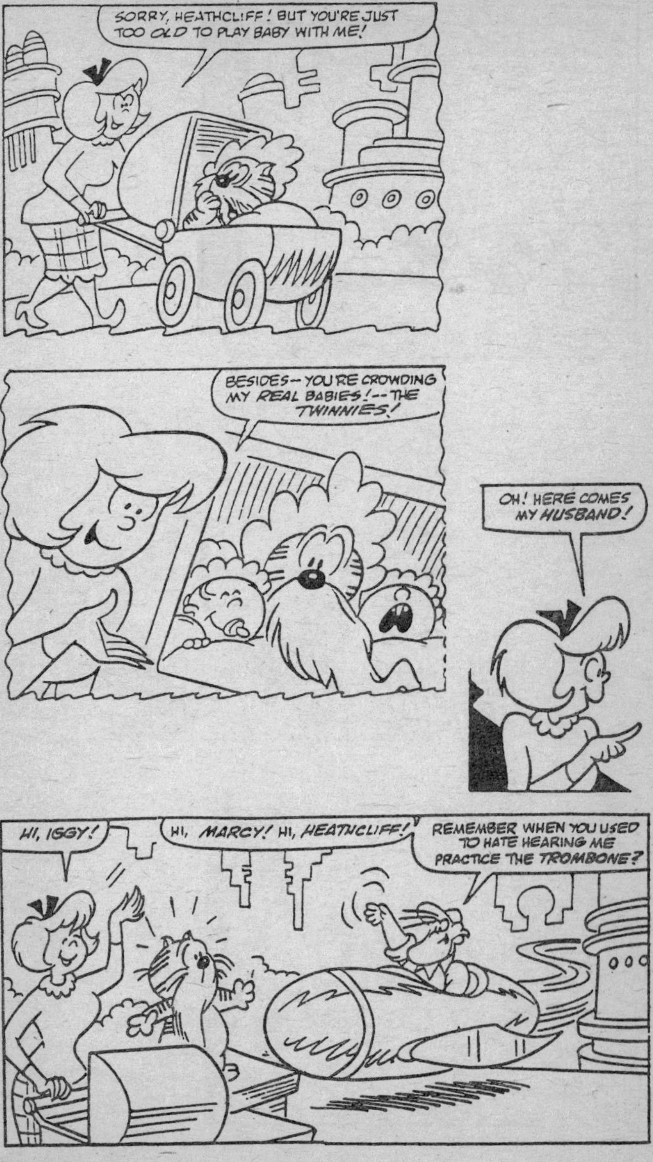

SORRY, HEATHCLIFF! BUT YOU'RE JUST TOO OLD TO PLAY BABY WITH ME!
BESIDES-- YOU'RE CROWDING MY REAL BABIES!-- THE TWINNIES!
OH! HERE COMES MY HUSBAND!
HI, IGGY!
HI, MARCY! HI, HEATHCLIFF!
REMEMBER WHEN YOU USED TO HATE HEARING ME PRACTICE THE TROMBONE?

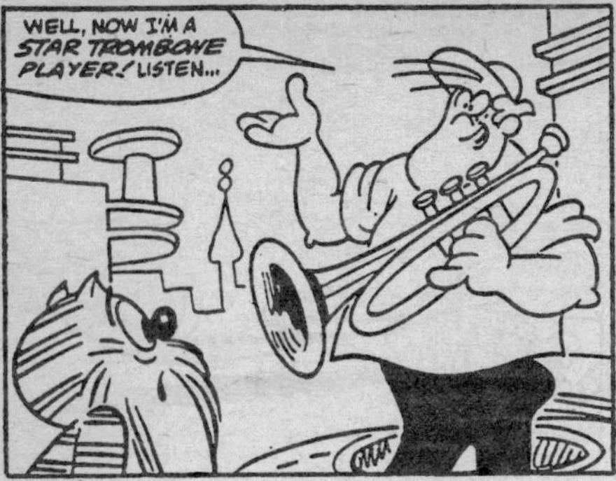
WELL, NOW I'M A STAR TROMBONE PLAYER! LISTEN...

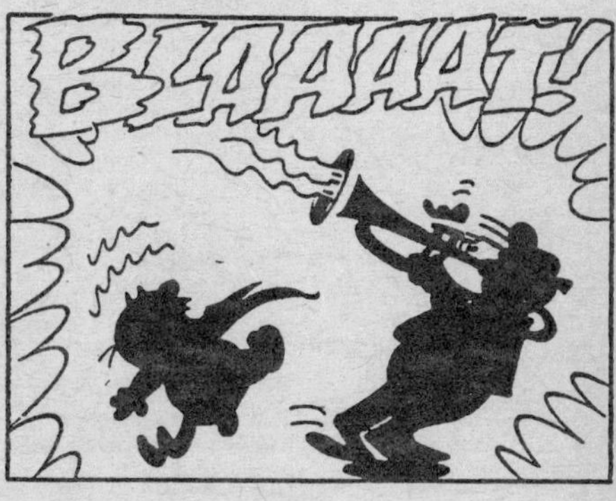
BLAAAAT!

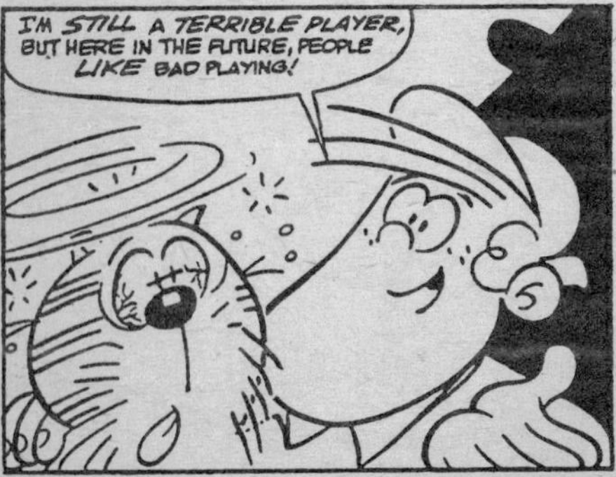
I'M STILL A TERRIBLE PLAYER, BUT HERE IN THE FUTURE, PEOPLE LIKE BAD PLAYING!

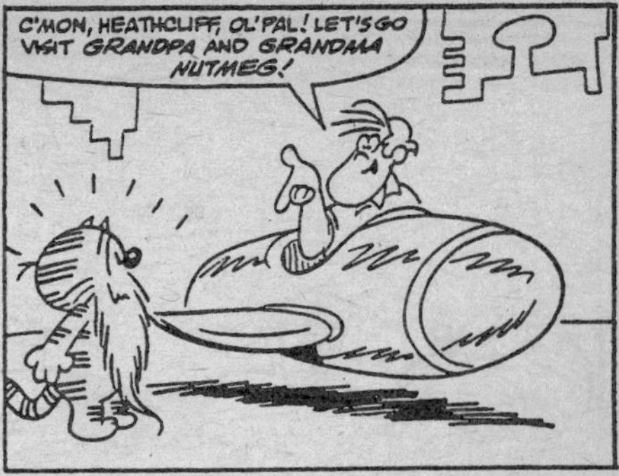
C'MON, HEATHCLIFF, OL' PAL! LET'S GO VISIT GRANDPA AND GRANDMA NUTMEG!

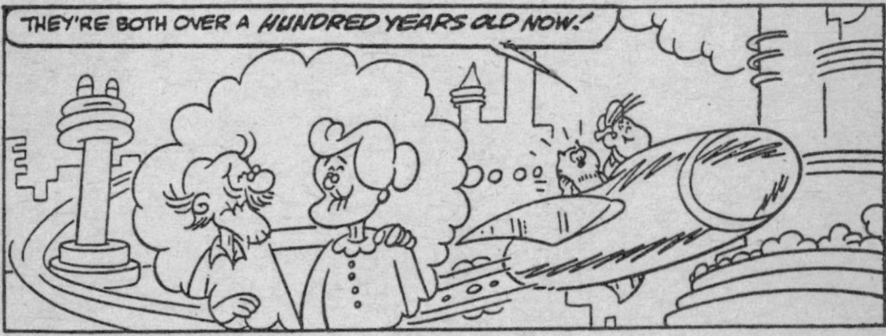
THEY'RE BOTH OVER A HUNDRED YEARS OLD NOW!

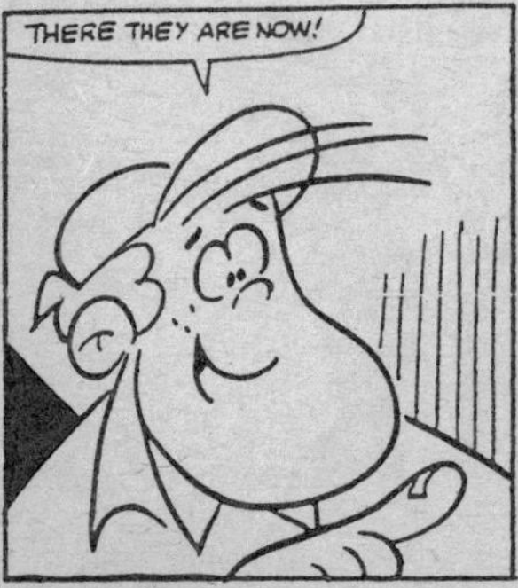
THERE THEY ARE NOW!

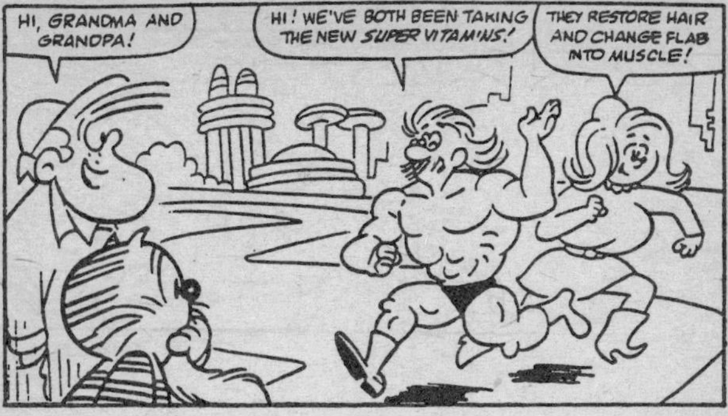
HI, GRANDMA AND GRANDPA!
HI! WE'VE BOTH BEEN TAKING THE NEW *SUPER VITAMINS!*
THEY RESTORE HAIR AND CHANGE FLAB INTO MUSCLE!

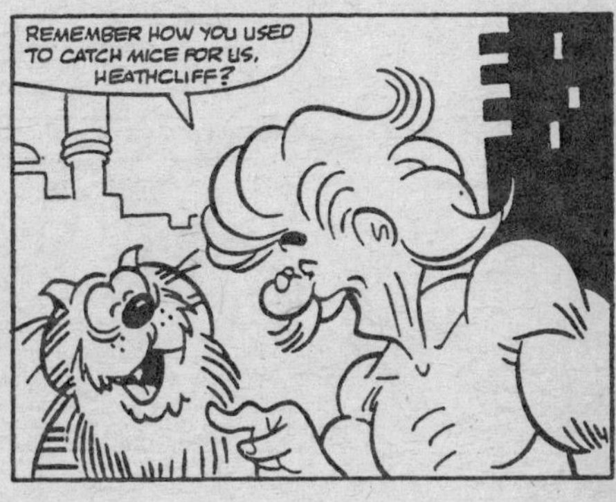
REMEMBER HOW YOU USED TO CATCH MICE FOR US, HEATHCLIFF?

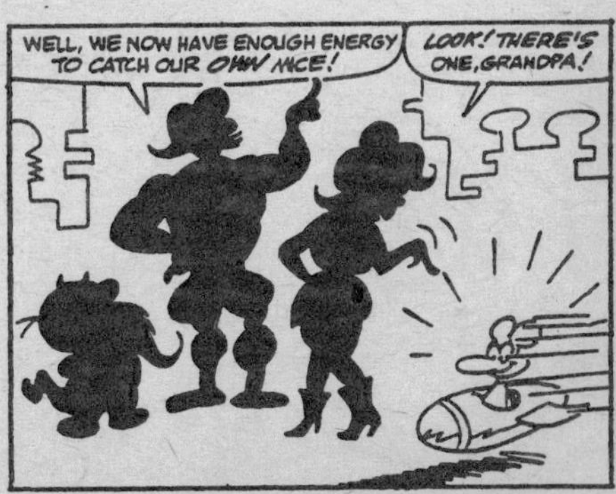
WELL, WE NOW HAVE ENOUGH ENERGY TO CATCH OUR *OWN* MICE!
LOOK! THERE'S ONE, GRANDPA!

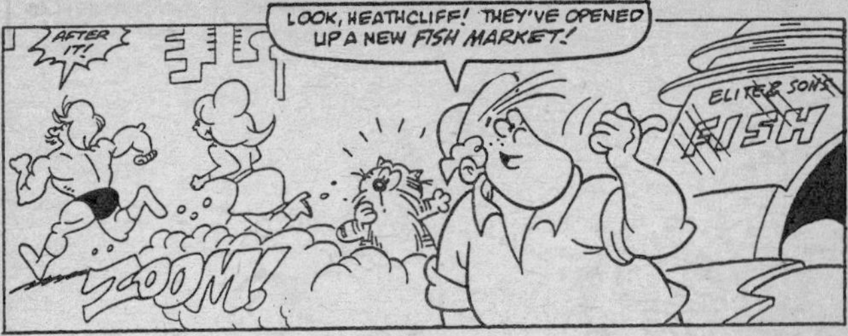
AFTER IT!
LOOK, HEATHCLIFF! THEY'VE OPENED UP A NEW FISH MARKET!
ELITE & SONS
FISH
ZOOM!

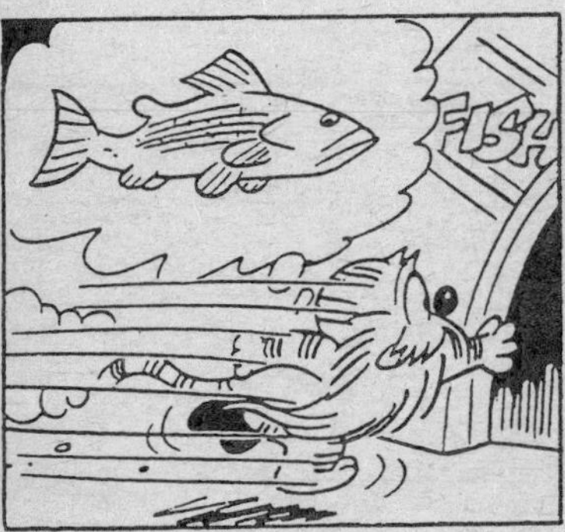
FISH

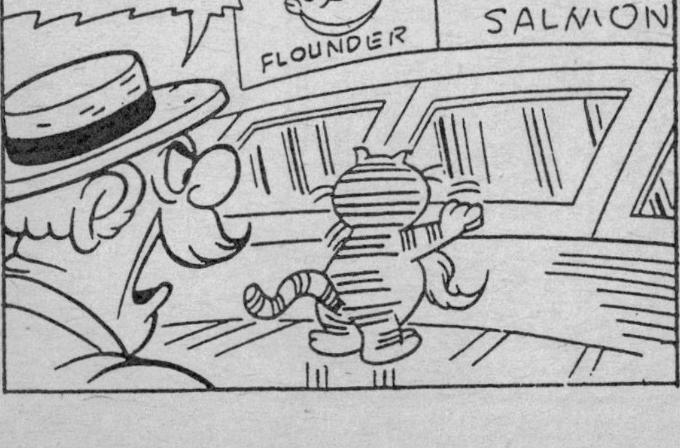
HEY, YOU! GET AWAY FROM THAT FISH!
FLOUNDER
SALMON

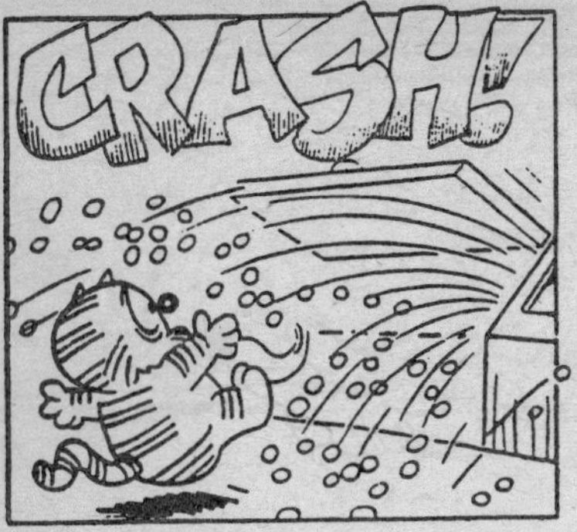
CRASH!

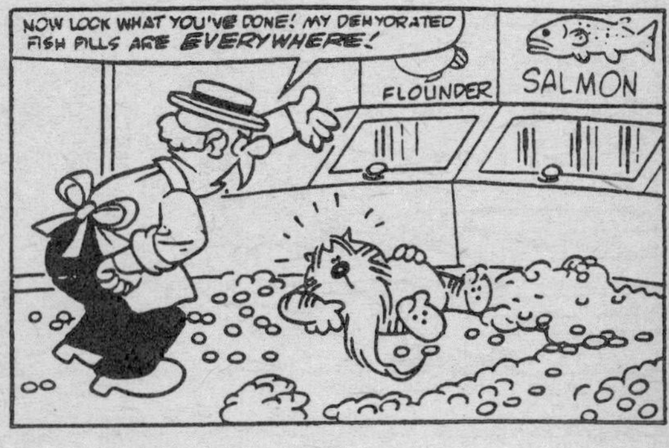
NOW LOOK WHAT YOU'VE DONE! MY DEHYDRATED FISH PILLS ARE EVERYWHERE!
FLOUNDER
SALMON

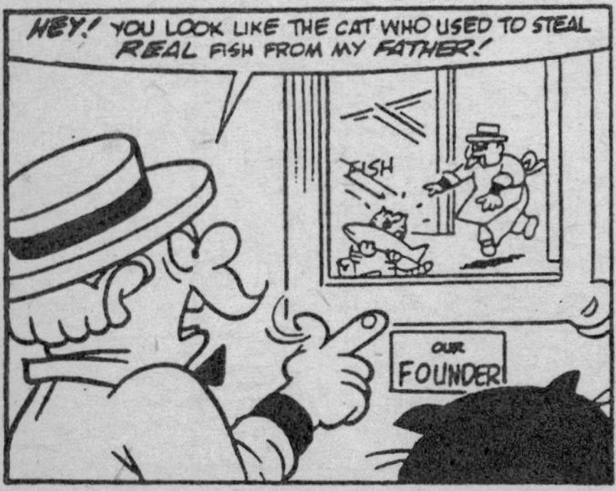
HEY! YOU LOOK LIKE THE CAT WHO USED TO STEAL REAL FISH FROM MY FATHER!
FISH
OUR FOUNDER

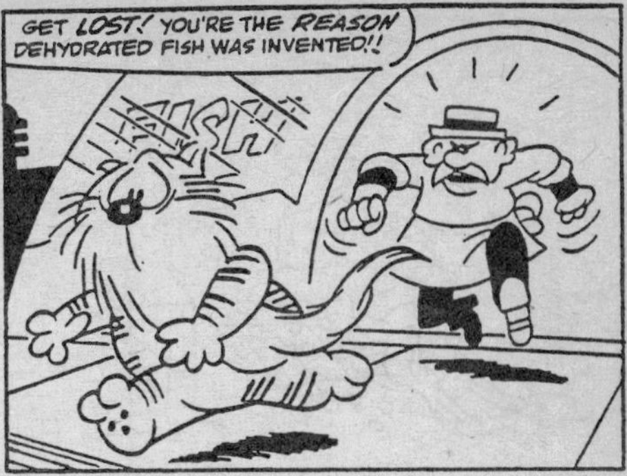
GET LOST! YOU'RE THE REASON DEHYDRATED FISH WAS INVENTED!!

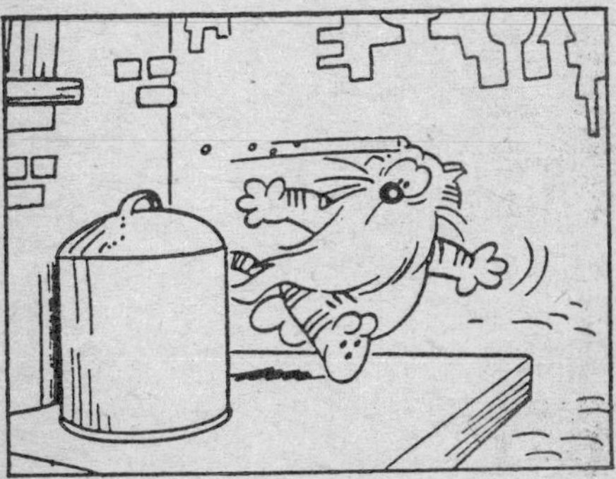

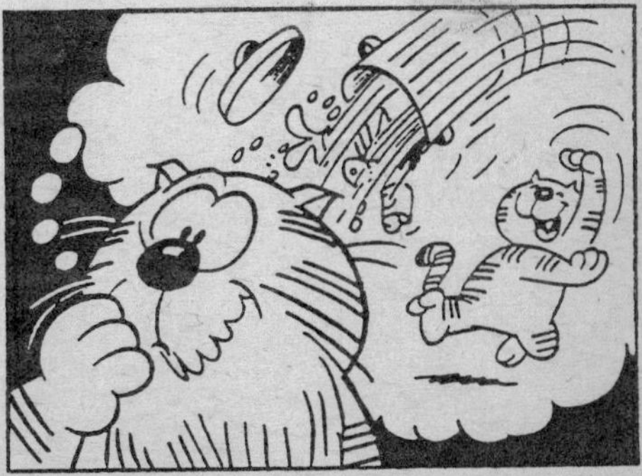

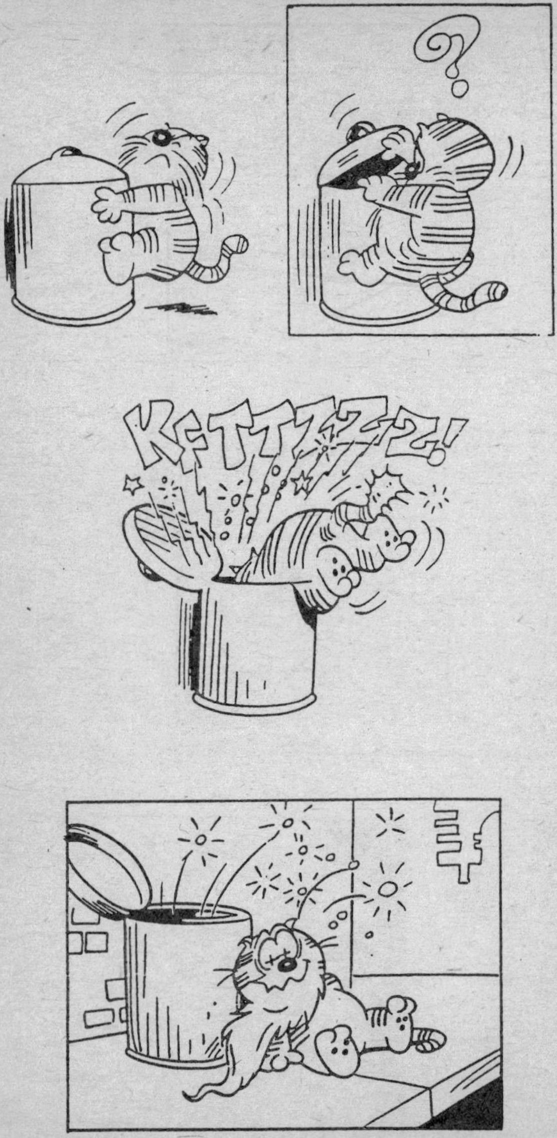
?
KFTTZZZ!

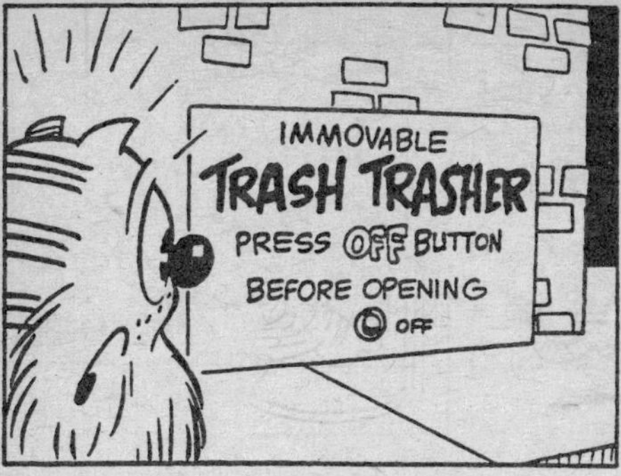
IMMOVABLE
TRASH TRASHER
PRESS OFF BUTTON
BEFORE OPENING
OFF

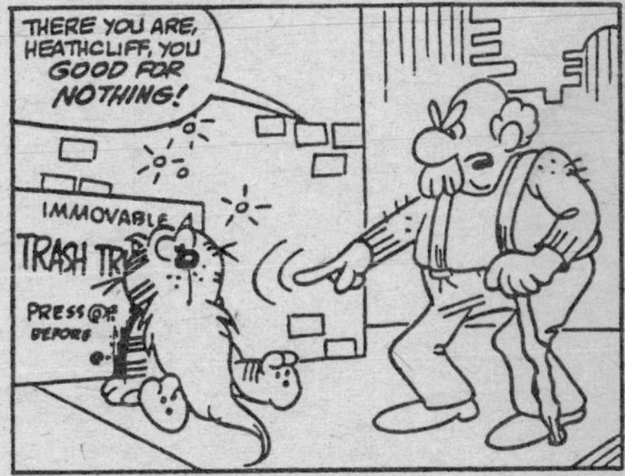
THERE YOU ARE, HEATHCLIFF, YOU GOOD FOR NOTHING!
IMMOVABLE
TRASH TR
PRESS
BEFORE

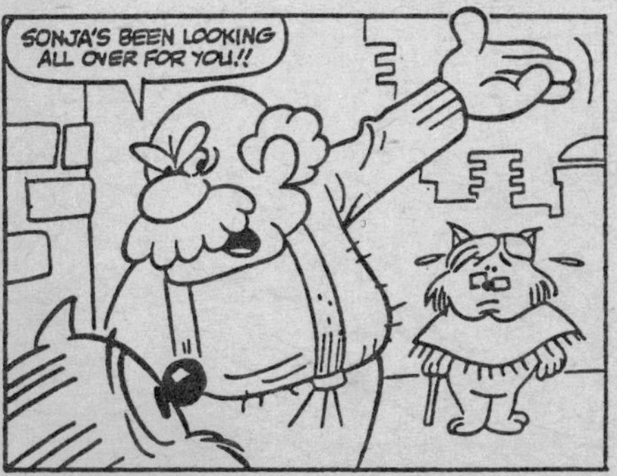
SONJA'S BEEN LOOKING ALL OVER FOR YOU!!

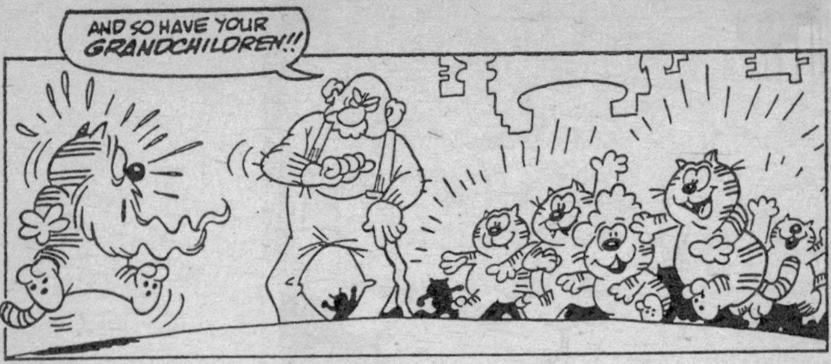
AND SO HAVE YOUR GRANDCHILDREN!!

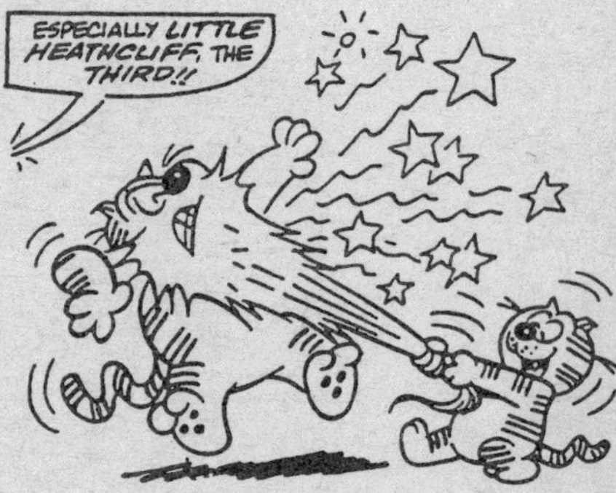
ESPECIALLY LITTLE HEATHCLIFF, THE THIRD!!

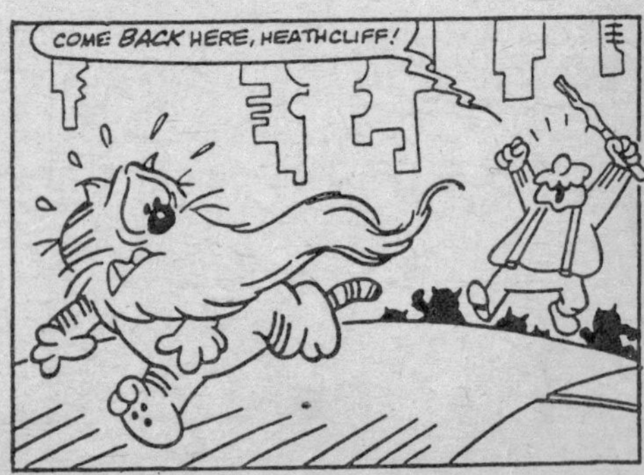
COME BACK HERE, HEATHCLIFF!

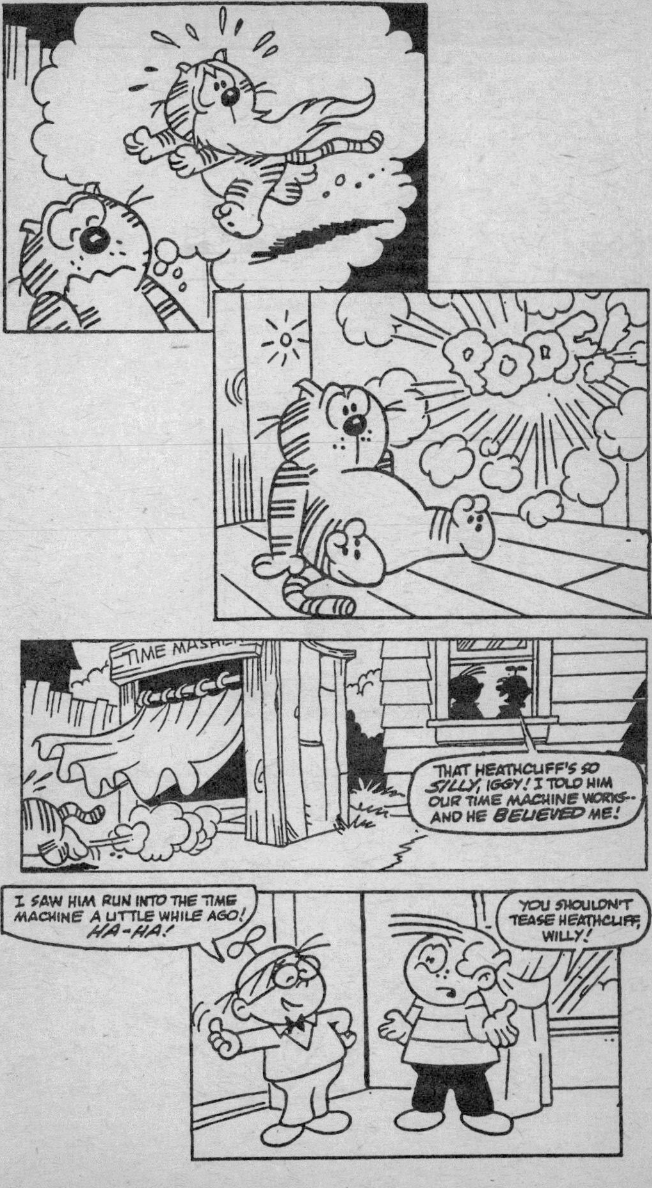
POOF!
TIME MASH
THAT HEATHCLIFF'S SO SILLY, IGGY! I TOLD HIM OUR TIME MACHINE WORKS-- AND HE BELIEVED ME!
I SAW HIM RUN INTO THE TIME MACHINE A LITTLE WHILE AGO! HA-HA!
YOU SHOULDN'T TEASE HEATHCLIFF, WILLY!

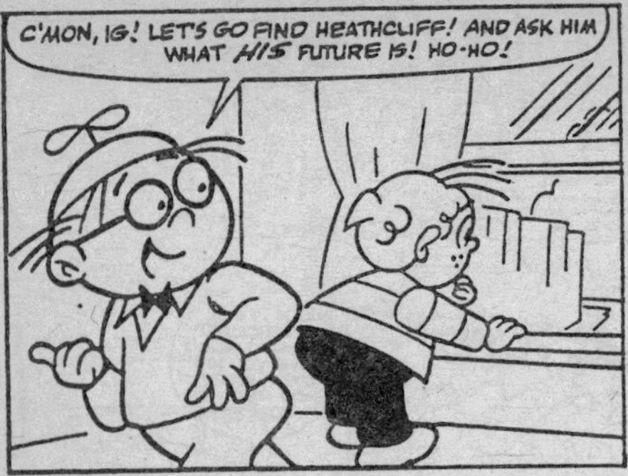
C'MON, IG! LET'S GO FIND HEATHCLIFF! AND ASK HIM WHAT *HIS* FUTURE IS! HO-HO!

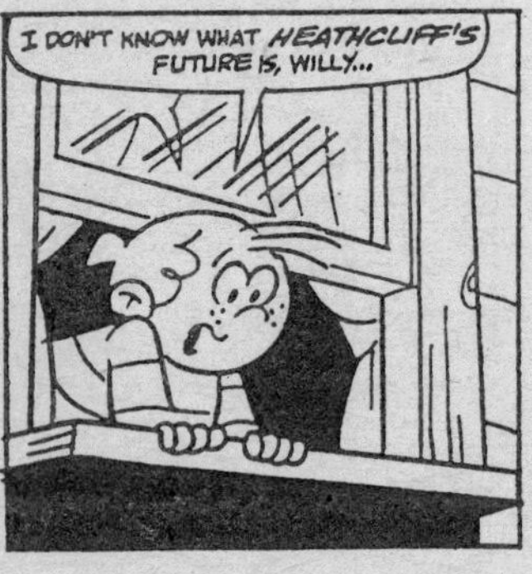
I DON'T KNOW WHAT *HEATHCLIFF'S* FUTURE IS, WILLY...

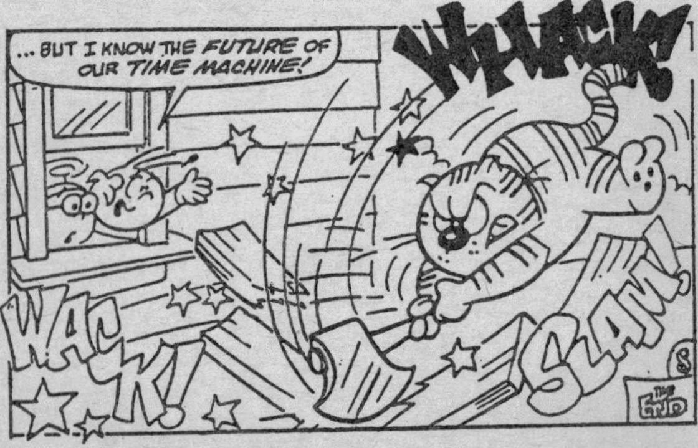
... BUT I KNOW THE *FUTURE* OF OUR *TIME MACHINE!*
WHACK!
WACK!
SLAM!
THE END

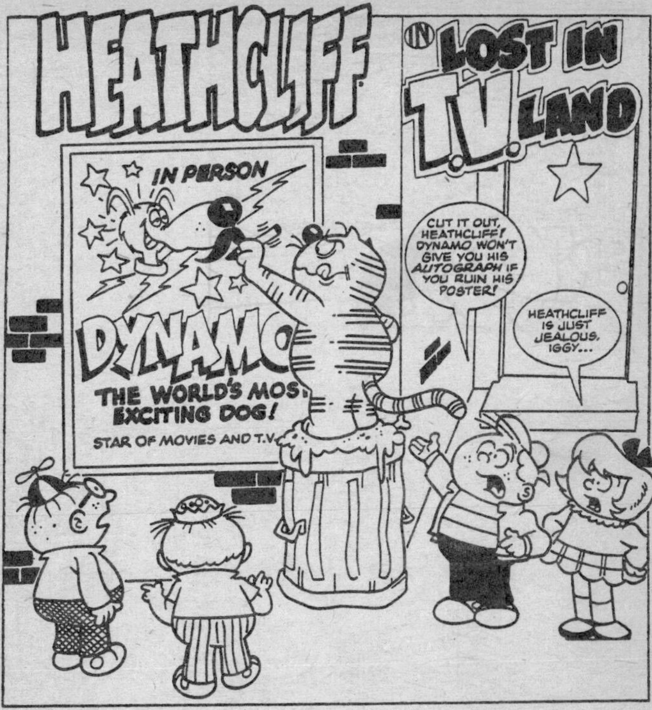
HEATHCLIFF
IN LOST IN T.V. LAND
IN PERSON
DYNAMO
THE WORLD'S MOST EXCITING DOG!
STAR OF MOVIES AND T.V.
CUT IT OUT, HEATHCLIFF! DYNAMO WON'T GIVE YOU HIS AUTOGRAPH IF YOU RUIN HIS POSTER!
HEATHCLIFF IS JUST JEALOUS, IGGY...

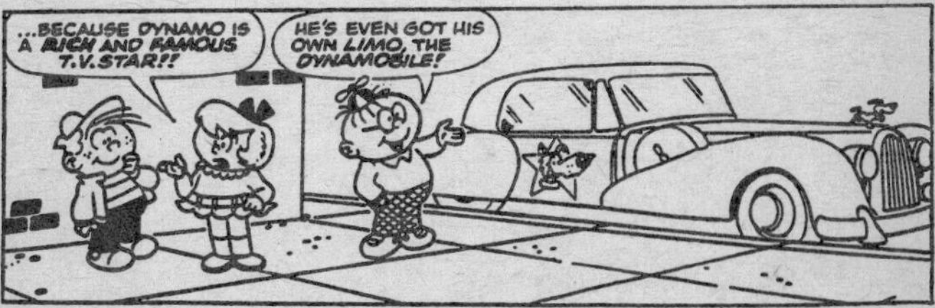
...BECAUSE DYNAMO IS A RICH AND FAMOUS T.V. STAR!!
HE'S EVEN GOT HIS OWN LIMO, THE DYNAMOBILE!

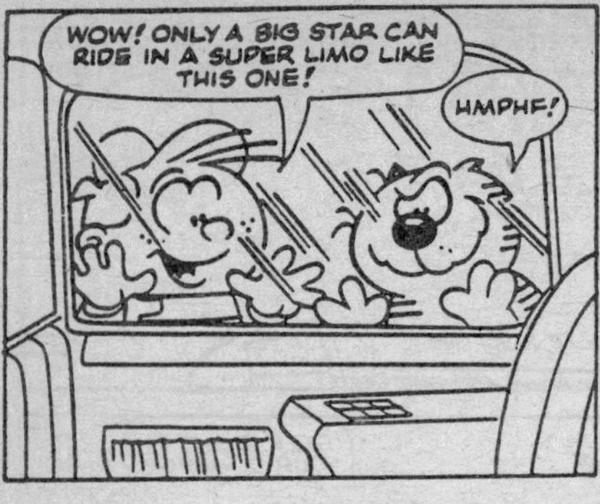
WOW! ONLY A BIG STAR CAN RIDE IN A SUPER LIMO LIKE THIS ONE!
HMPHF!

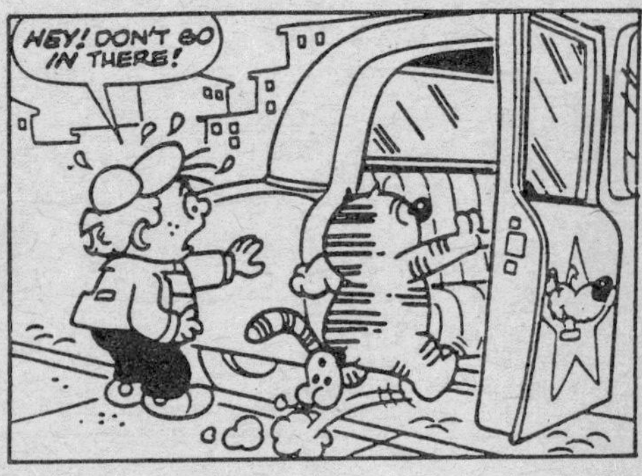
HEY! DON'T GO IN THERE!

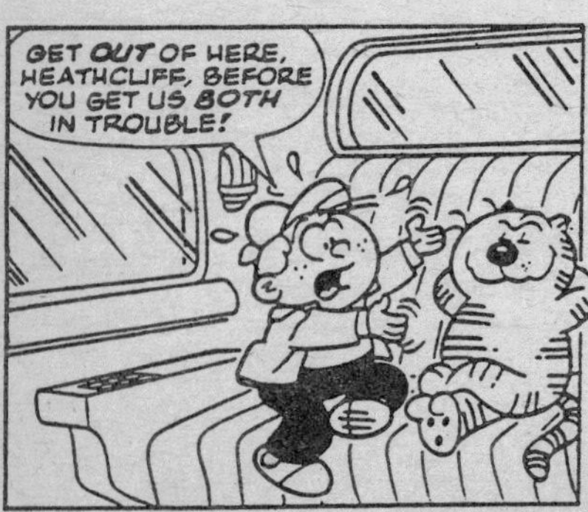
GET *OUT* OF HERE, HEATHCLIFF, BEFORE YOU GET US *BOTH* IN TROUBLE!

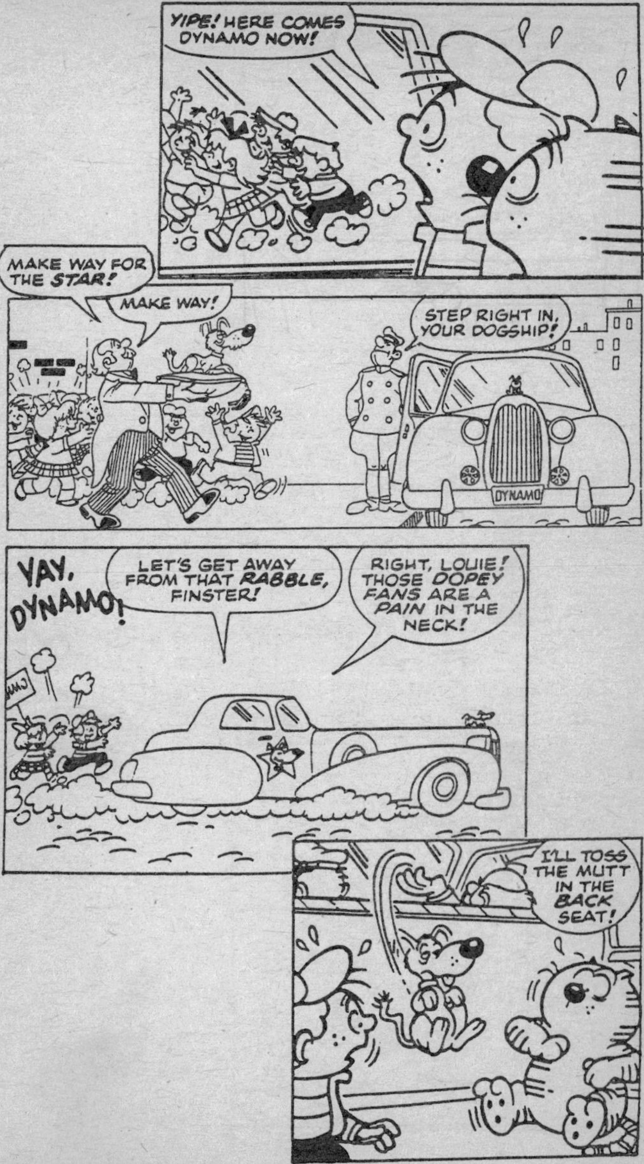
YIPE! HERE COMES DYNAMO NOW!
MAKE WAY FOR THE STAR!
MAKE WAY!
STEP RIGHT IN, YOUR DOGSHIP!
DYNAMO
YAY, DYNAMO!
LET'S GET AWAY FROM THAT RABBLE, FINSTER!
RIGHT, LOUIE! THOSE DOPEY FANS ARE A PAIN IN THE NECK!
I'LL TOSS THE MUTT IN THE BACK SEAT!

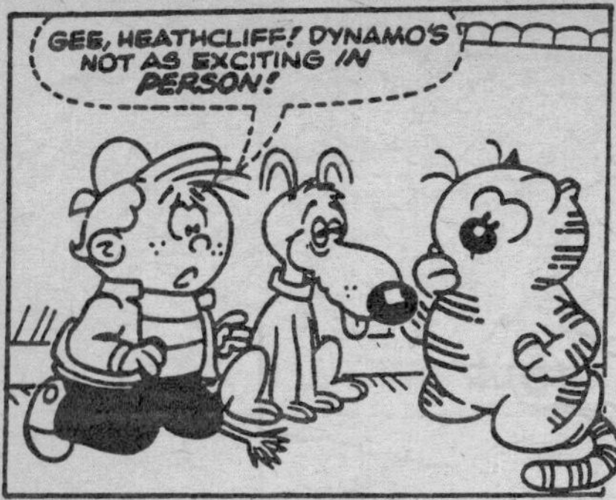
GEE, HEATHCLIFF! DYNAMO'S NOT AS EXCITING *IN PERSON!*

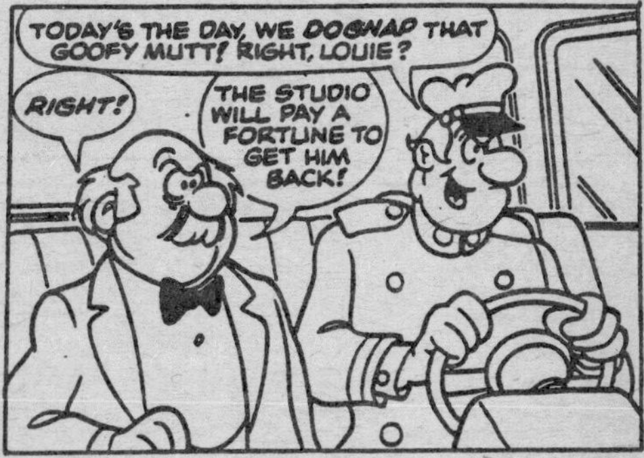
TODAY'S THE DAY, WE *DOGNAP* THAT GOOFY MUTT! RIGHT, LOUIE?
RIGHT!
THE STUDIO WILL PAY A FORTUNE TO GET HIM BACK!

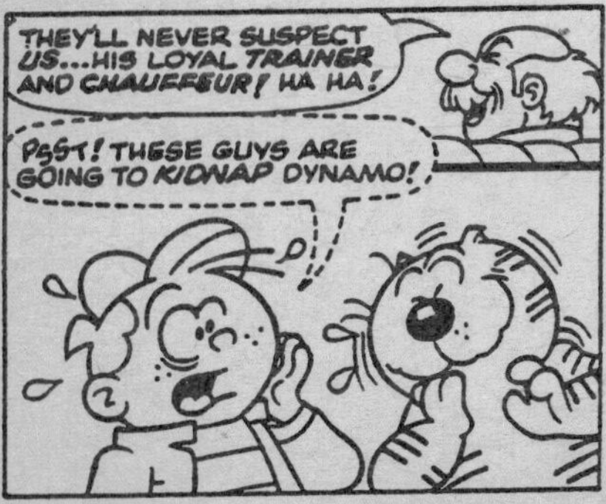
THEY'LL NEVER SUSPECT *US*...HIS LOYAL *TRAINER* AND *CHAUFFEUR!* HA HA!
PSST! THESE GUYS ARE GOING TO *KIDNAP* DYNAMO!

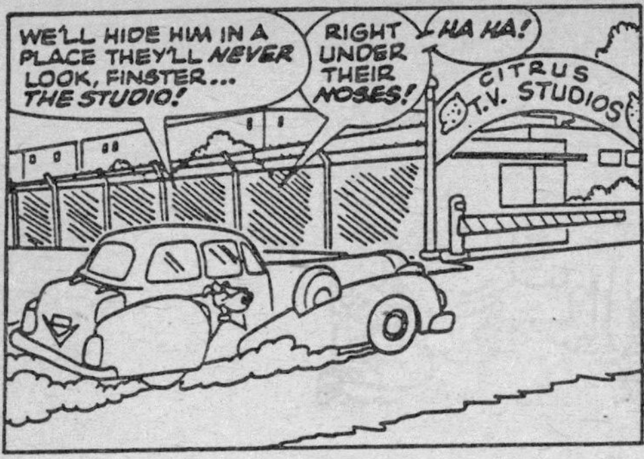
WE'LL HIDE HIM IN A PLACE THEY'LL *NEVER* LOOK, FINSTER... *THE STUDIO!*
RIGHT UNDER THEIR *NOSES!*
HA HA!
CITRUS T.V. STUDIOS

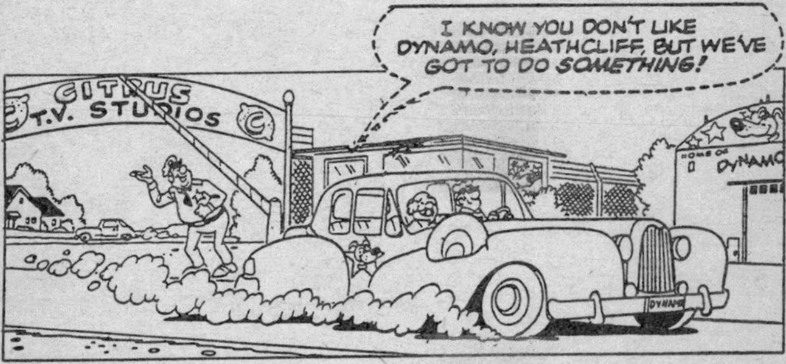
I KNOW YOU DON'T LIKE DYNAMO, HEATHCLIFF, BUT WE'VE GOT TO DO *SOMETHING!*
CITRUS T.V. STUDIOS
DYNAMO

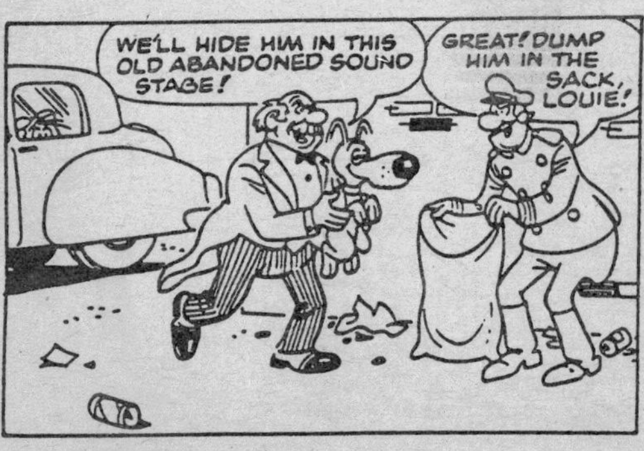
WE'LL HIDE HIM IN THIS OLD ABANDONED SOUND STAGE!
GREAT! DUMP HIM IN THE SACK, LOUIE!

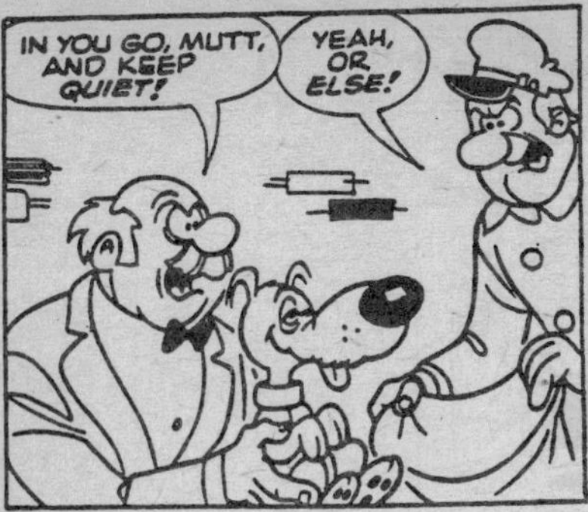
IN YOU GO, MUTT, AND KEEP QUIET!
YEAH, OR ELSE!

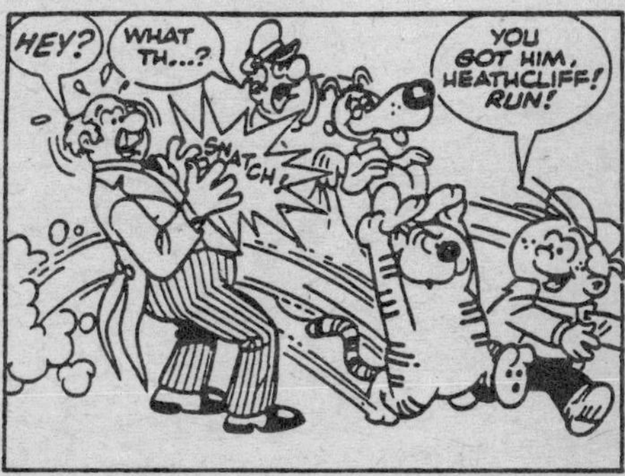
HEY?
WHAT TH...?
SNATCH!
YOU GOT HIM, HEATHCLIFF! RUN!

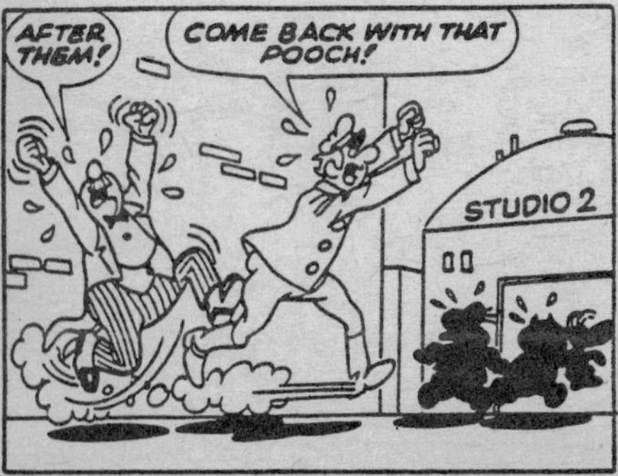
AFTER THEM!
COME BACK WITH THAT POOCH!
STUDIO 2

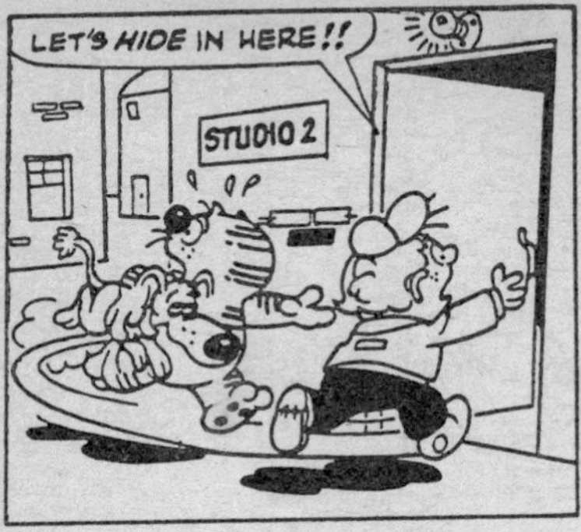
LET'S HIDE IN HERE!!
STUDIO 2

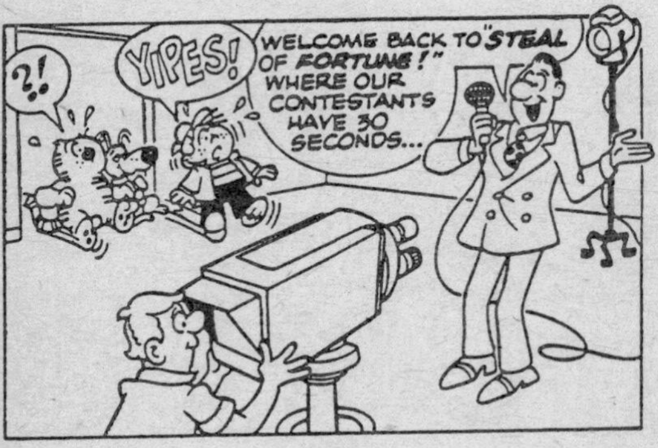
?!
YIPES!
WELCOME BACK TO "STEAL OF FORTUNE!" WHERE OUR CONTESTANTS HAVE 30 SECONDS...

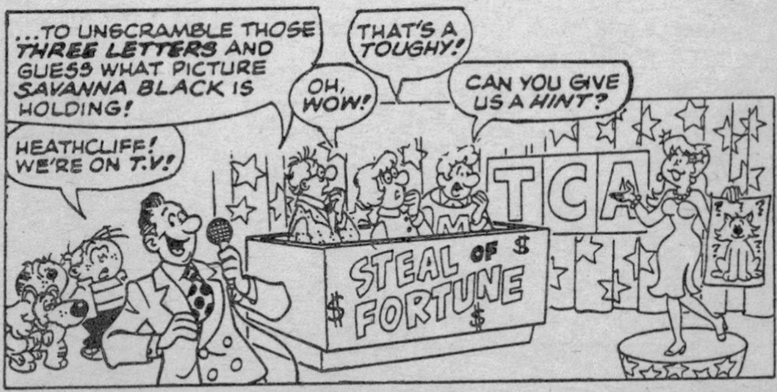
...TO UNSCRAMBLE THOSE THREE LETTERS AND GUESS WHAT PICTURE SAVANNA BLACK IS HOLDING!
HEATHCLIFF! WE'RE ON T.V!
OH, WOW!
THAT'S A TOUGHY!
CAN YOU GIVE US A HINT?
T C A
STEAL OF FORTUNE

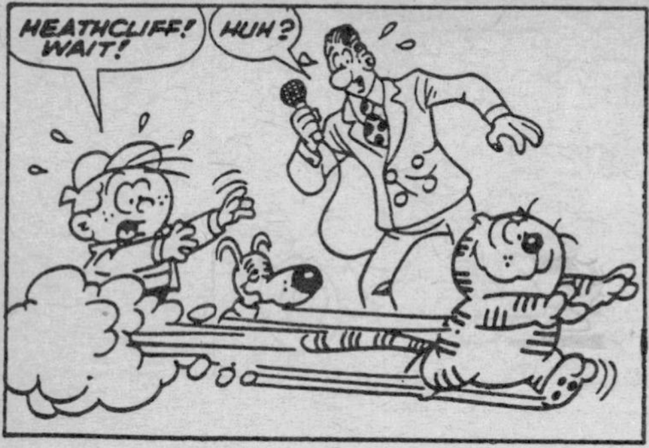
HEATHCLIFF! WAIT!
HUH?

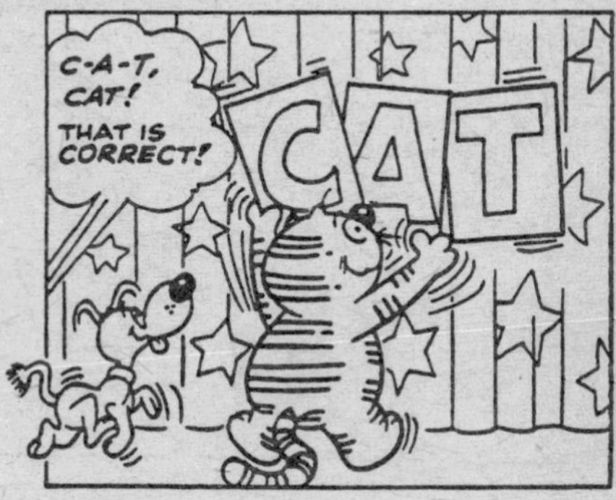
C-A-T, CAT!
THAT IS CORRECT!
CAT

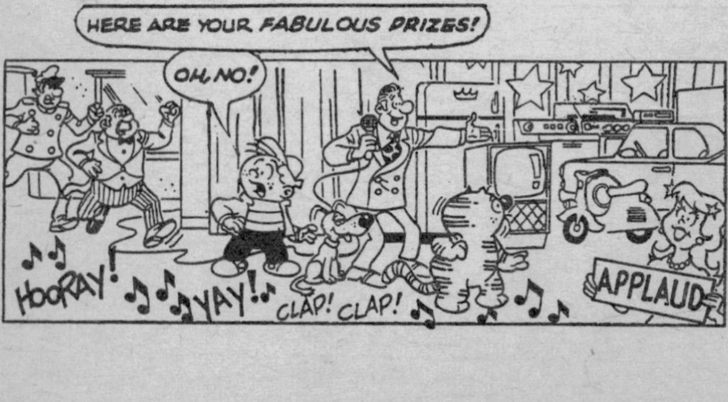
HERE ARE YOUR FABULOUS PRIZES!
OH, NO!
HOORAY!
YAY!
CLAP! CLAP!
APPLAUD

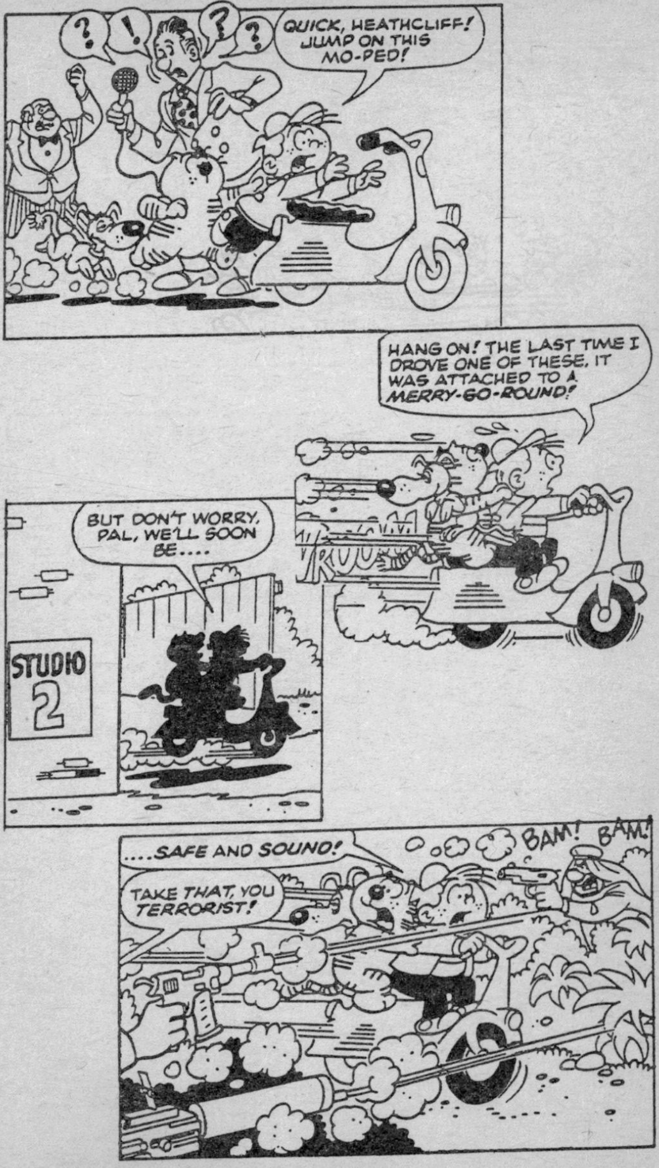
?
!
?
?
QUICK, HEATHCLIFF! JUMP ON THIS MO-PED!
HANG ON! THE LAST TIME I DROVE ONE OF THESE, IT WAS ATTACHED TO A MERRY-GO-ROUND!
BUT DON'T WORRY, PAL, WE'LL SOON BE....
STUDIO 2
....SAFE AND SOUND!
BAM! BAM!
TAKE THAT, YOU TERRORIST!

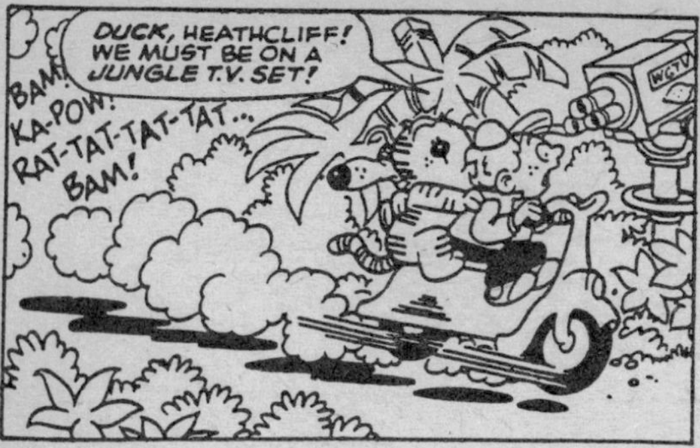
DUCK, HEATHCLIFF! WE MUST BE ON A JUNGLE T.V. SET!
BAM! KA-POW! RAT-TAT-TAT-TAT... BAM!
WCTV

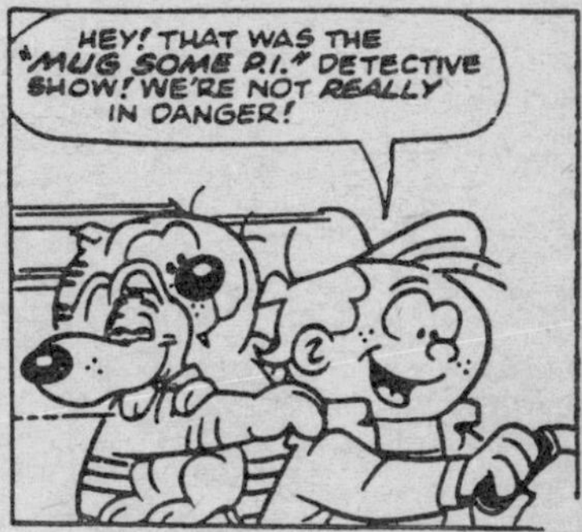
HEY! THAT WAS THE "MUG SOME P.I." DETECTIVE SHOW! WE'RE NOT REALLY IN DANGER!

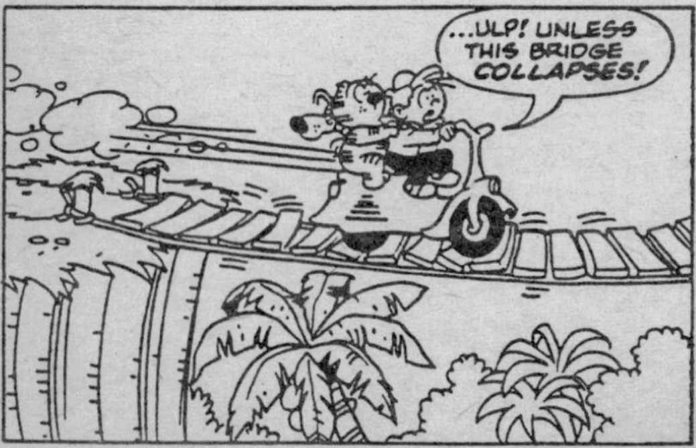
...ULP! UNLESS THIS BRIDGE COLLAPSES!

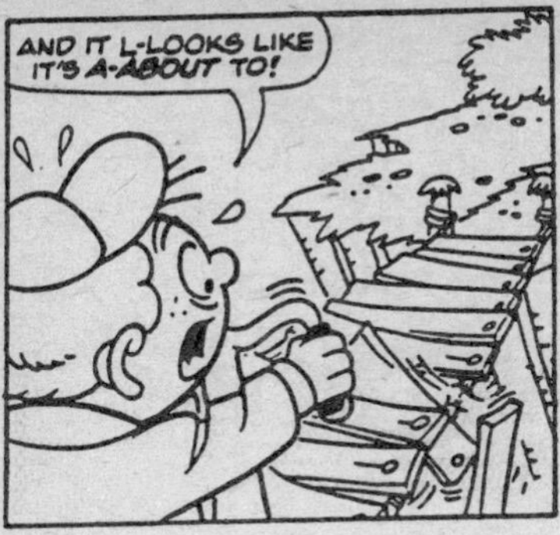
AND IT L-LOOKS LIKE IT'S A-ABOUT TO!

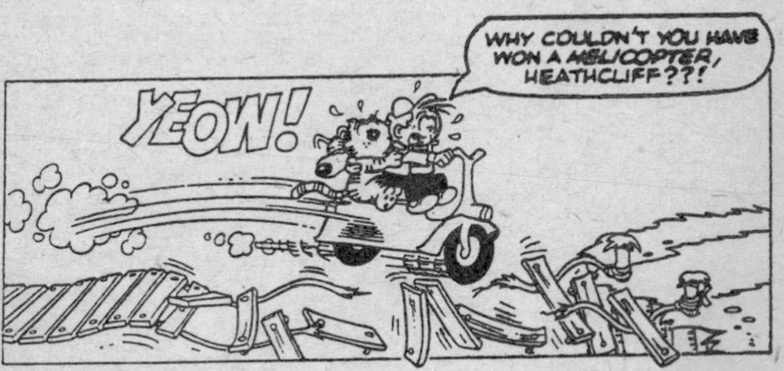
YEOW!
WHY COULDN'T YOU HAVE WON A HELICOPTER, HEATHCLIFF??!

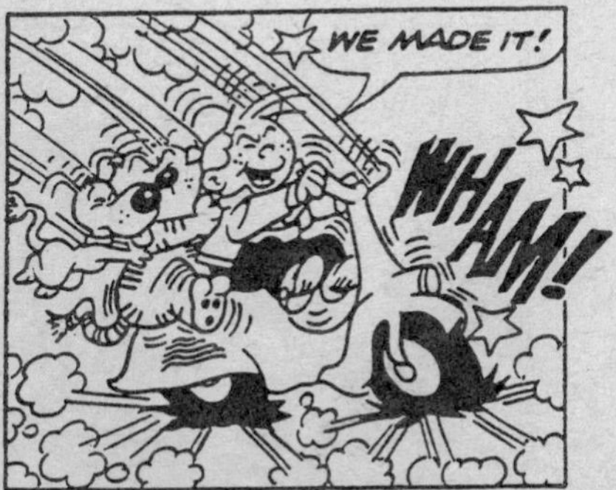
WE MADE IT!
WHAM!

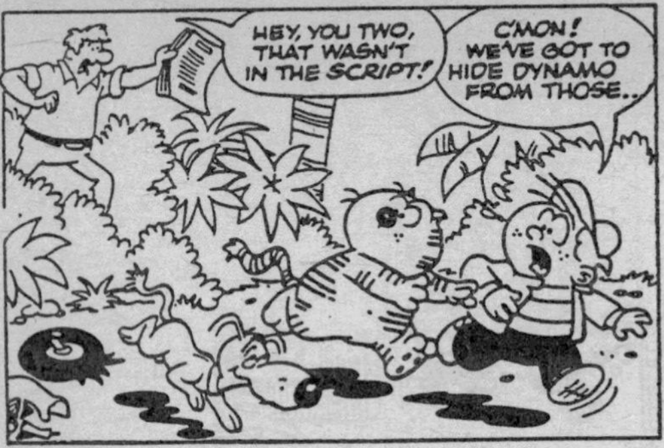
HEY, YOU TWO, THAT WASN'T IN THE *SCRIPT!*
C'MON! WE'VE GOT TO HIDE DYNAMO FROM THOSE...

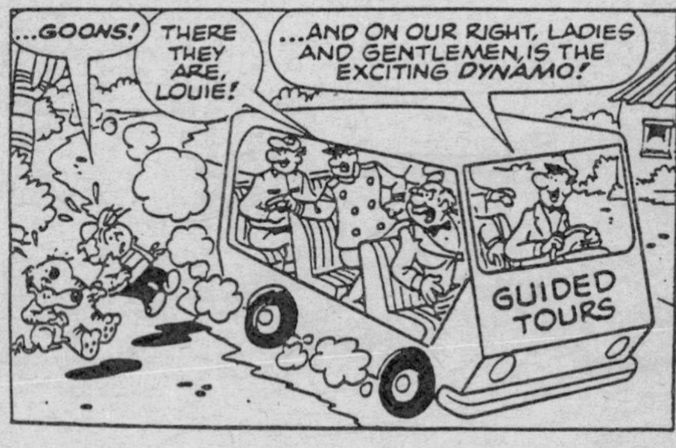
...GOONS!
THERE THEY ARE, LOUIE!
...AND ON OUR RIGHT, LADIES AND GENTLEMEN, IS THE EXCITING *DYNAMO!*
GUIDED TOURS

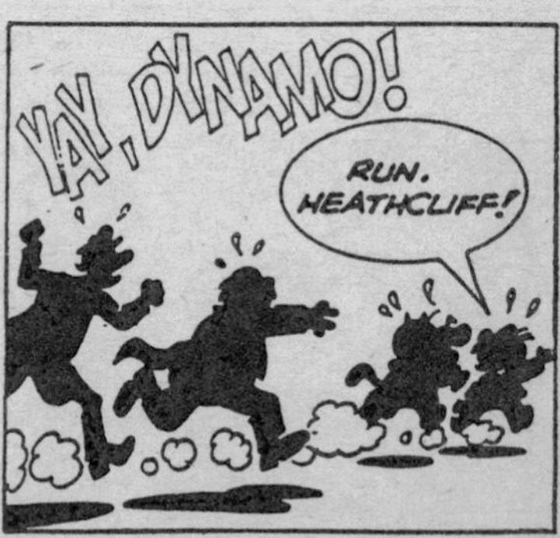
YAY, DYNAMO!
RUN. HEATHCLIFF!

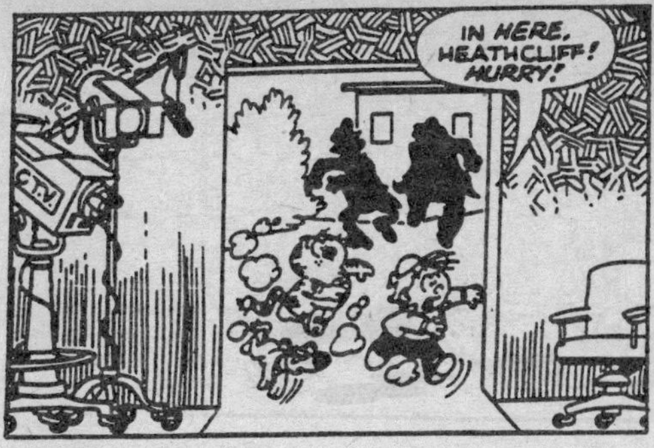
IN HERE, HEATHCLIFF! HURRY!
C.T.V.

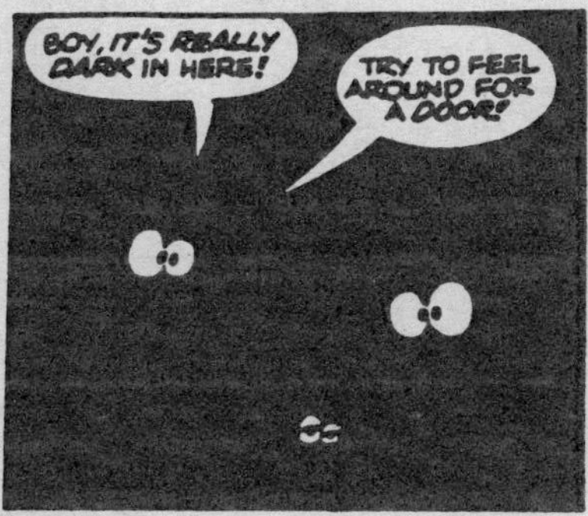
BOY, IT'S REALLY DARK IN HERE!
TRY TO FEEL AROUND FOR A DOOR!

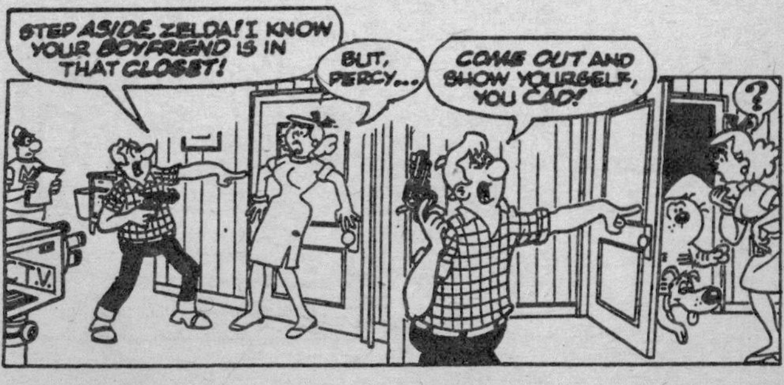
STEP ASIDE, ZELDA! I KNOW YOUR BOYFRIEND IS IN THAT CLOSET!
BUT, PERCY...
COME OUT AND SHOW YOURSELF, YOU CAD!
?
C.T.V.

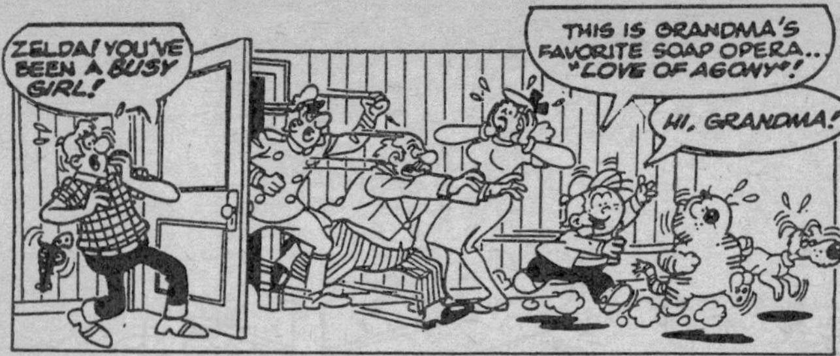
ZELDA! YOU'VE BEEN A BUSY GIRL!
THIS IS GRANDMA'S FAVORITE SOAP OPERA.. "LOVE OF AGONY"!
HI, GRANDMA!

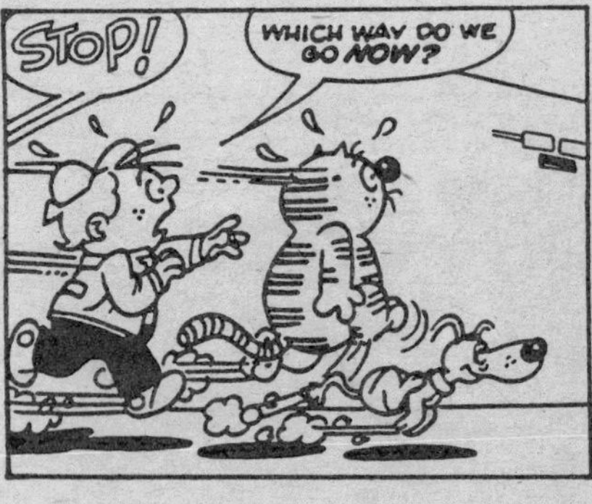
STOP!
WHICH WAY DO WE GO NOW?

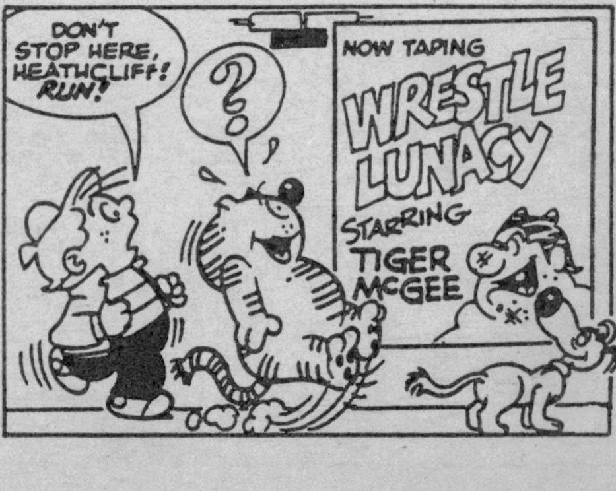
DON'T STOP HERE, HEATHCLIFF! RUN!
?
NOW TAPING
WRESTLE LUNACY
STARRING
TIGER McGEE

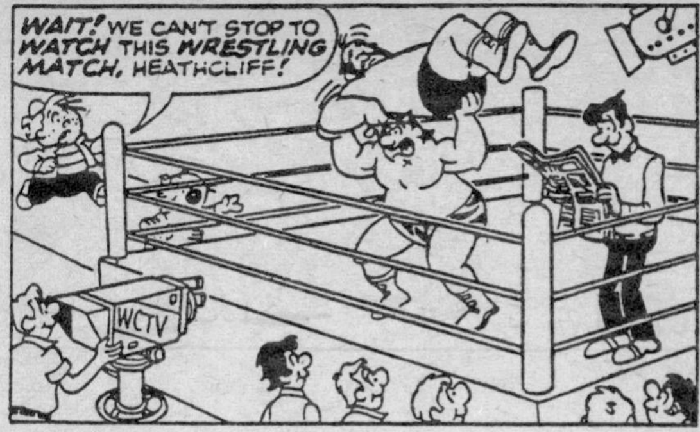
WAIT! WE CAN'T STOP TO WATCH THIS WRESTLING MATCH, HEATHCLIFF!
WCTV

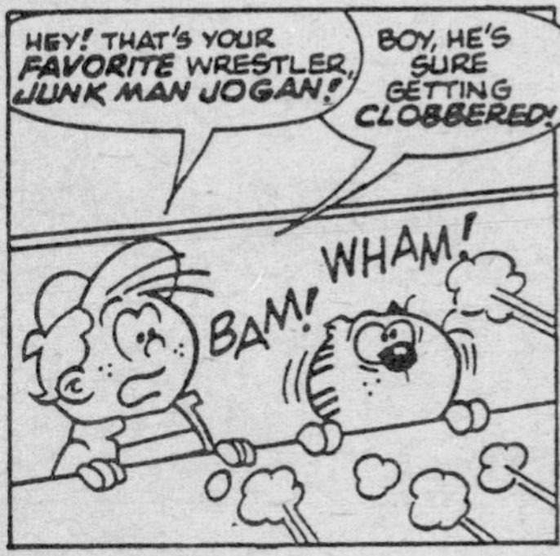
HEY! THAT'S YOUR FAVORITE WRESTLER, JUNK MAN JOGAN!
BOY, HE'S SURE GETTING CLOBBERED!
WHAM!
BAM!

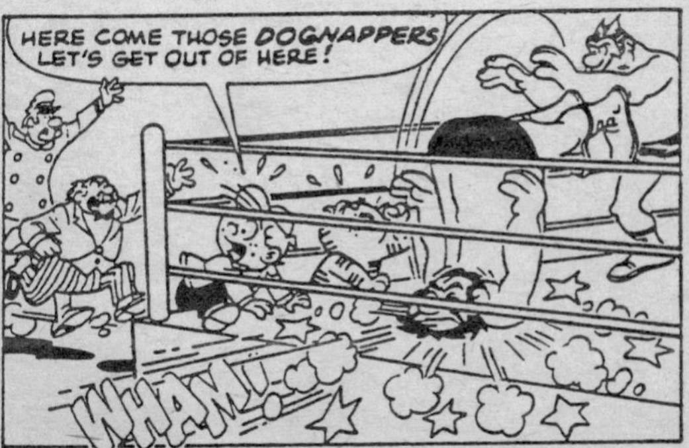
HERE COME THOSE DOGNAPPERS LET'S GET OUT OF HERE!
WHAM!

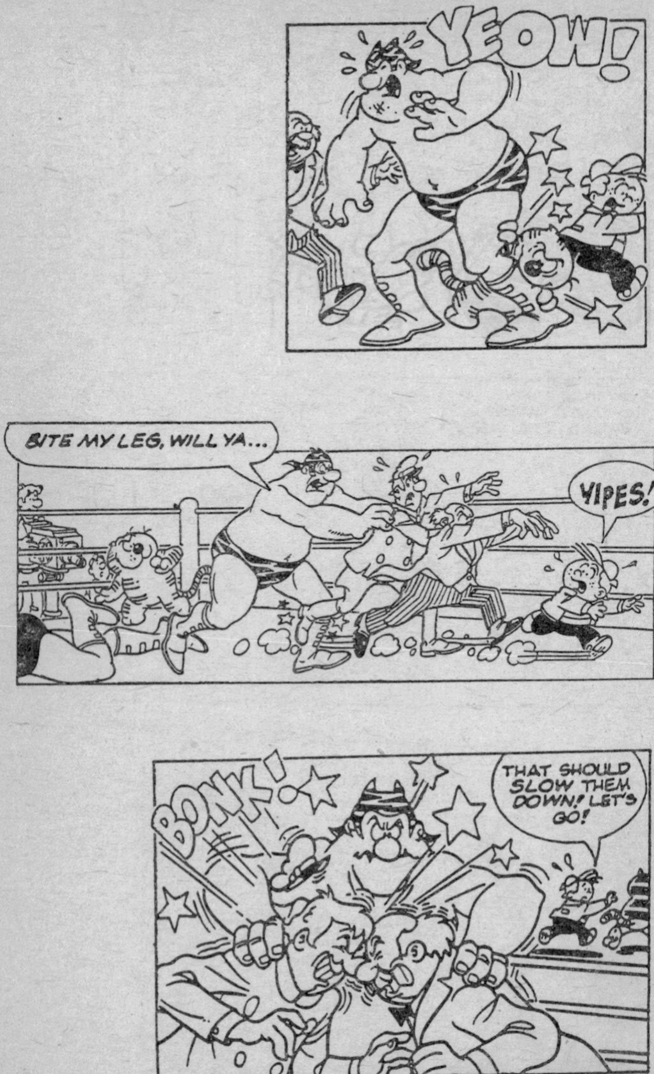
YEOW!
BITE MY LEG, WILL YA...
YIPES!
BONK!
THAT SHOULD SLOW THEM DOWN! LET'S GO!

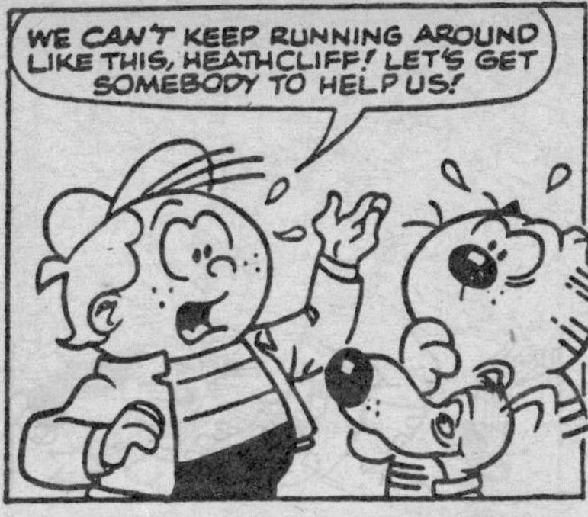
WE CAN'T KEEP RUNNING AROUND LIKE THIS, HEATHCLIFF! LET'S GET SOMEBODY TO HELP US!

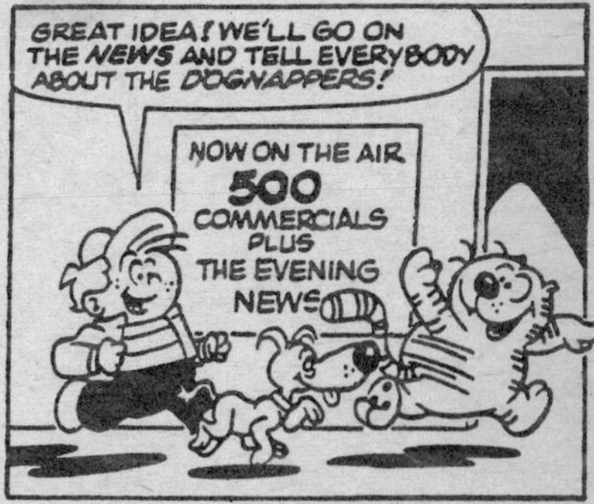
GREAT IDEA! WE'LL GO ON THE NEWS AND TELL EVERYBODY ABOUT THE DOGNAPPERS!
NOW ON THE AIR 500 COMMERCIALS PLUS THE EVENING NEWS

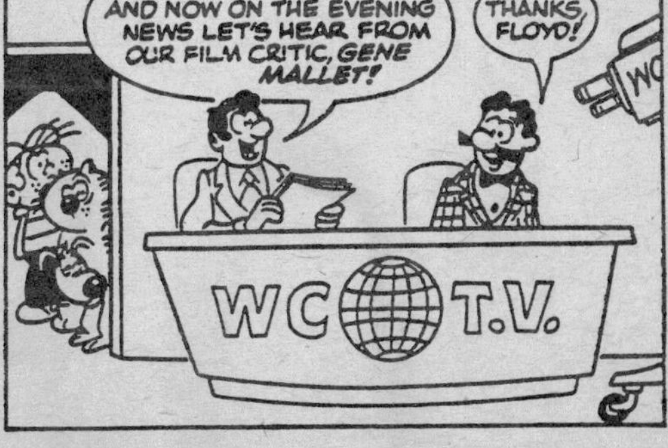
AND NOW ON THE EVENING NEWS LET'S HEAR FROM OUR FILM CRITIC, GENE MALLET!
THANKS, FLOYD!
WC T.V.

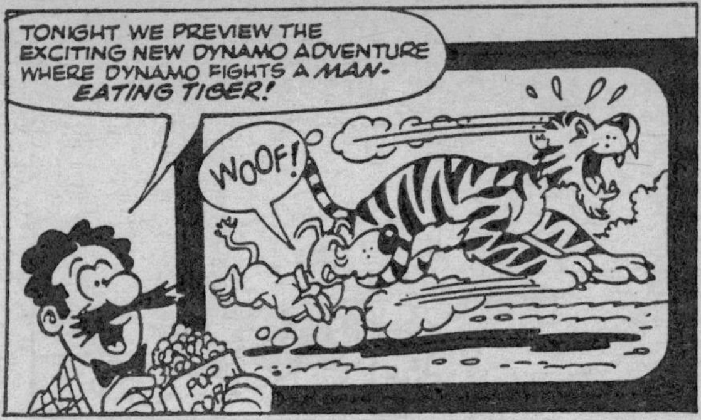
TONIGHT WE PREVIEW THE EXCITING NEW DYNAMO ADVENTURE WHERE DYNAMO FIGHTS A *MAN-EATING TIGER!*
WOOF!
POP CORN

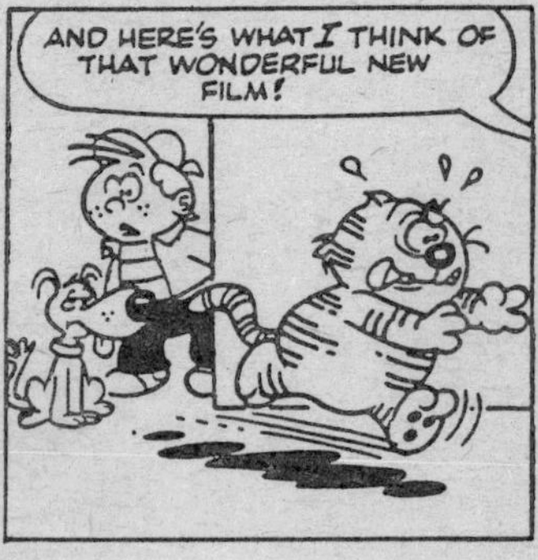
AND HERE'S WHAT *I* THINK OF THAT WONDERFUL NEW FILM!

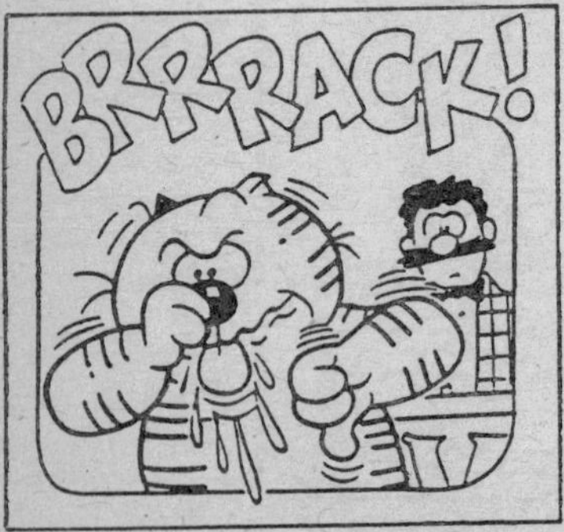
BRRRACK!

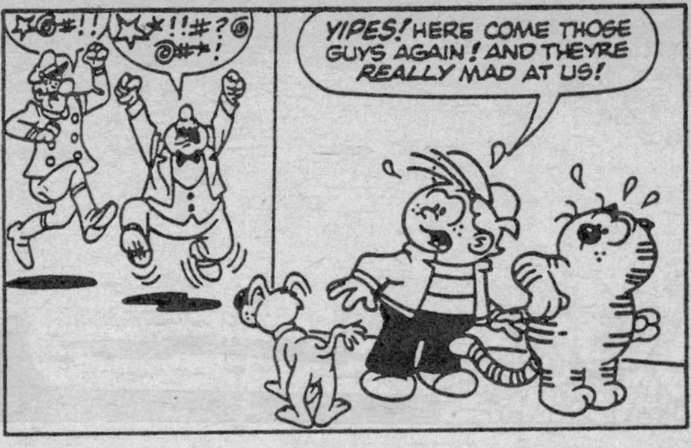
YIPES! HERE COME THOSE GUYS AGAIN! AND THEYRE REALLY MAD AT US!

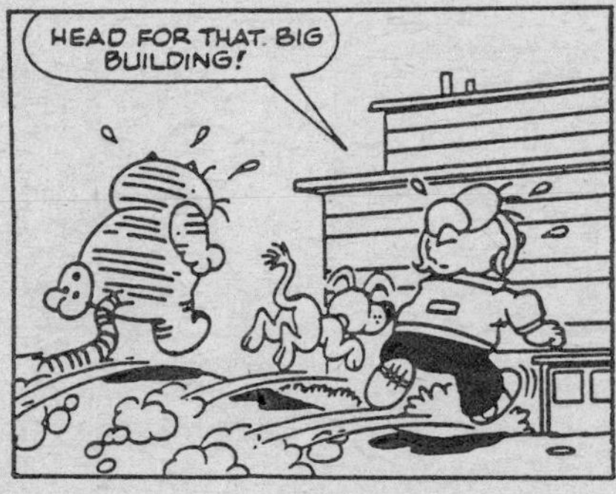
HEAD FOR THAT BIG BUILDING!

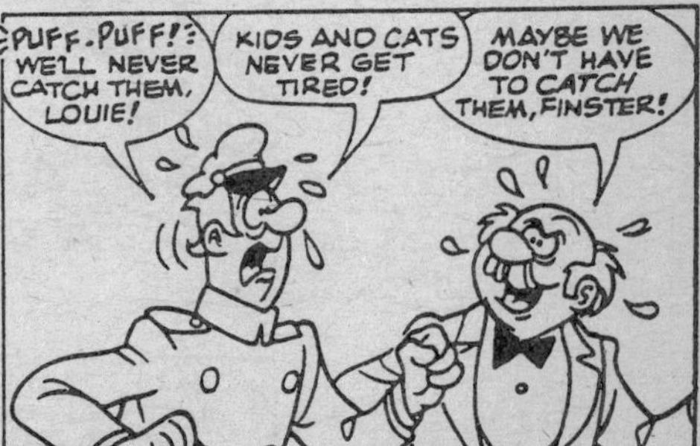
PUFF-PUFF! WE'LL NEVER CATCH THEM, LOUIE!
KIDS AND CATS NEVER GET TIRED!
MAYBE WE DON'T HAVE TO CATCH THEM, FINSTER!

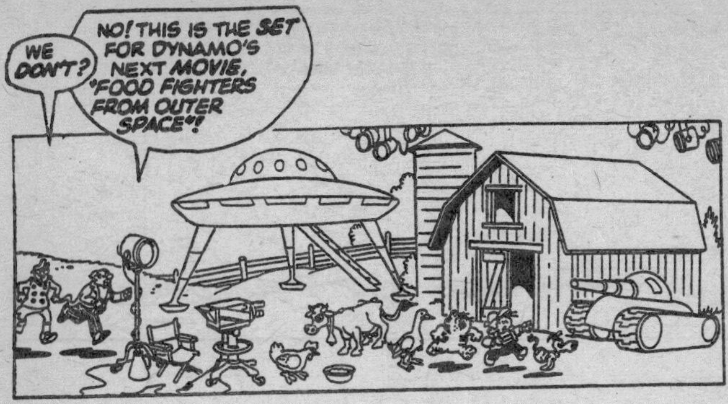
WE DON'T?
NO! THIS IS THE SET FOR DYNAMO'S NEXT MOVIE, "FOOD FIGHTERS FROM OUTER SPACE"!

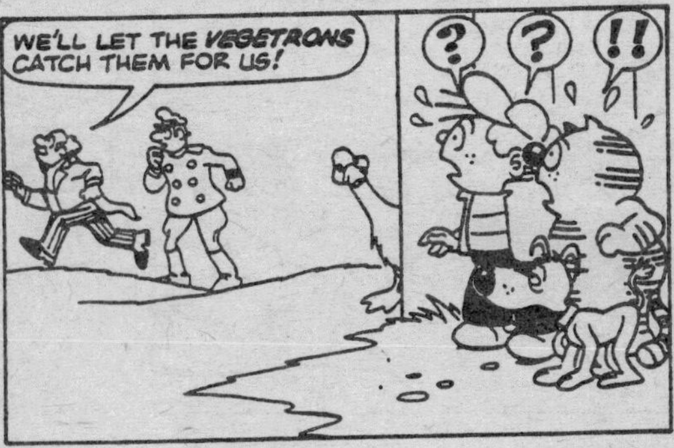
WE'LL LET THE VEGETRONS CATCH THEM FOR US!
?
?
!!

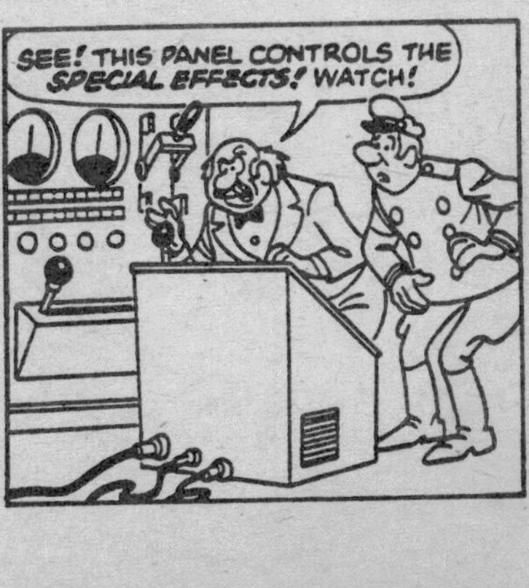
SEE! THIS PANEL CONTROLS THE SPECIAL EFFECTS! WATCH!

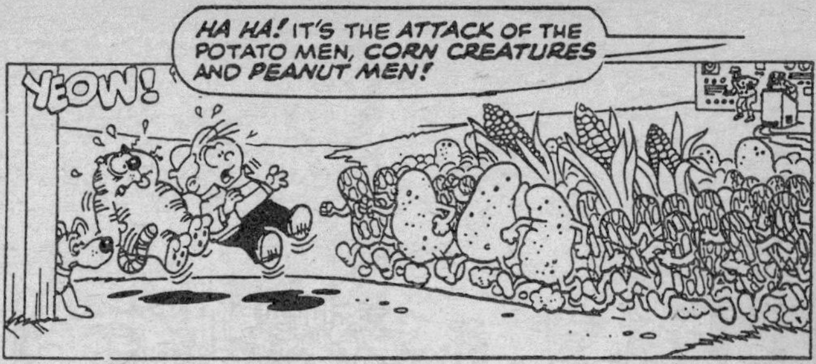
HA HA! IT'S THE ATTACK OF THE POTATO MEN, CORN CREATURES AND PEANUT MEN!
YEOW!

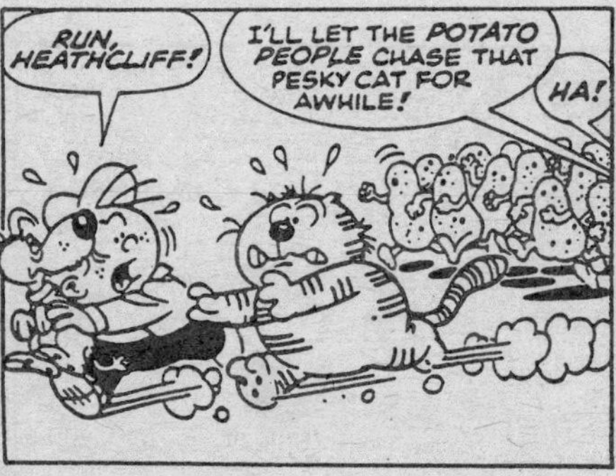
RUN, HEATHCLIFF!
I'LL LET THE POTATO PEOPLE CHASE THAT PESKY CAT FOR AWHILE!
HA!

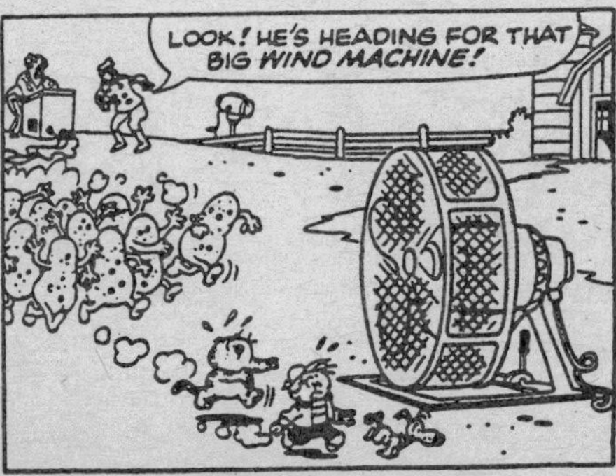
LOOK! HE'S HEADING FOR THAT BIG WIND MACHINE!

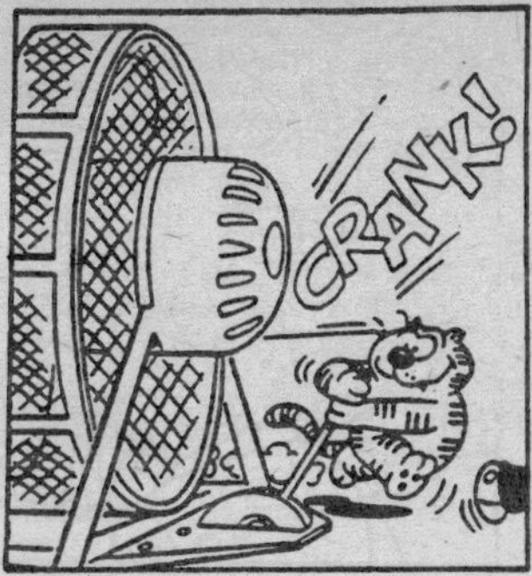
CRANK!

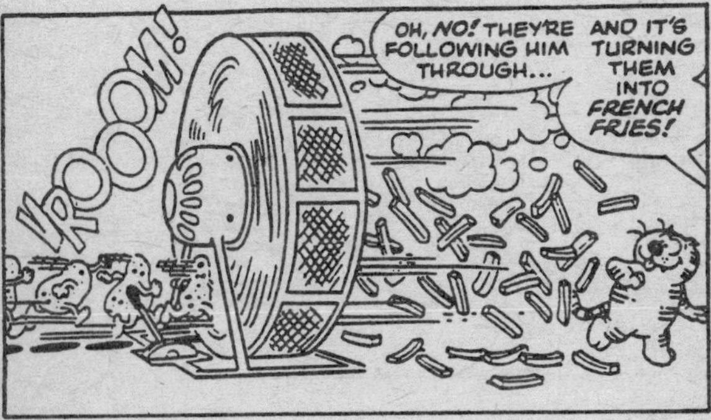
VROOOM!
OH, NO! THEY'RE FOLLOWING HIM THROUGH...
AND IT'S TURNING THEM INTO FRENCH FRIES!

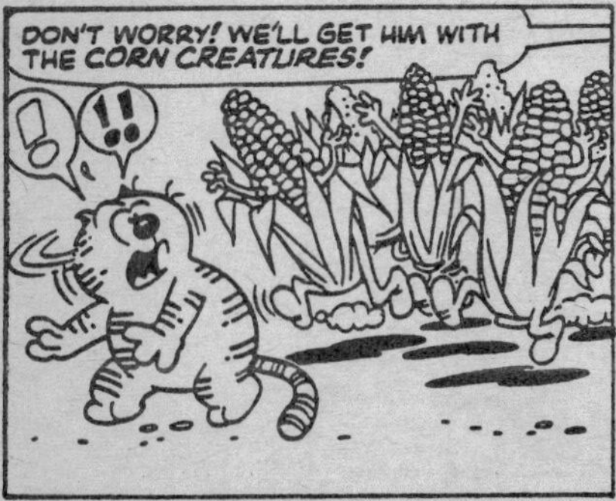
DON'T WORRY! WE'LL GET HIM WITH THE CORN CREATURES!
!
!!

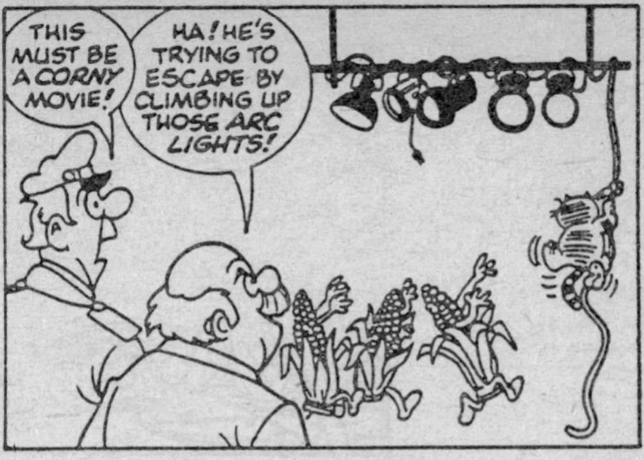
THIS MUST BE A CORNY MOVIE!
HA! HE'S TRYING TO ESCAPE BY CLIMBING UP THOSE ARC LIGHTS!

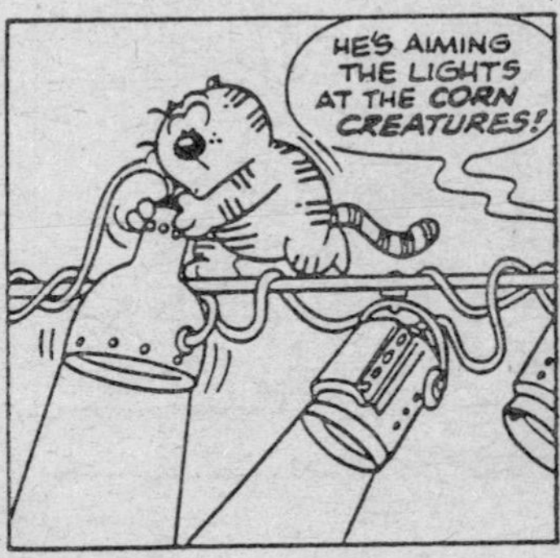
HE'S AIMING THE LIGHTS AT THE CORN CREATURES!

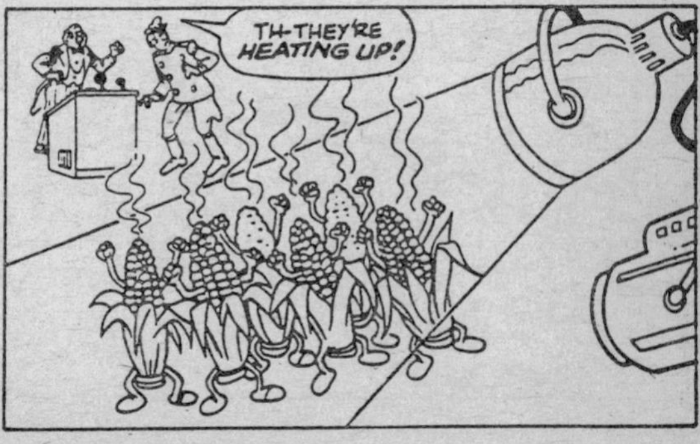
TH-THEY'RE HEATING UP!

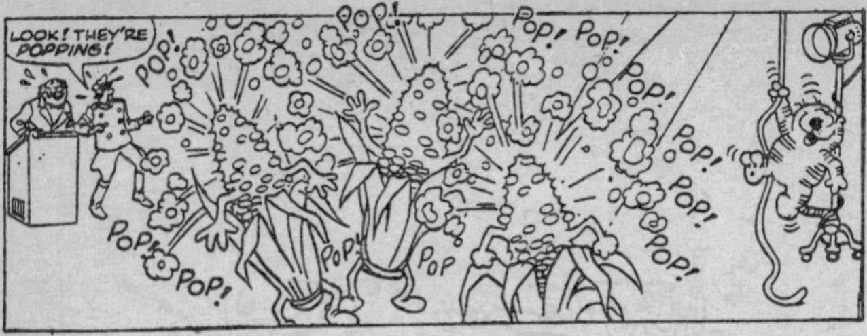
LOOK! THEY'RE POPPING!
POP! POP! POP! POP! POP! POP! POP! POP! POP! POP! POP POP! POP!

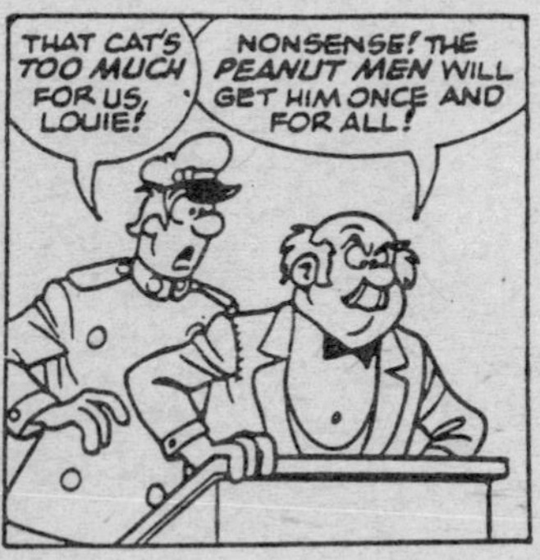
THAT CAT'S TOO MUCH FOR US, LOUIE!
NONSENSE! THE PEANUT MEN WILL GET HIM ONCE AND FOR ALL!

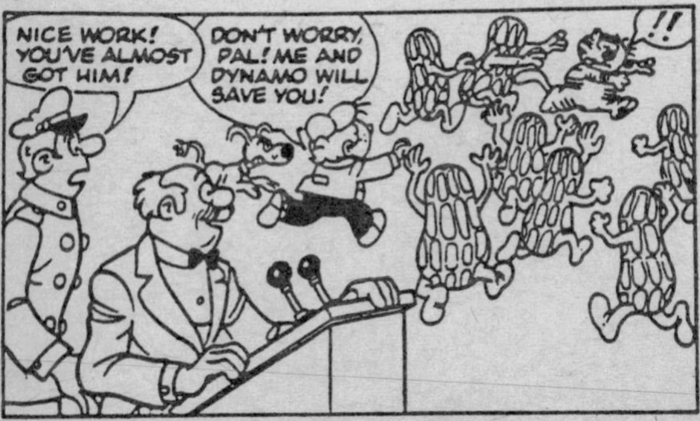
NICE WORK! YOU'VE ALMOST GOT HIM!
DON'T WORRY, PAL! ME AND DYNAMO WILL SAVE YOU!
!!

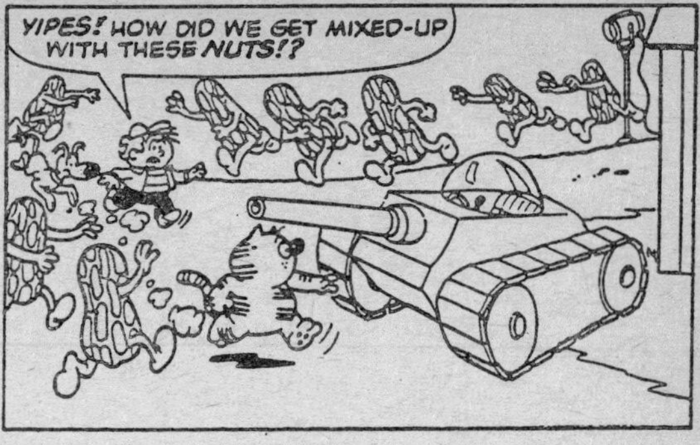
YIPES! HOW DID WE GET MIXED-UP WITH THESE NUTS!?

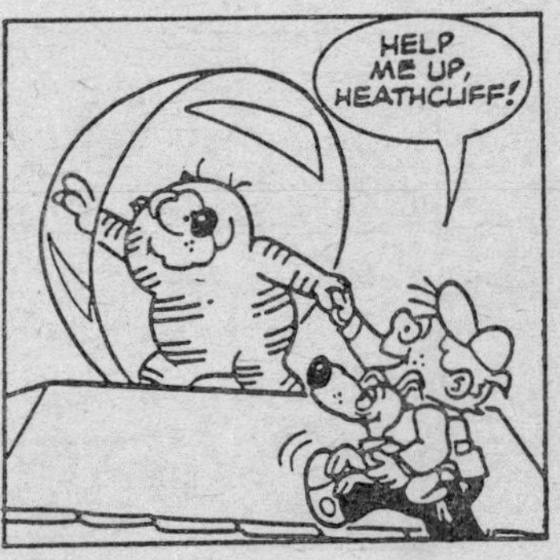
HELP ME UP, HEATHCLIFF!

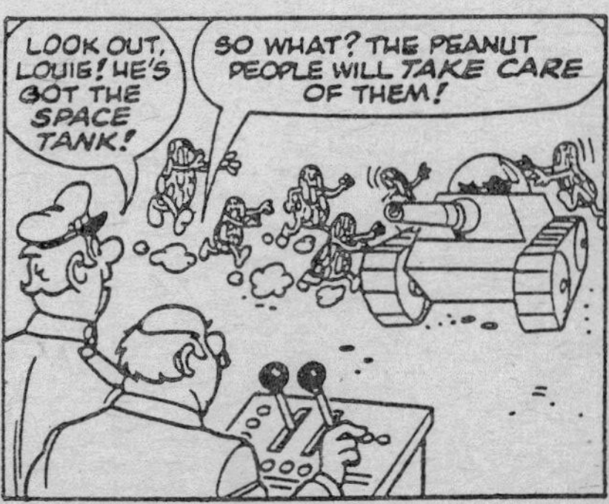
LOOK OUT, LOUIE! HE'S GOT THE SPACE TANK!
SO WHAT? THE PEANUT PEOPLE WILL TAKE CARE OF THEM!

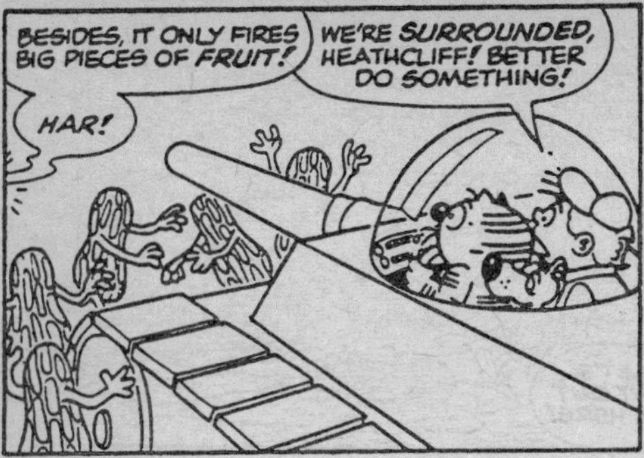
BESIDES, IT ONLY FIRES BIG PIECES OF *FRUIT!*
WE'RE *SURROUNDED,* HEATHCLIFF! BETTER DO SOMETHING!
HAR!

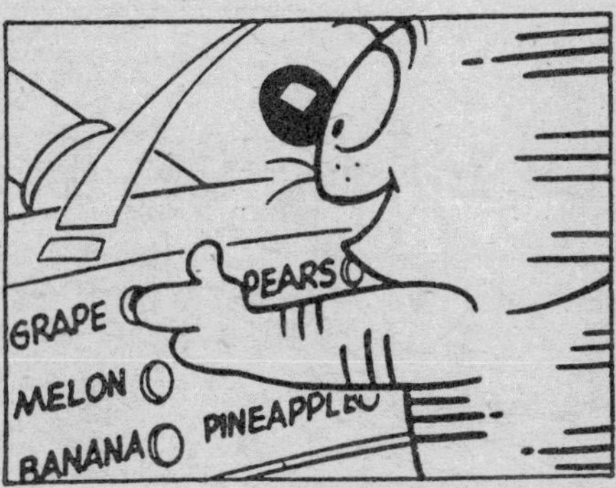
PEARS
GRAPE
MELON
BANANA
PINEAPPLE

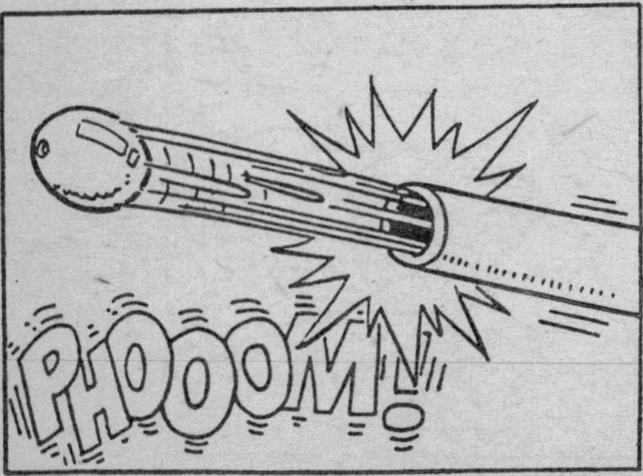
PHOOOM!

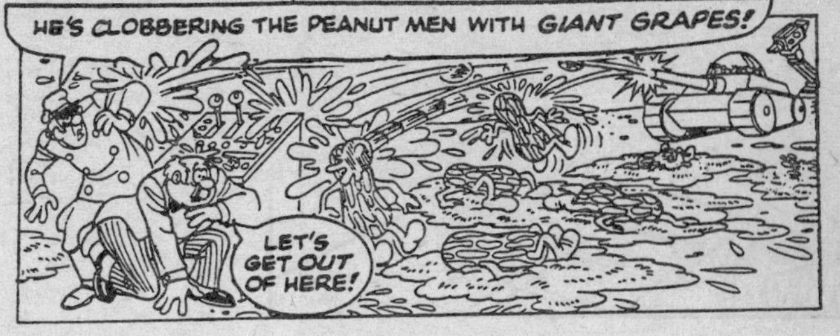
HE'S CLOBBERING THE PEANUT MEN WITH GIANT GRAPES!
LET'S GET OUT OF HERE!

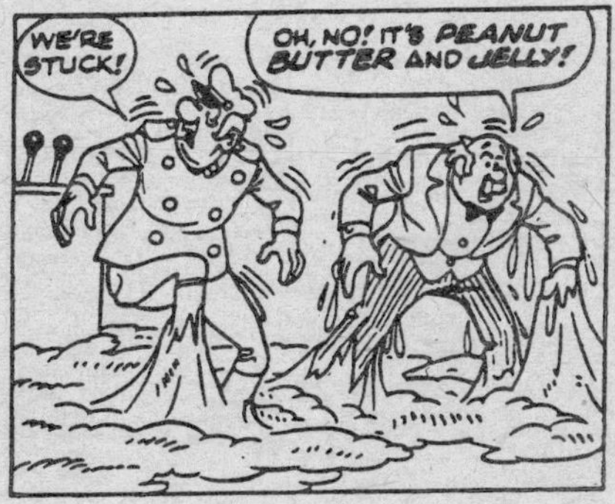
WE'RE STUCK!
OH, NO! IT'S PEANUT BUTTER AND JELLY!

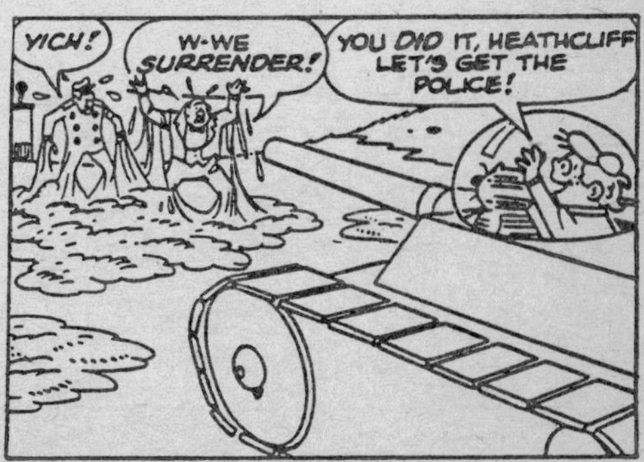
YICH!
W-WE SURRENDER!
YOU DID IT, HEATHCLIFF LET'S GET THE POLICE!

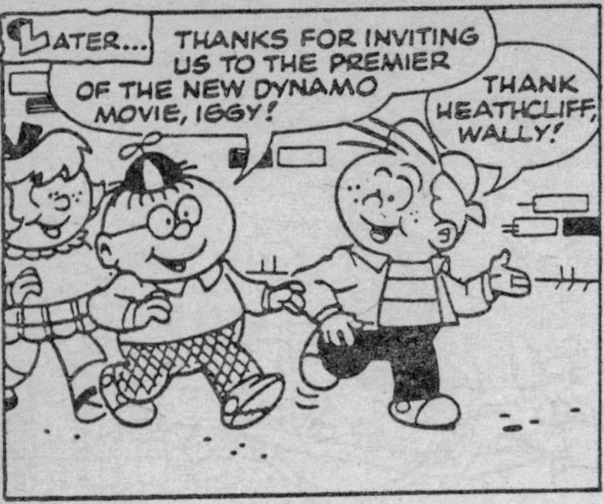
LATER...
THANKS FOR INVITING US TO THE PREMIER OF THE NEW DYNAMO MOVIE, IGGY!
THANK HEATHCLIFF, WALLY!

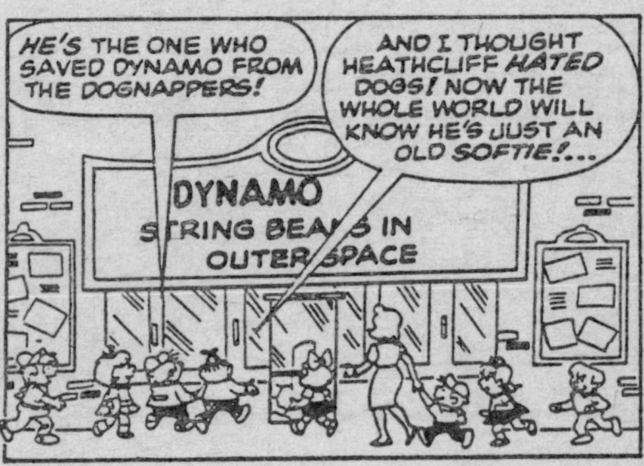
HE'S THE ONE WHO SAVED DYNAMO FROM THE DOGNAPPERS!
AND I THOUGHT HEATHCLIFF HATED DOGS! NOW THE WHOLE WORLD WILL KNOW HE'S JUST AN OLD SOFTIE!...
DYNAMO
STRING BEANS IN OUTER SPACE

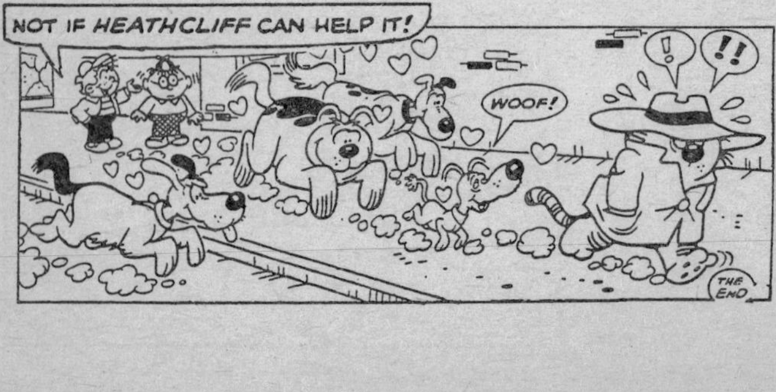
NOT IF HEATHCLIFF CAN HELP IT!
WOOF!
!
!!
THE END

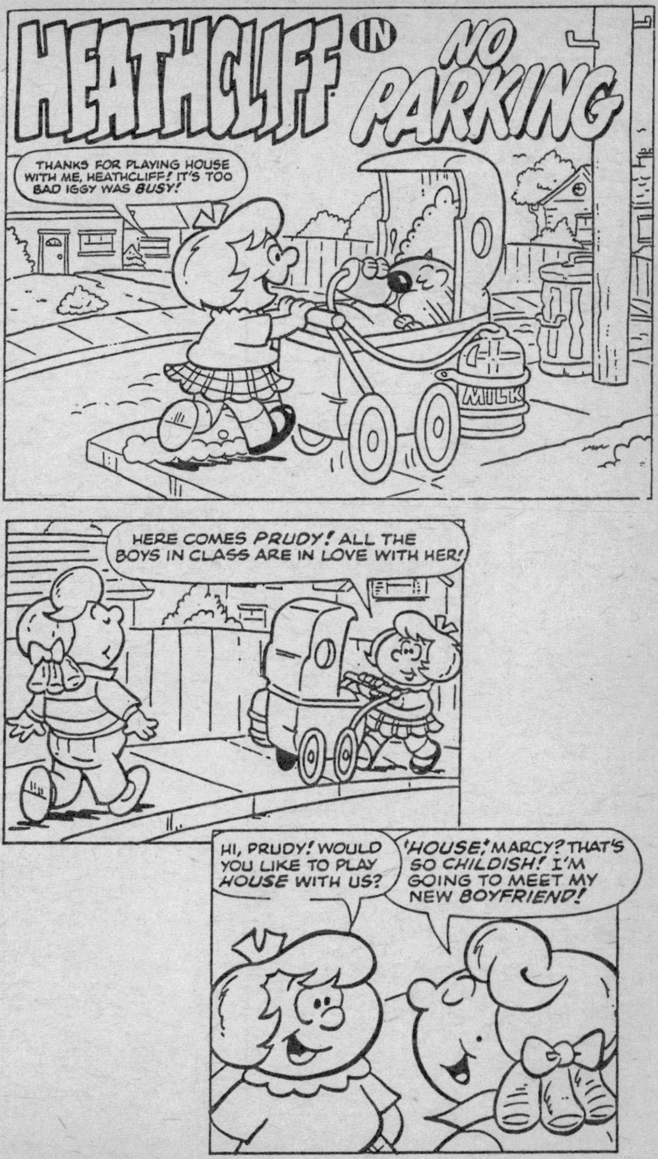
HEATHCLIFF IN NO PARKING
THANKS FOR PLAYING HOUSE WITH ME, HEATHCLIFF! IT'S TOO BAD IGGY WAS BUSY!
MILK
HERE COMES PRUDY! ALL THE BOYS IN CLASS ARE IN LOVE WITH HER!
HI, PRUDY! WOULD YOU LIKE TO PLAY HOUSE WITH US?
'HOUSE,' MARCY? THAT'S SO CHILDISH! I'M GOING TO MEET MY NEW BOYFRIEND!

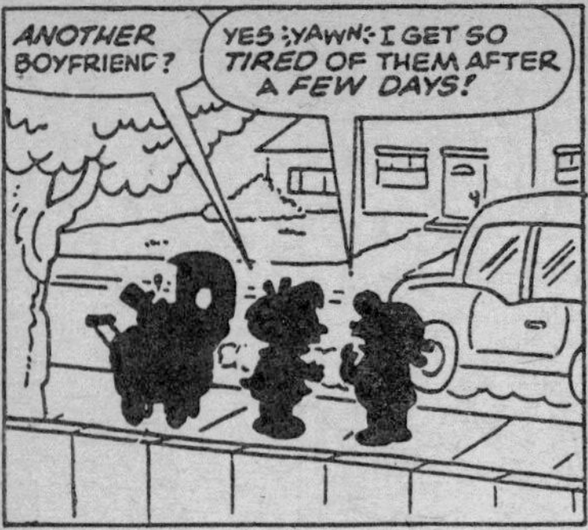
ANOTHER BOYFRIEND?
YES :YAWN: I GET SO TIRED OF THEM AFTER A FEW DAYS!

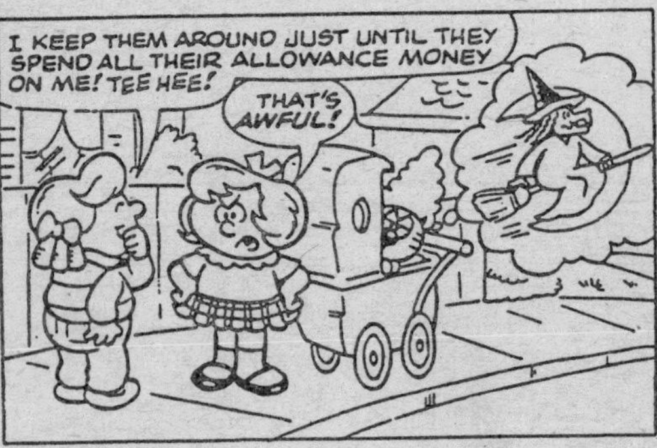
I KEEP THEM AROUND JUST UNTIL THEY SPEND ALL THEIR ALLOWANCE MONEY ON ME! TEE HEE!
THAT'S AWFUL!

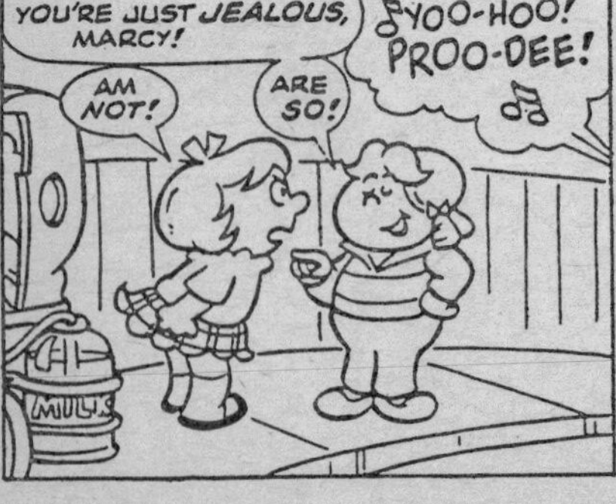
YOU'RE JUST JEALOUS, MARCY!
AM NOT!
ARE SO!
YOO-HOO! PROO-DEE!
MILLS

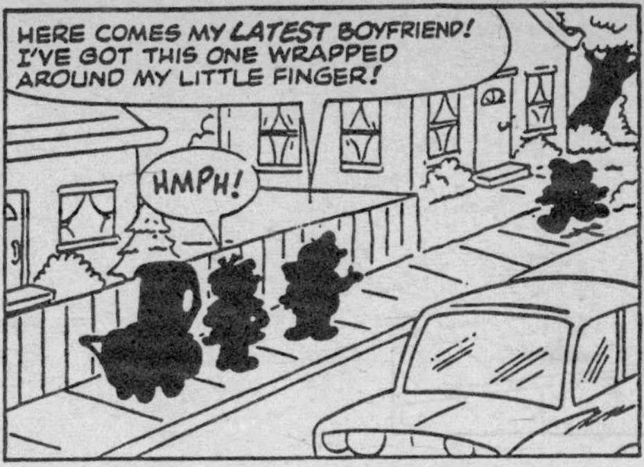
HERE COMES MY *LATEST* BOYFRIEND! I'VE GOT THIS ONE WRAPPED AROUND MY LITTLE FINGER!
HMPH!

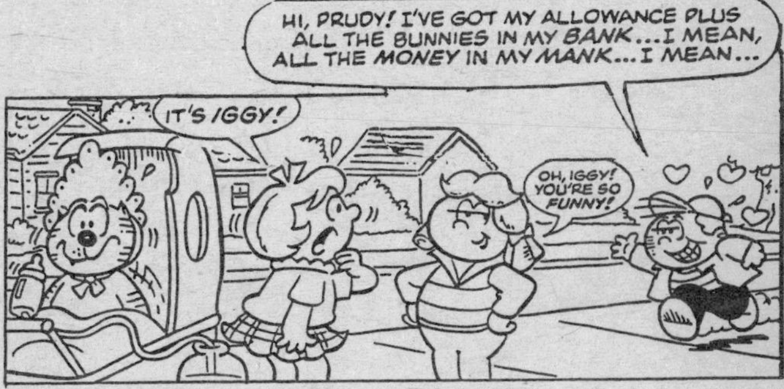
HI, PRUDY! I'VE GOT MY ALLOWANCE PLUS ALL THE BUNNIES IN MY *BANK*... I MEAN, ALL THE *MONEY* IN MY *MANK*... I MEAN...
IT'S *IGGY!*
OH, IGGY! YOU'RE SO *FUNNY!*

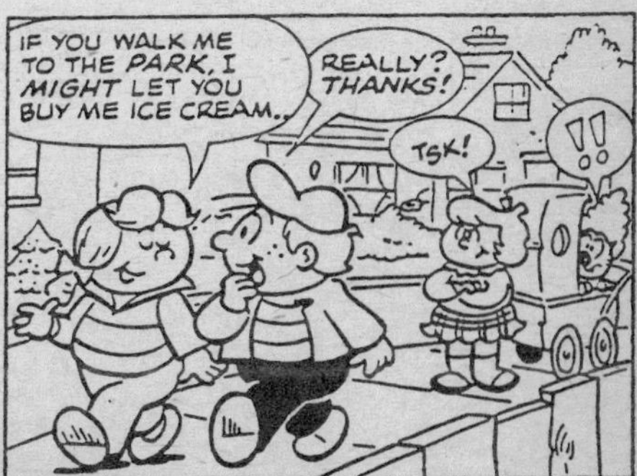
IF YOU WALK ME TO THE *PARK*, I *MIGHT* LET YOU BUY ME ICE CREAM...
REALLY? THANKS!
TSK!
!!

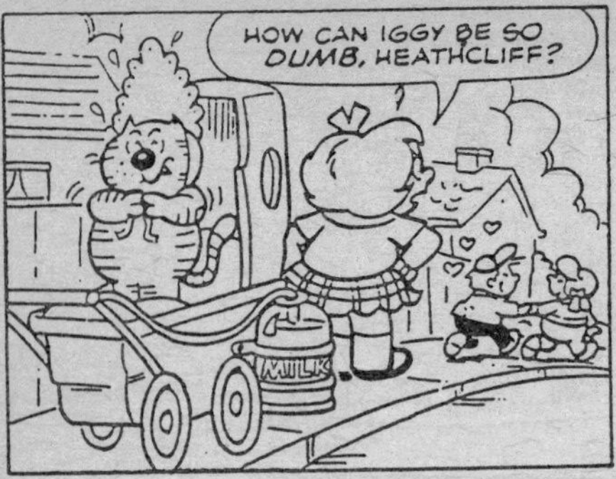
HOW CAN IGGY BE SO *DUMB*, HEATHCLIFF?
MILK

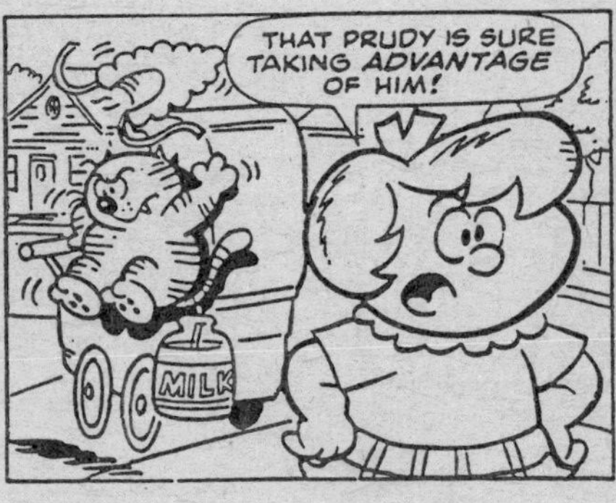
THAT PRUDY IS SURE TAKING *ADVANTAGE* OF HIM!
MILK

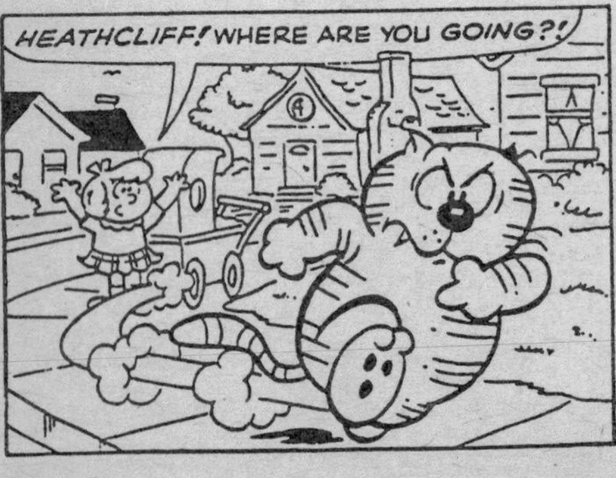
HEATHCLIFF! WHERE ARE YOU *GOING?!*

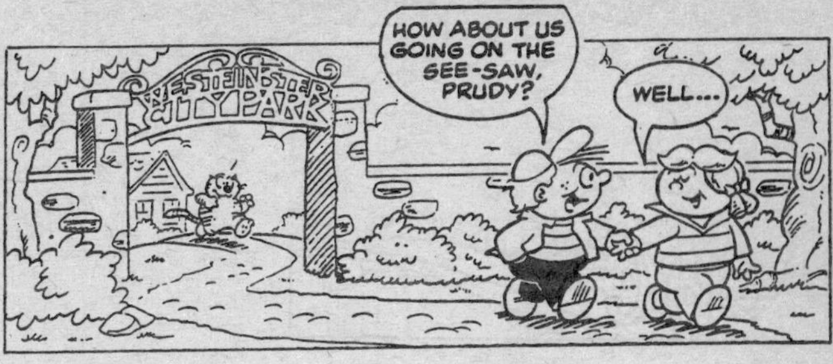
HOW ABOUT US GOING ON THE SEE-SAW, PRUDY?
WELL...

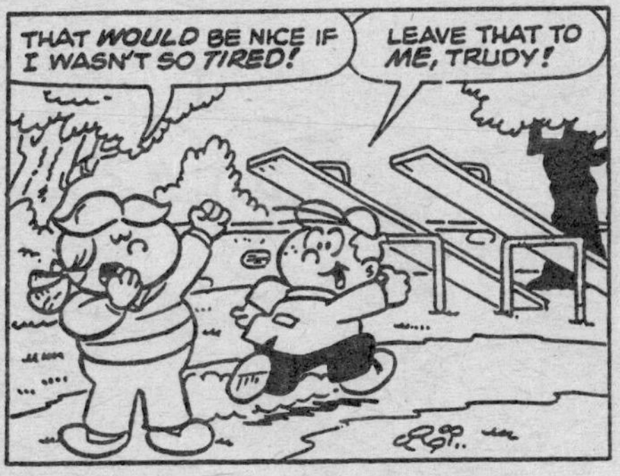
THAT *WOULD* BE NICE IF I WASN'T SO *TIRED!*
LEAVE THAT TO *ME*, TRUDY!

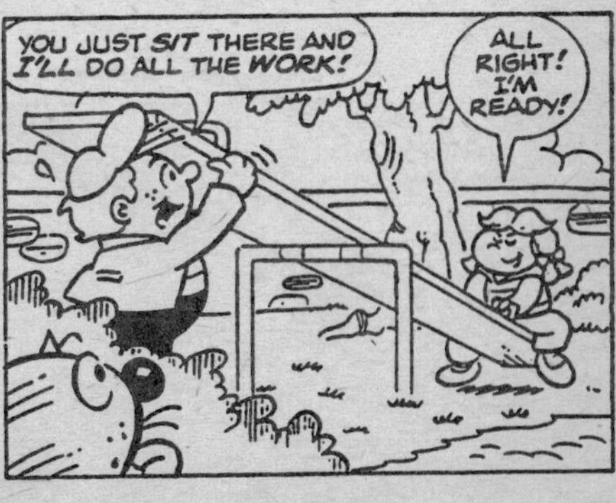
YOU JUST *SIT* THERE AND *I'LL* DO ALL THE *WORK!*
ALL RIGHT! I'M READY!

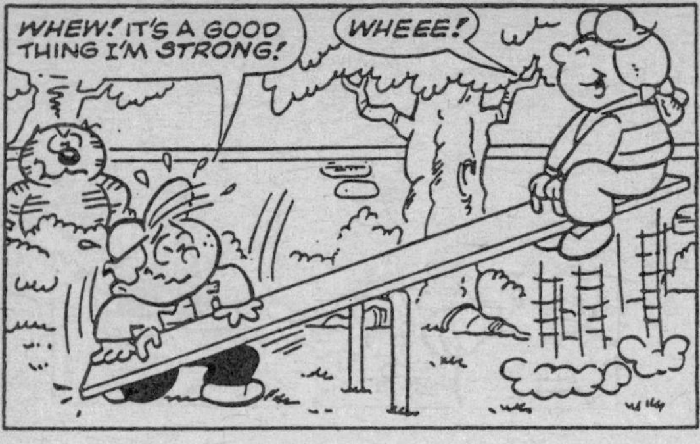
WHEW! IT'S A GOOD THING I'M STRONG!
WHEEE!

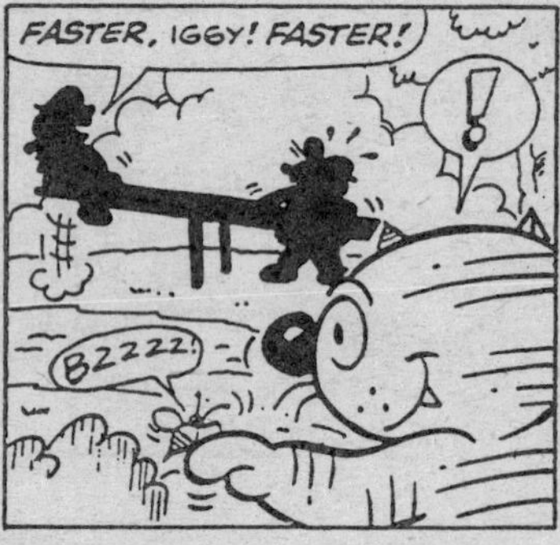
FASTER, IGGY! FASTER!
!
BZZZZ!

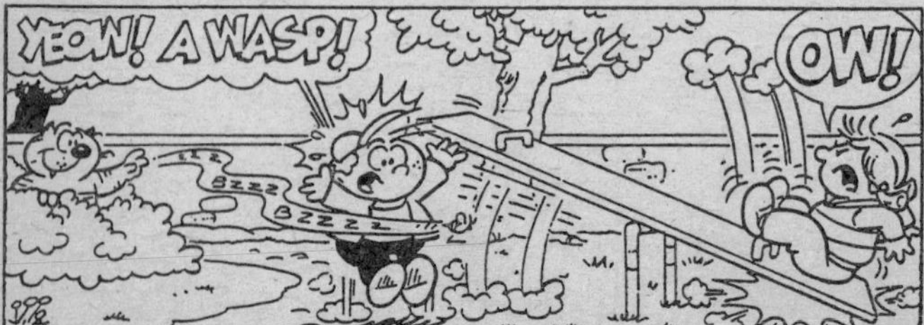
YEOW! A WASP!
BZZZ
BZZZZ
OW!

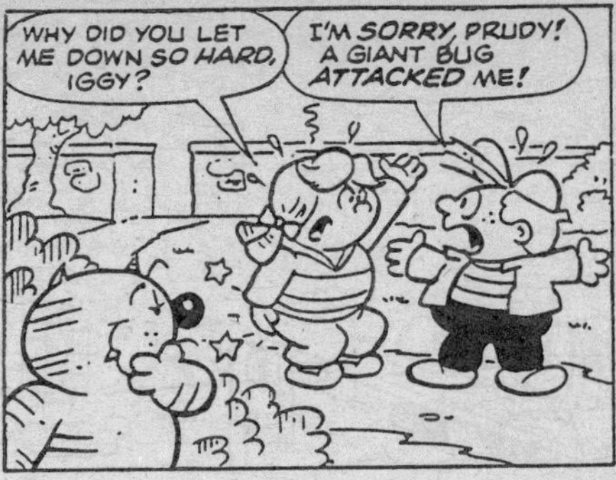
WHY DID YOU LET ME DOWN SO HARD, IGGY?
I'M SORRY, PRUDY! A GIANT BUG ATTACKED ME!

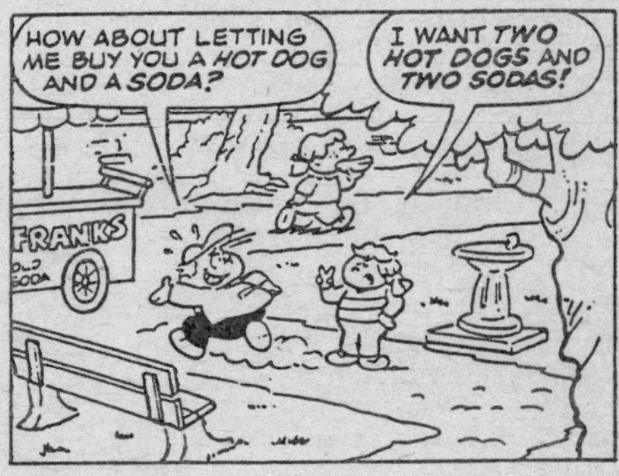
HOW ABOUT LETTING ME BUY YOU A HOT DOG AND A SODA?
I WANT TWO HOT DOGS AND TWO SODAS!
FRANKS

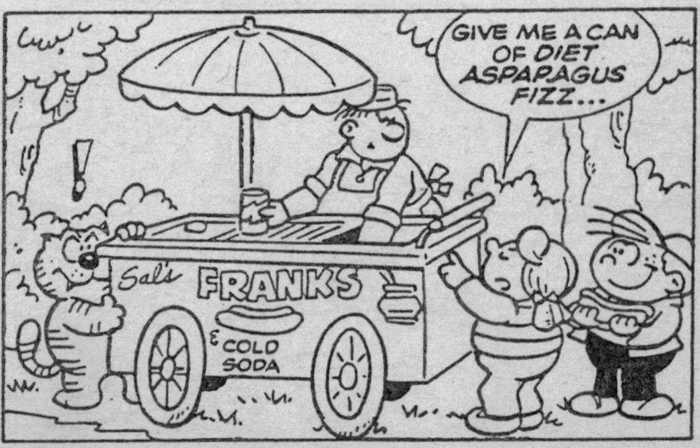
GIVE ME A CAN OF DIET ASPARAGUS FIZZ...
!
Sal's FRANKS
COLD SODA

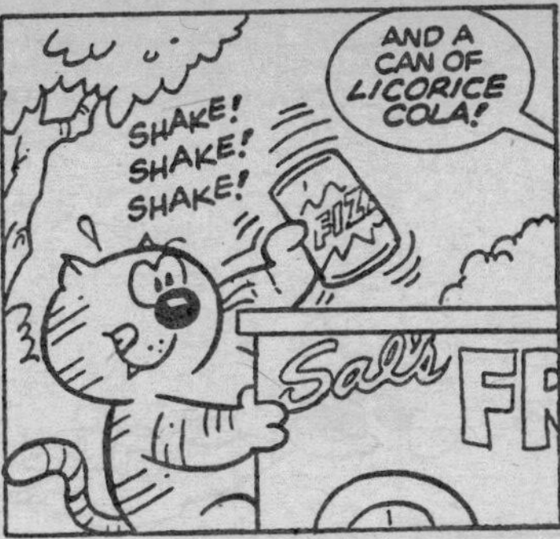
AND A CAN OF LICORICE COLA!
SHAKE! SHAKE! SHAKE!
FIZZ
Sal's FR

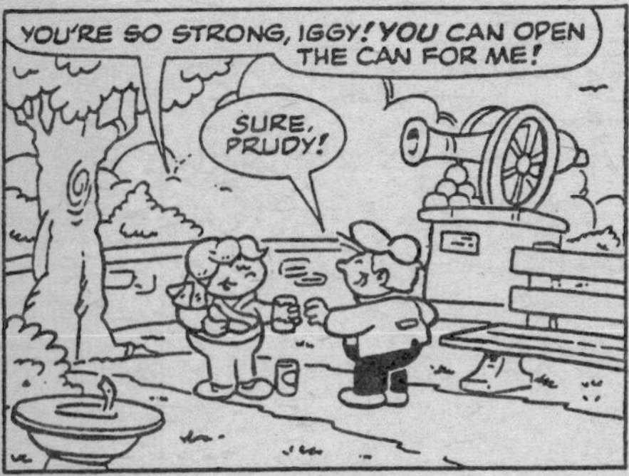
YOU'RE SO STRONG, IGGY! YOU CAN OPEN THE CAN FOR ME!
SURE, PRUDY!

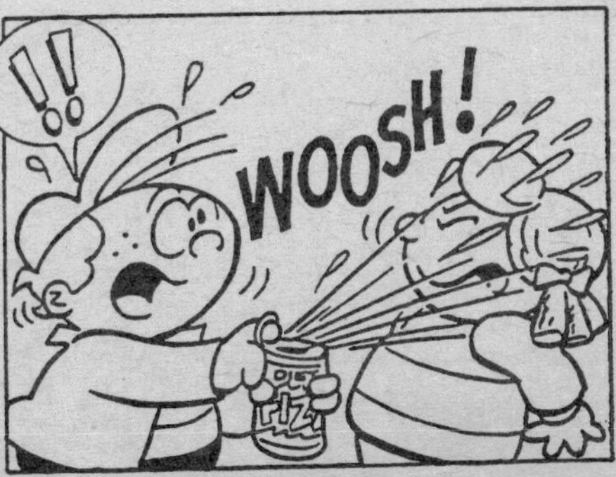
!!
WOOSH!
DIET FIZZ

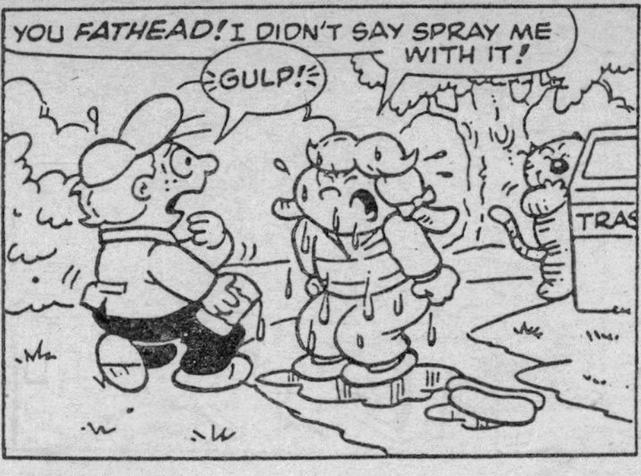
YOU FATHEAD! I DIDN'T SAY SPRAY ME WITH IT!
GULP!
TRAS

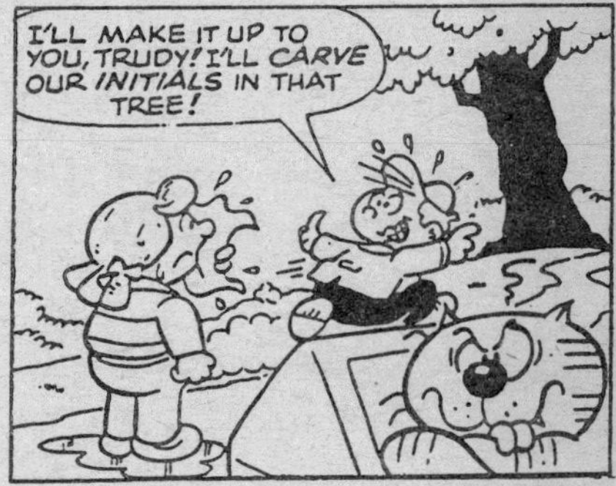
I'LL MAKE IT UP TO YOU, TRUDY! I'LL CARVE OUR INITIALS IN THAT TREE!

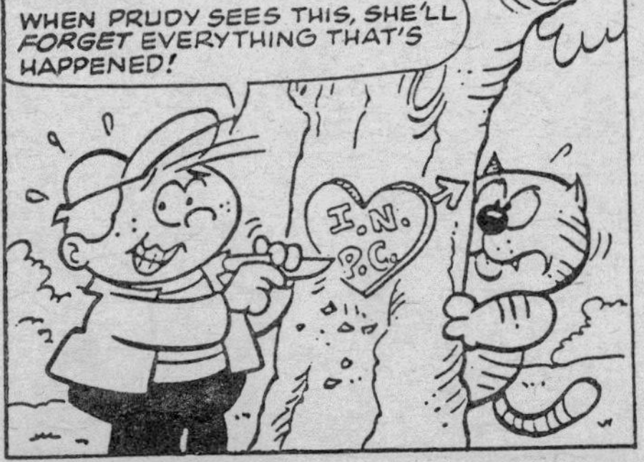
WHEN PRUDY SEES THIS, SHE'LL FORGET EVERYTHING THAT'S HAPPENED!
I. N.
P. C.

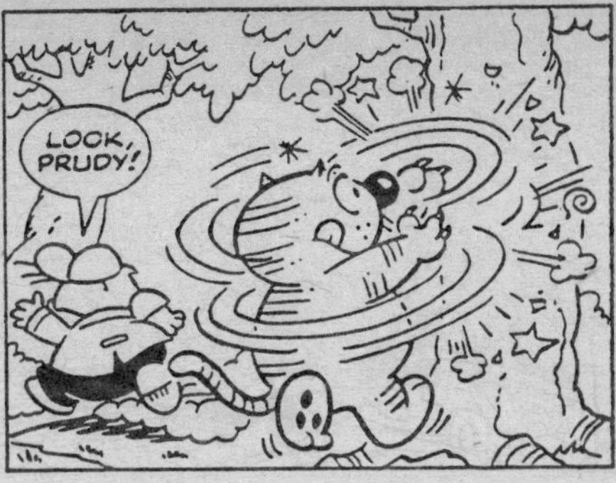
LOOK, PRUDY!

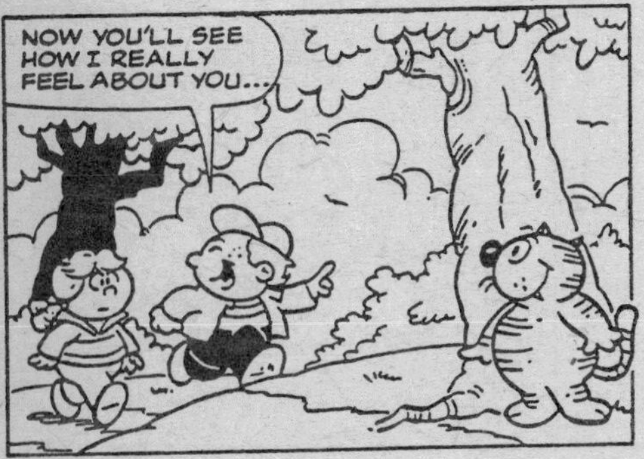
NOW YOU'LL SEE HOW I REALLY FEEL ABOUT YOU...

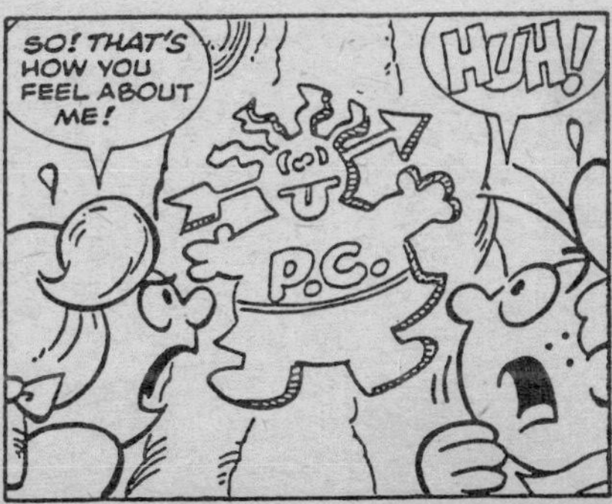
SO! THAT'S HOW YOU FEEL ABOUT ME!
HUH!
P.C.

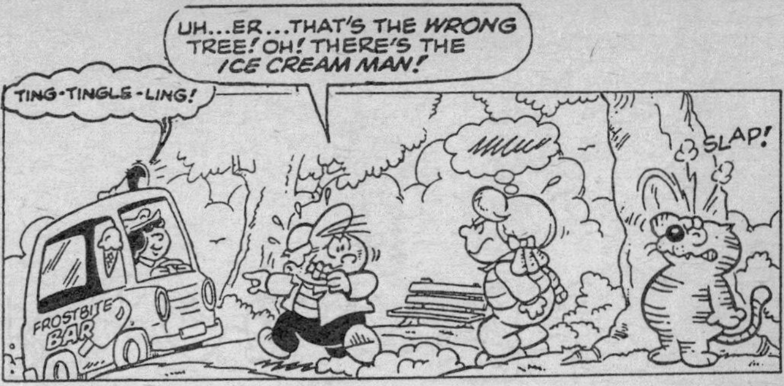
TING-TINGLE-LING!
UH...ER...THAT'S THE *WRONG* TREE! OH! THERE'S THE *ICE CREAM MAN!*
SLAP!
FROSTBITE BAR

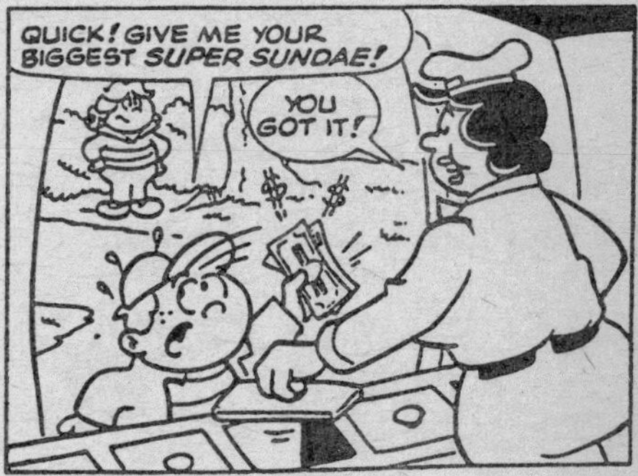
QUICK! GIVE ME YOUR BIGGEST *SUPER SUNDAE!*
YOU GOT IT!

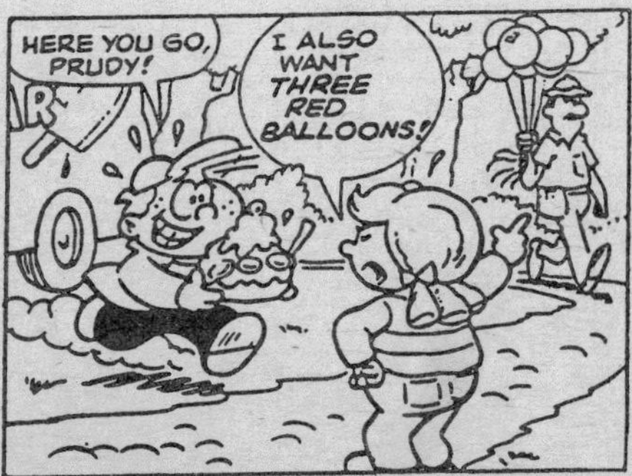
HERE YOU GO, PRUDY!
I ALSO WANT *THREE RED BALLOONS!*

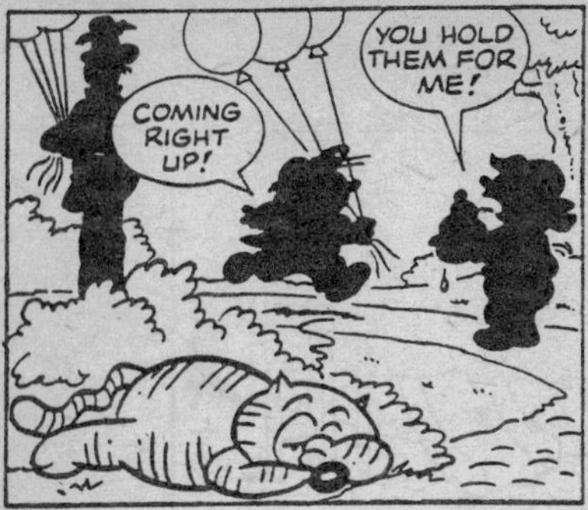
COMING RIGHT UP!
YOU HOLD THEM FOR ME!

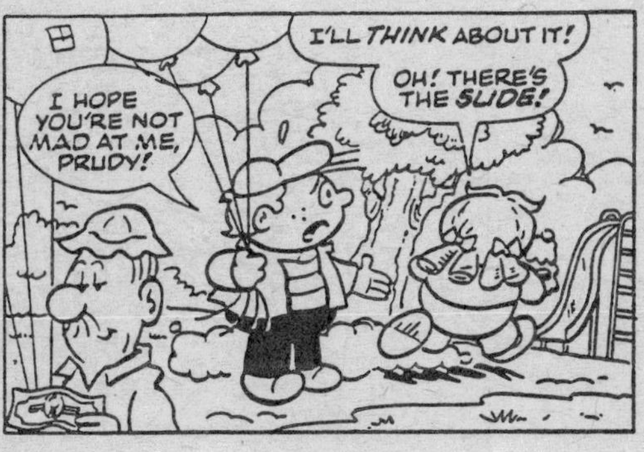
I HOPE YOU'RE NOT MAD AT ME, PRUDY!
I'LL *THINK* ABOUT IT!
OH! THERE'S THE *SLIDE!*

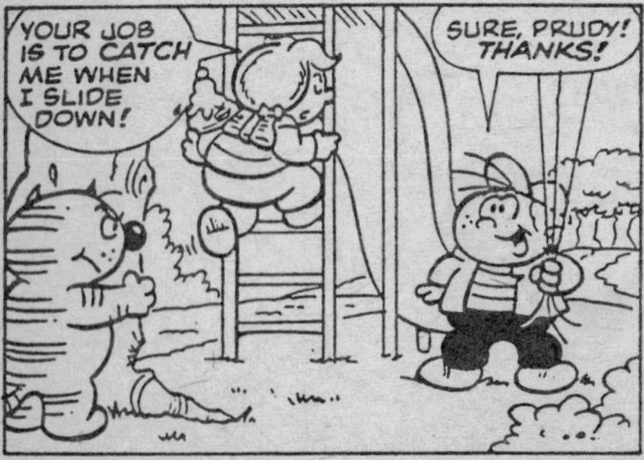
YOUR JOB IS TO CATCH ME WHEN I SLIDE DOWN!
SURE, PRUDY! *THANKS!*

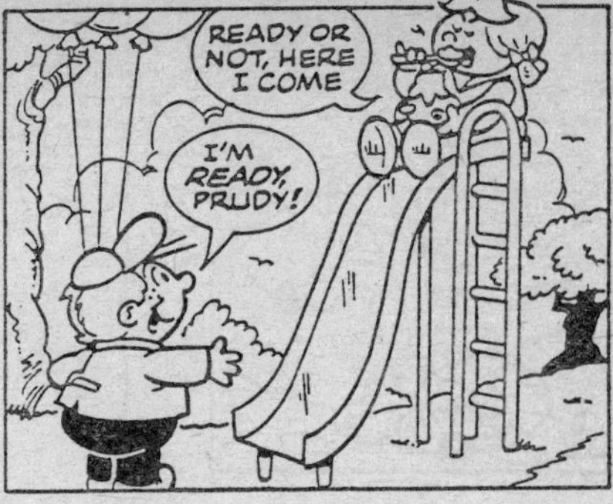
READY OR NOT, HERE I COME
I'M *READY*, PRUDY!

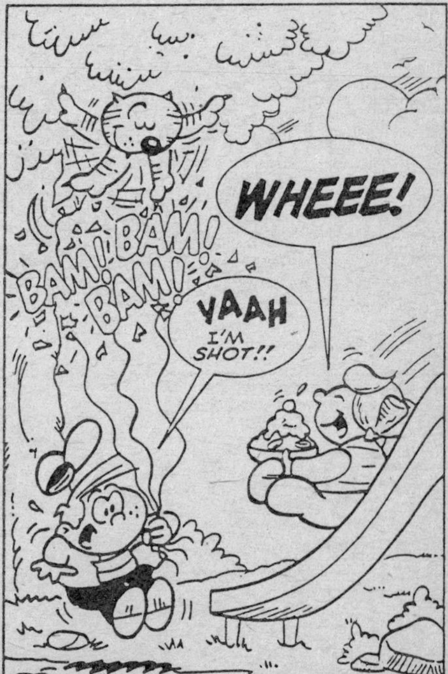
WHEEE!
BAM! BAM! BAM! BAM!
YAAH I'M *SHOT!!*

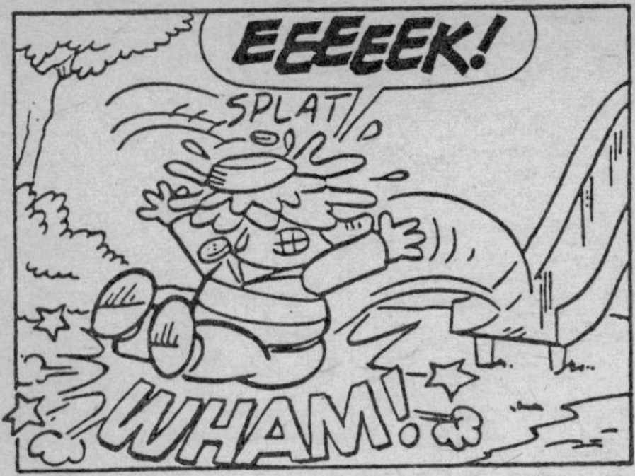
EEEEEK!
SPLAT
WHAM!

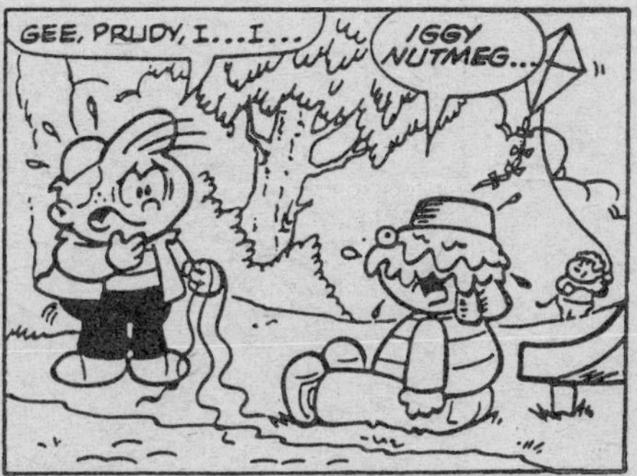
GEE, PRUDY, I...I...
IGGY NUTMEG...

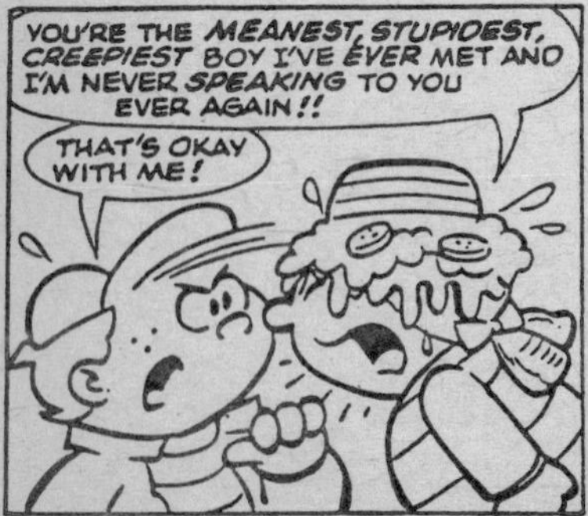
YOU'RE THE MEANEST, STUPIDEST, CREEPIEST BOY I'VE EVER MET AND I'M NEVER SPEAKING TO YOU EVER AGAIN!!
THAT'S OKAY WITH ME!

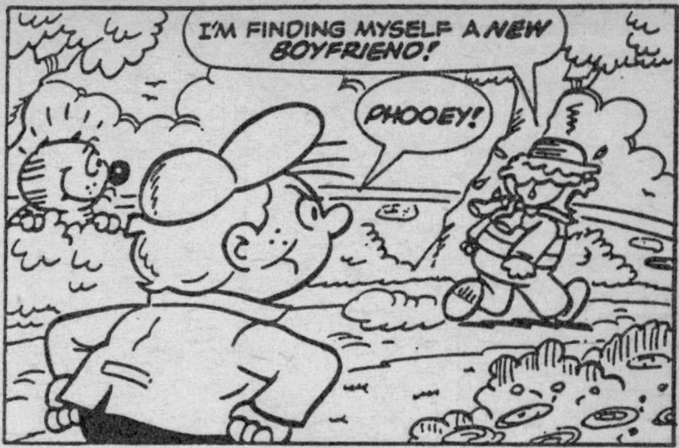
I'M FINDING MYSELF A *NEW* BOYFRIEND!
PHOOEY!

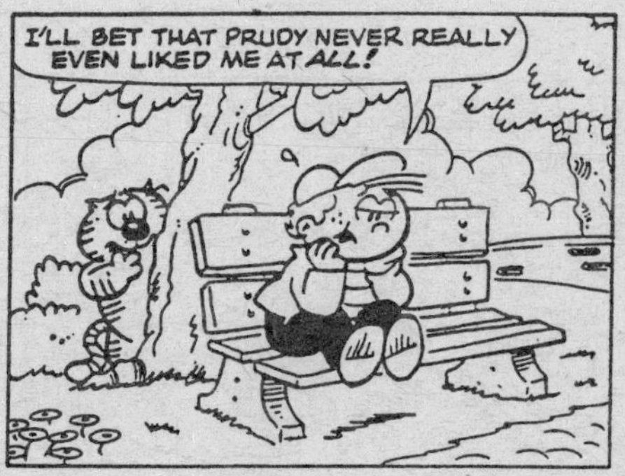
I'LL BET THAT PRUDY NEVER REALLY EVEN LIKED ME AT *ALL!*

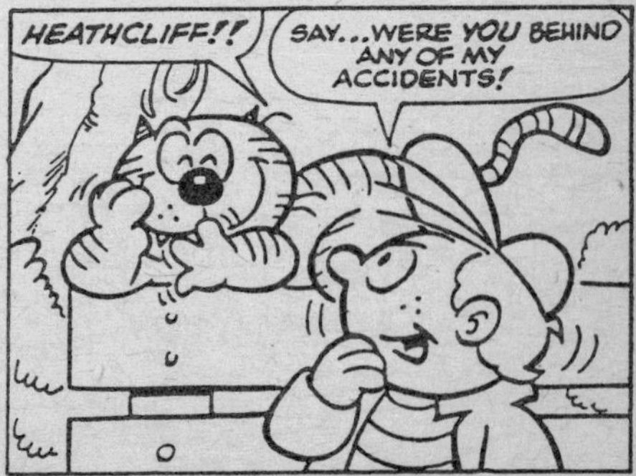
HEATHCLIFF!!
SAY...WERE *YOU* BEHIND ANY OF MY ACCIDENTS!

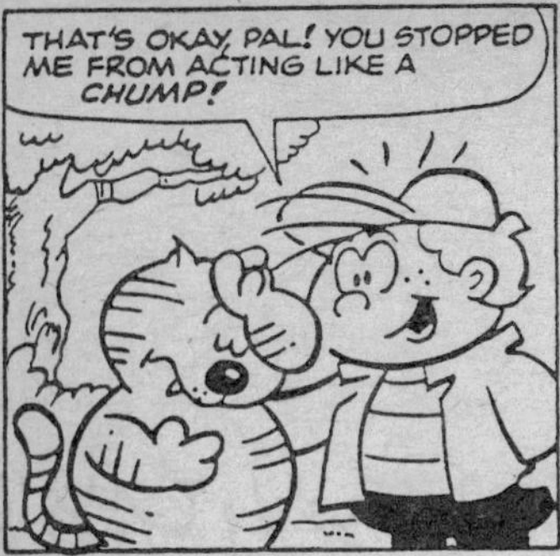
THAT'S OKAY, PAL! YOU STOPPED ME FROM ACTING LIKE A *CHUMP!*

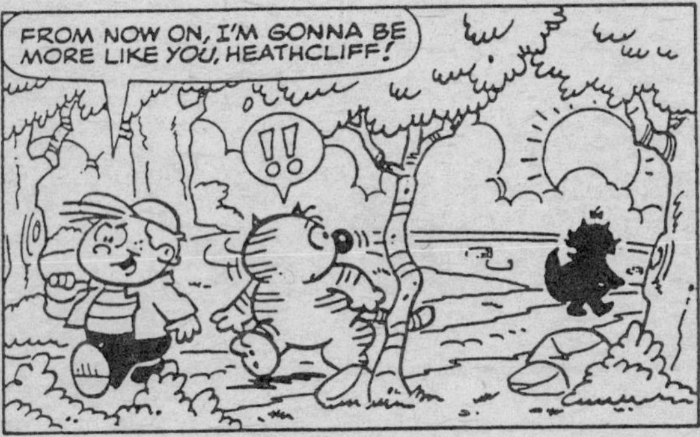
FROM NOW ON, I'M GONNA BE MORE LIKE *YOU*, HEATHCLIFF!
!!

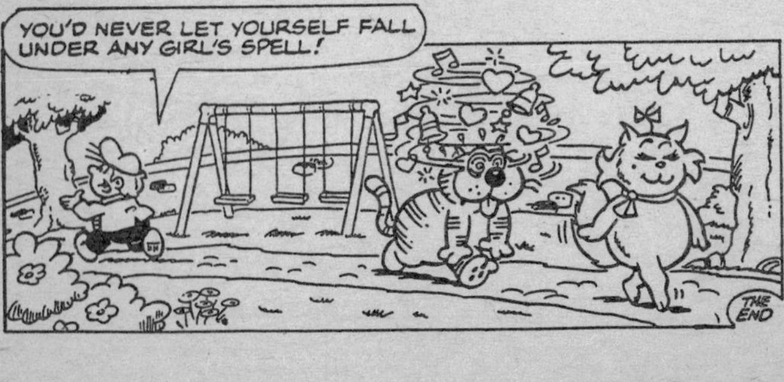
YOU'D NEVER LET YOURSELF FALL UNDER ANY GIRL'S SPELL!
THE END

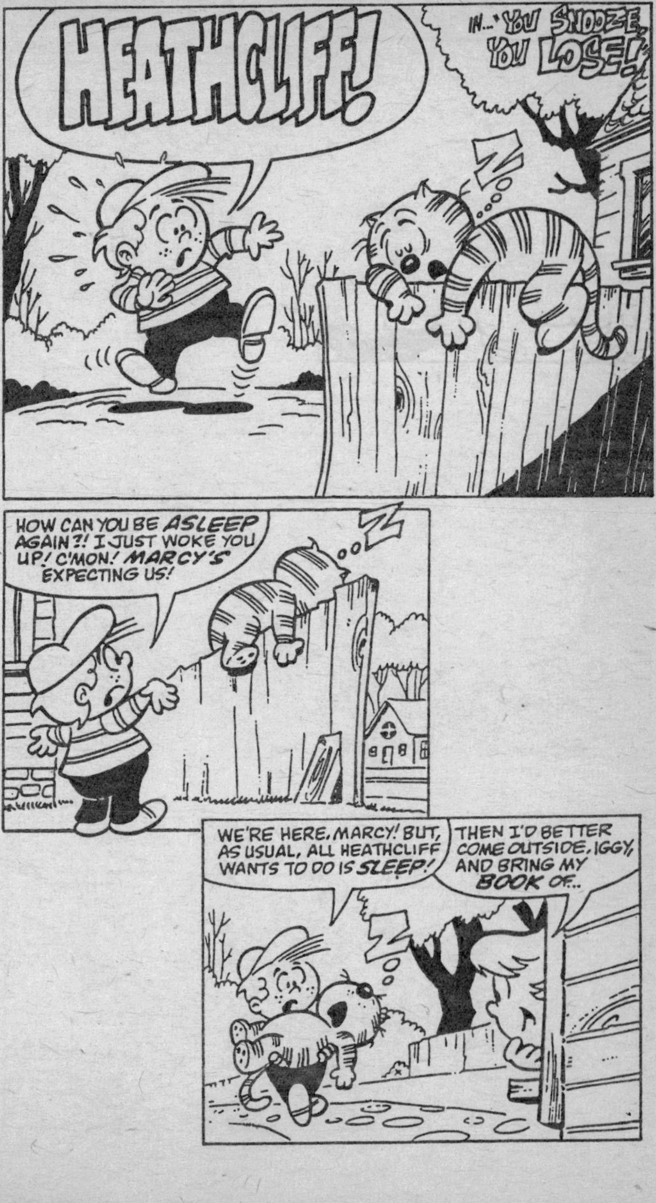
HEATHCLIFF!
IN... "YOU SNOOZE, YOU LOSE!"
Z
HOW CAN YOU BE ASLEEP AGAIN?! I JUST WOKE YOU UP! C'MON! MARCY'S EXPECTING US!
Z
WE'RE HERE, MARCY! BUT, AS USUAL, ALL HEATHCLIFF WANTS TO DO IS SLEEP!
THEN I'D BETTER COME OUTSIDE, IGGY, AND BRING MY BOOK OF...
Z

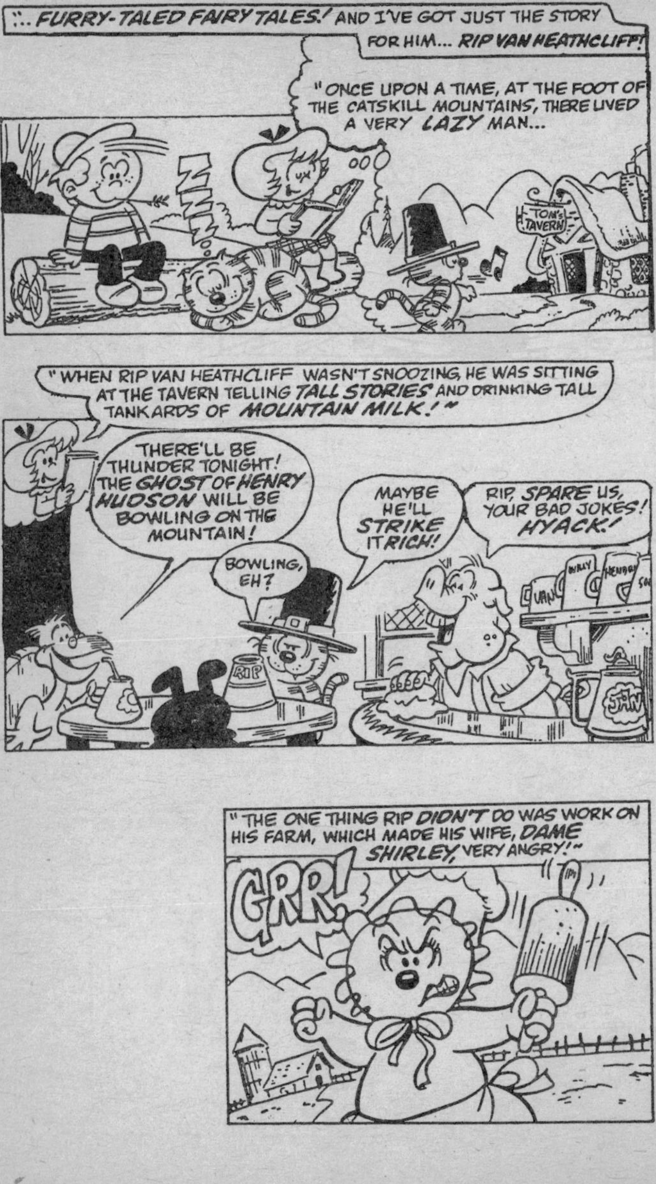
"... FURRY-TALED FAIRY TALES!" AND I'VE GOT JUST THE STORY FOR HIM... RIP VAN HEATHCLIFF!
"ONCE UPON A TIME, AT THE FOOT OF THE CATSKILL MOUNTAINS, THERE LIVED A VERY LAZY MAN...
ZZZ
TOM'S TAVERN
"WHEN RIP VAN HEATHCLIFF WASN'T SNOOZING, HE WAS SITTING AT THE TAVERN TELLING TALL STORIES AND DRINKING TALL TANKARDS OF MOUNTAIN MILK!"
THERE'LL BE THUNDER TONIGHT! THE GHOST OF HENRY HUDSON WILL BE BOWLING ON THE MOUNTAIN!
BOWLING, EH?
MAYBE HE'LL STRIKE IT RICH!
RIP, SPARE US, YOUR BAD JOKES! HYACK!
RIP
VAN
"THE ONE THING RIP DIDN'T DO WAS WORK ON HIS FARM, WHICH MADE HIS WIFE, DAME SHIRLEY, VERY ANGRY!"
GRR!

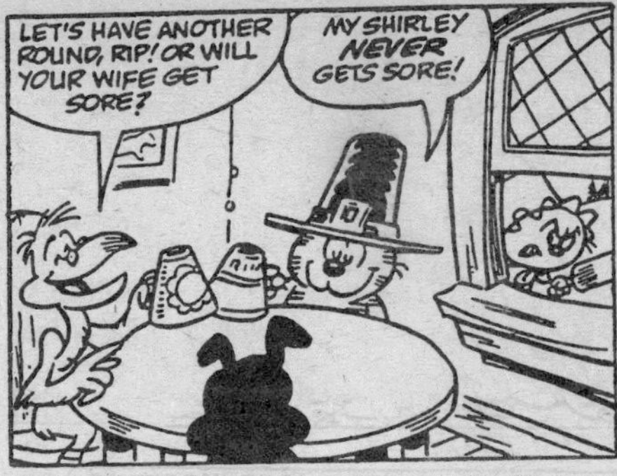
LET'S HAVE ANOTHER ROUND, RIP! OR WILL YOUR WIFE GET SORE?
MY SHIRLEY *NEVER* GETS SORE!

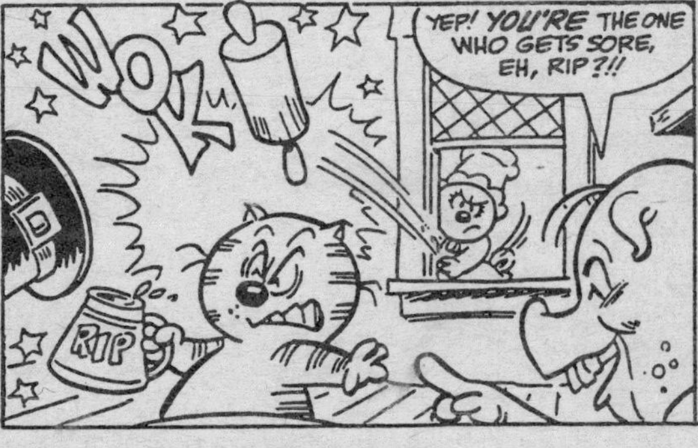
WOK
YEP! *YOU'RE* THE ONE WHO GETS SORE, EH, RIP?!!
RIP

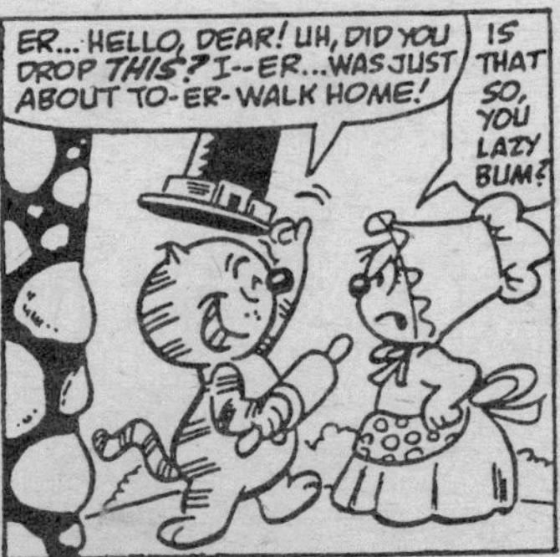
ER... HELLO, DEAR! UH, DID YOU DROP *THIS?* I--ER...WAS JUST ABOUT TO-ER-WALK HOME!
IS THAT SO, YOU LAZY BUM?

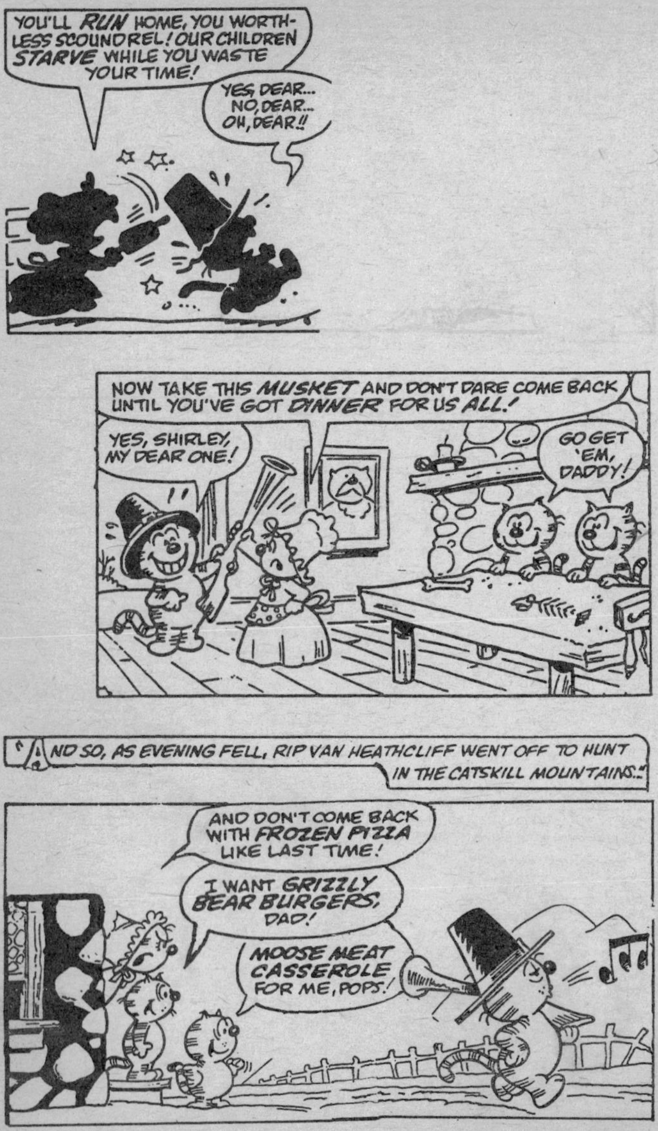
YOU'LL RUN HOME, YOU WORTHLESS SCOUNDREL! OUR CHILDREN STARVE WHILE YOU WASTE YOUR TIME!
YES, DEAR... NO, DEAR... OH, DEAR!!
NOW TAKE THIS MUSKET AND DON'T DARE COME BACK UNTIL YOU'VE GOT DINNER FOR US ALL!
YES, SHIRLEY, MY DEAR ONE!
GO GET 'EM, DADDY!
AND SO, AS EVENING FELL, RIP VAN HEATHCLIFF WENT OFF TO HUNT IN THE CATSKILL MOUNTAINS...
AND DON'T COME BACK WITH FROZEN PIZZA LIKE LAST TIME!
I WANT GRIZZLY BEAR BURGERS, DAD!
MOOSE MEAT CASSEROLE FOR ME, POPS!

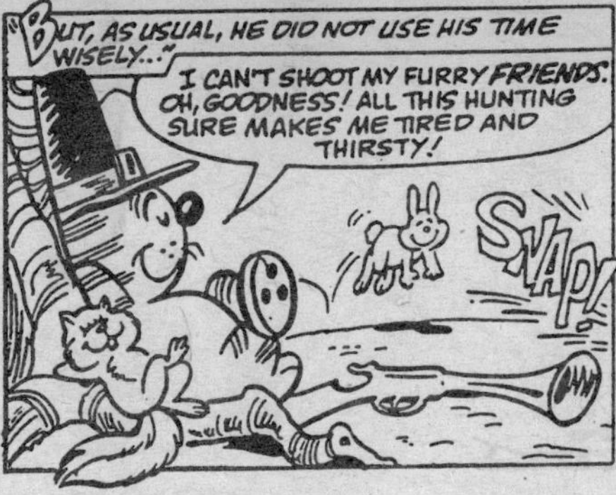
"But, as usual, he did not use his time wisely..."
I can't shoot my furry friends! Oh, goodness! All this hunting sure makes me tired and thirsty!
SNAP!

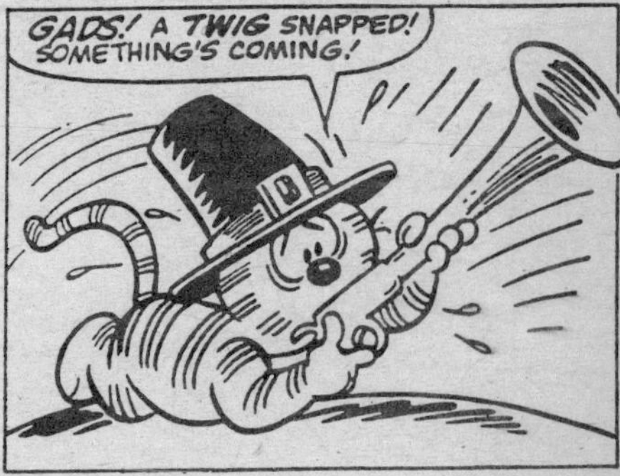
GADS! A TWIG SNAPPED! SOMETHING'S COMING!

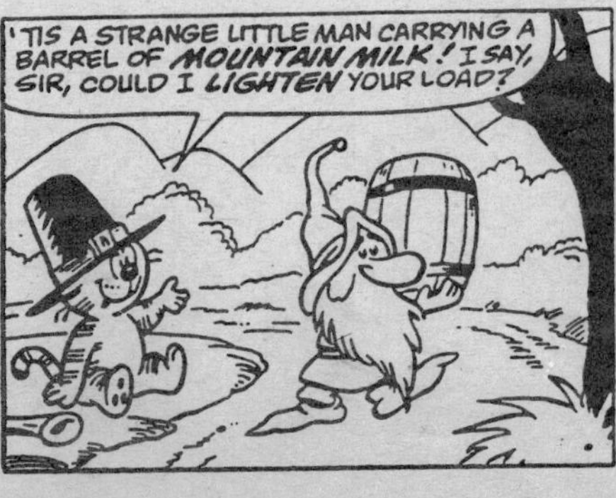
'TIS A STRANGE LITTLE MAN CARRYING A BARREL OF MOUNTAIN MILK! I SAY, SIR, COULD I LIGHTEN YOUR LOAD?

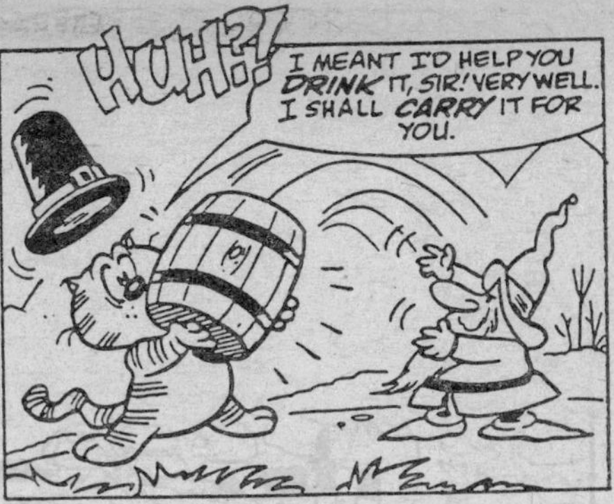
HUH?!
I MEANT I'D HELP YOU DRINK IT, SIR! VERY WELL. I SHALL CARRY IT FOR YOU.

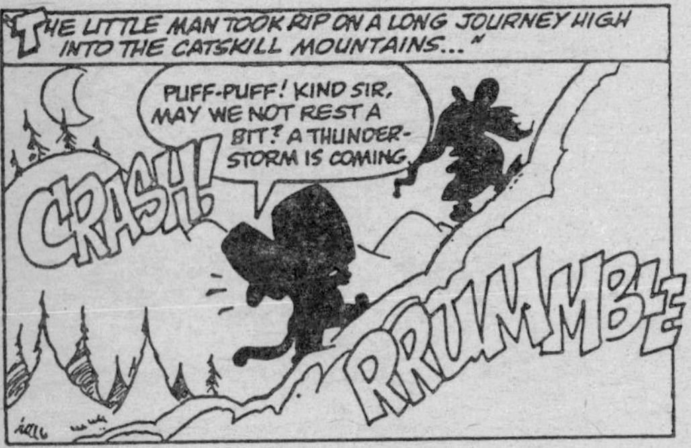
"THE LITTLE MAN TOOK RIP ON A LONG JOURNEY HIGH INTO THE CATSKILL MOUNTAINS..."
PUFF-PUFF! KIND SIR, MAY WE NOT REST A BIT? A THUNDER-STORM IS COMING.
CRASH!
RRUMMBLE

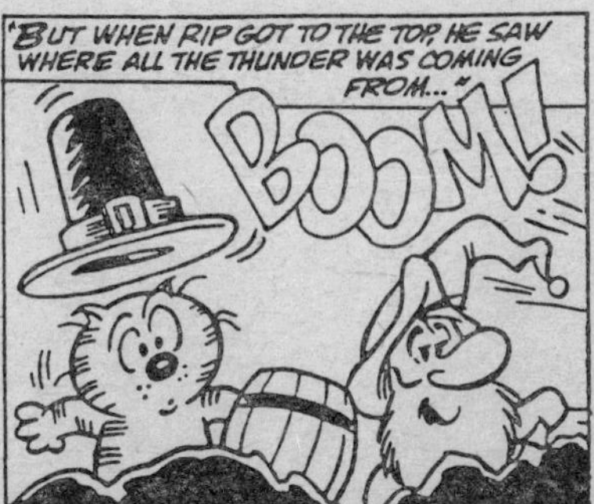
"BUT WHEN RIP GOT TO THE TOP, HE SAW WHERE ALL THE THUNDER WAS COMING FROM..."
BOOOM!

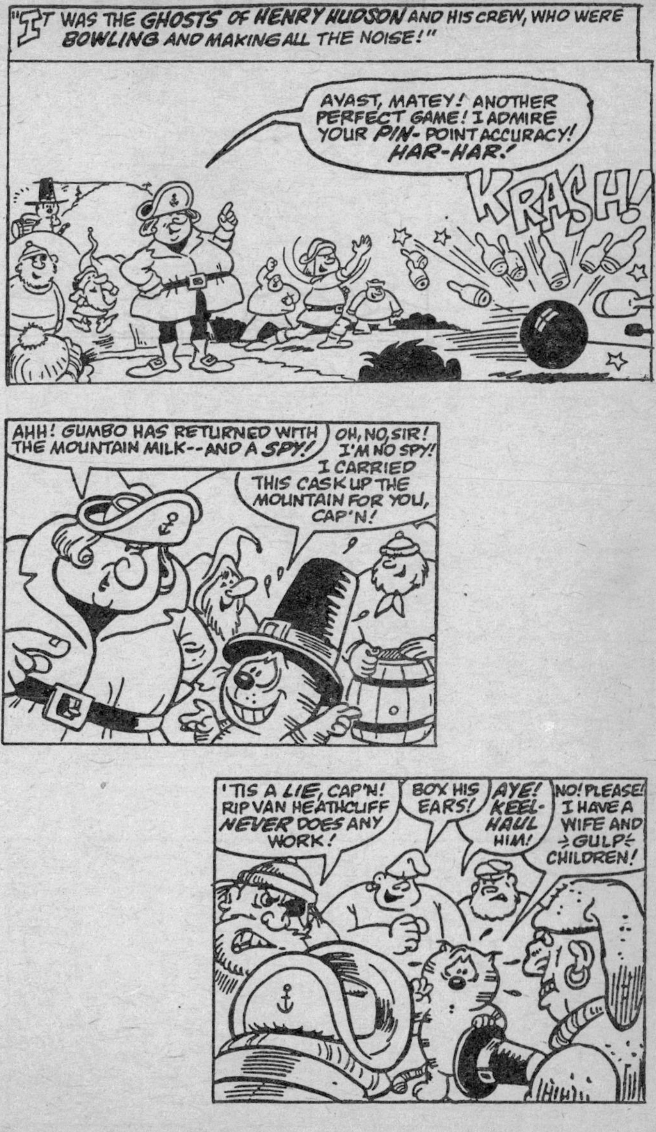
"IT WAS THE GHOSTS OF HENRY HUDSON AND HIS CREW, WHO WERE BOWLING AND MAKING ALL THE NOISE!"
AVAST, MATEY! ANOTHER PERFECT GAME! I ADMIRE YOUR PIN-POINT ACCURACY! HAR-HAR!
KRASH!
AHH! GUMBO HAS RETURNED WITH THE MOUNTAIN MILK--AND A SPY!
OH, NO, SIR! I'M NO SPY! I CARRIED THIS CASK UP THE MOUNTAIN FOR YOU, CAP'N!
'TIS A LIE, CAP'N! RIP VAN HEATHCLIFF NEVER DOES ANY WORK!
BOX HIS EARS!
AYE! KEEL-HAUL HIM!
NO! PLEASE! I HAVE A WIFE AND GULP CHILDREN!

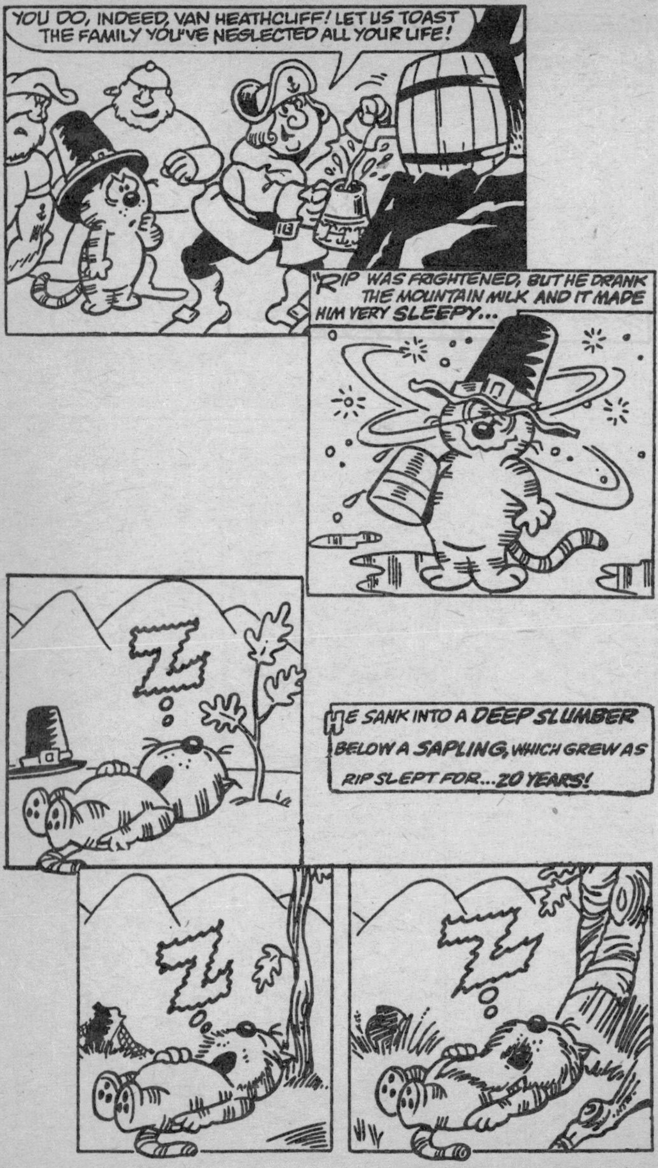
YOU DO, INDEED, VAN HEATHCLIFF! LET US TOAST THE FAMILY YOU'VE NEGLECTED ALL YOUR LIFE!
"RIP WAS FRIGHTENED, BUT HE DRANK THE MOUNTAIN MILK AND IT MADE HIM VERY SLEEPY...
HE SANK INTO A DEEP SLUMBER BELOW A SAPLING, WHICH GREW AS RIP SLEPT FOR...20 YEARS!
Z
Z
Z

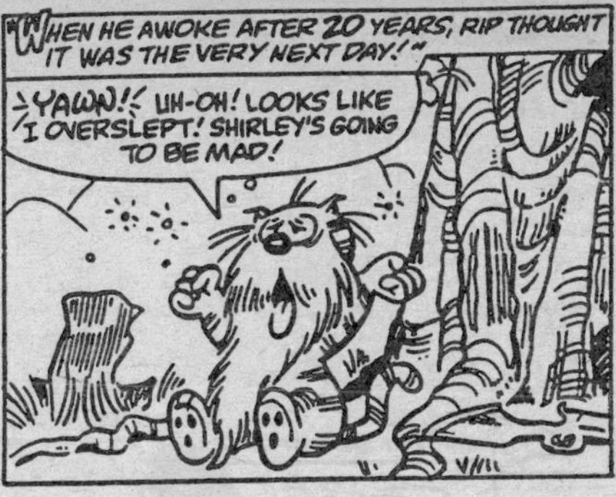
"WHEN HE AWOKE AFTER 20 YEARS, RIP THOUGHT IT WAS THE VERY NEXT DAY!"
YAWN! UH-OH! LOOKS LIKE I OVERSLEPT! SHIRLEY'S GOING TO BE MAD!

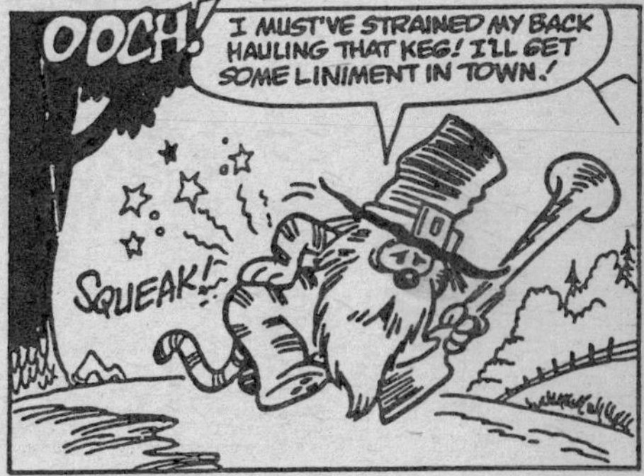
OOCH!
I MUST'VE STRAINED MY BACK HAULING THAT KEG! I'LL GET SOME LINIMENT IN TOWN!
SQUEAK!

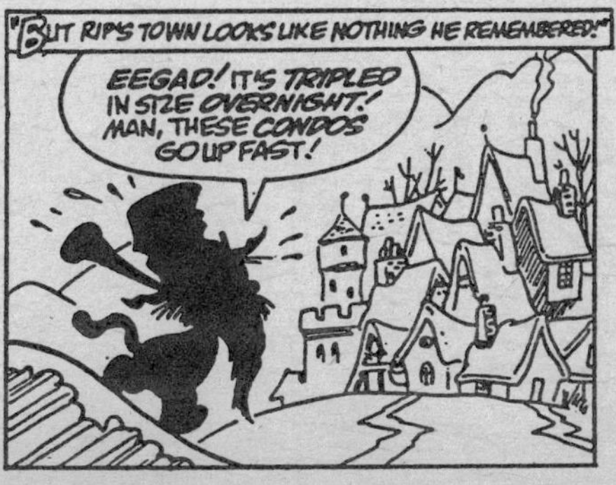
"BUT RIP'S TOWN LOOKS LIKE NOTHING HE REMEMBERED!"
EEGAD! IT'S TRIPLED IN SIZE OVERNIGHT! MAN, THESE CONDOS GO UP FAST!

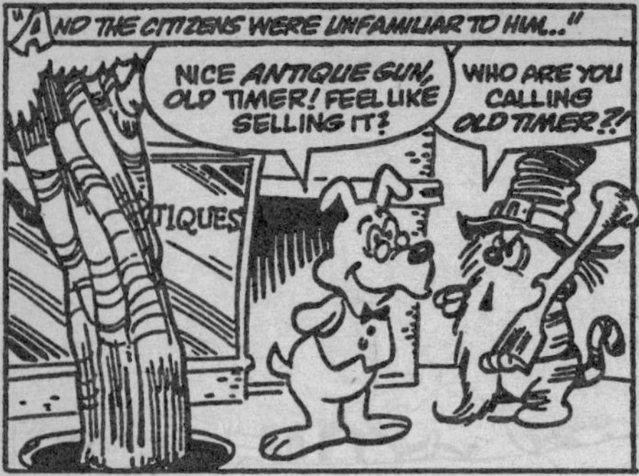
"AND THE CITIZENS WERE UNFAMILIAR TO HIM..."
NICE ANTIQUE GUN, OLD TIMER! FEEL LIKE SELLING IT?
WHO ARE YOU CALLING OLD TIMER?!
ANTIQUES

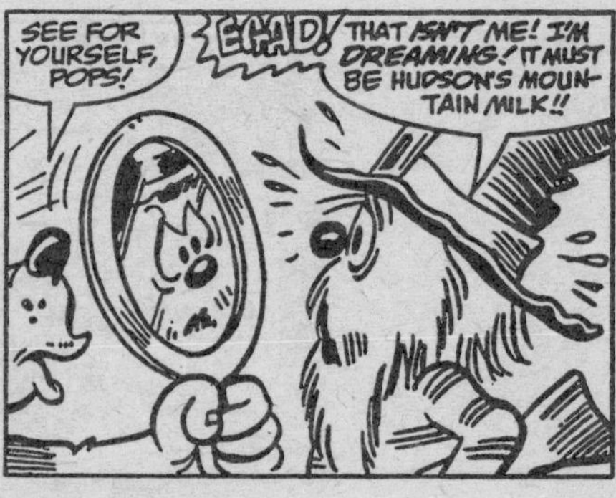
SEE FOR YOURSELF, POPS!
EGAD! THAT ISN'T ME! I'M DREAMING! IT MUST BE HUDSON'S MOUNTAIN MILK!!

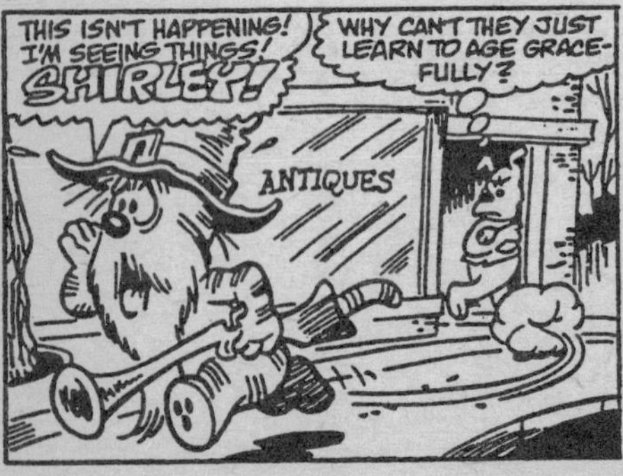
THIS ISN'T HAPPENING! I'M SEEING THINGS! SHIRLEY!
WHY CAN'T THEY JUST LEARN TO AGE GRACEFULLY?
ANTIQUES

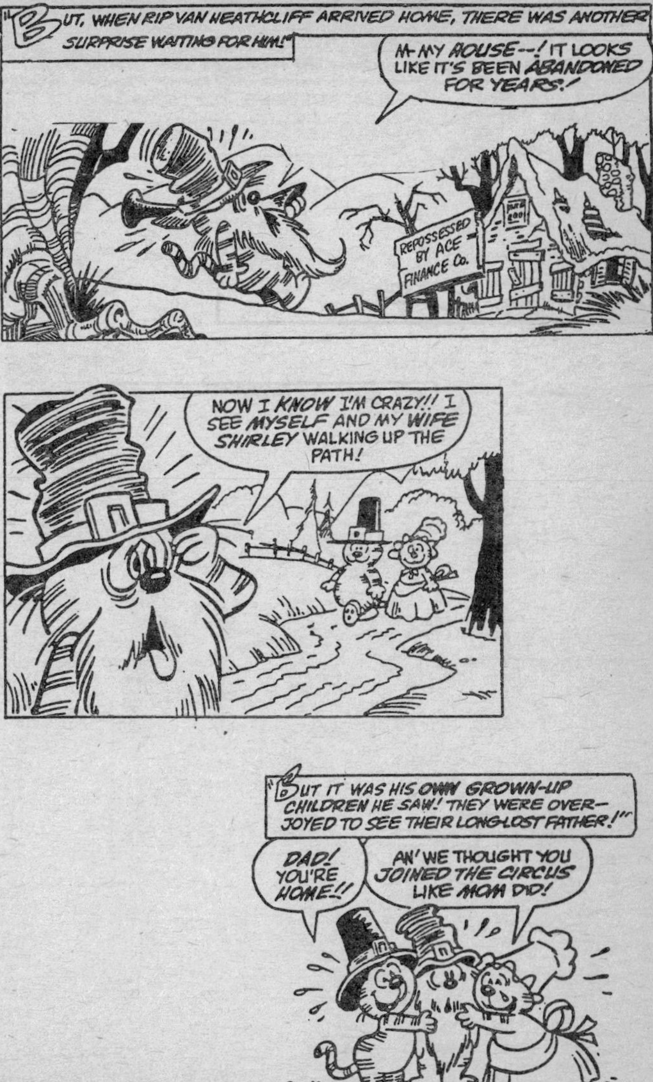
"BUT, WHEN RIP VAN HEATHCLIFF ARRIVED HOME, THERE WAS ANOTHER SURPRISE WAITING FOR HIM!"
M-MY HOUSE--! IT LOOKS LIKE IT'S BEEN ABANDONED FOR YEARS!
REPOSSESSED BY ACE FINANCE Co.
NOW I KNOW I'M CRAZY!! I SEE MYSELF AND MY WIFE SHIRLEY WALKING UP THE PATH!
"BUT IT WAS HIS OWN GROWN-UP CHILDREN HE SAW! THEY WERE OVER-JOYED TO SEE THEIR LONG-LOST FATHER!"
DAD! YOU'RE HOME!!
AN' WE THOUGHT YOU JOINED THE CIRCUS LIKE MOM DID!

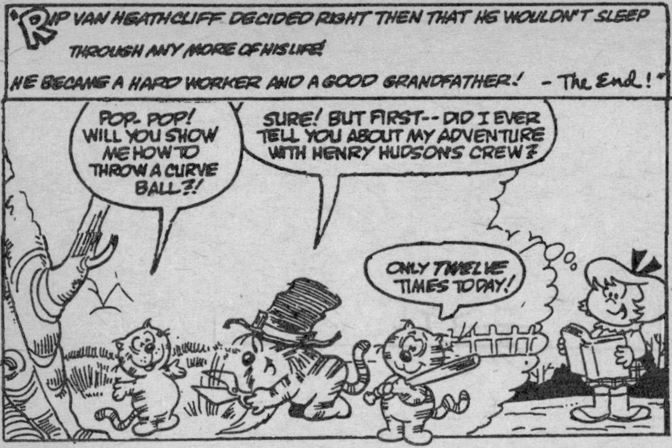
"RIP VAN HEATHCLIFF DECIDED RIGHT THEN THAT HE WOULDN'T SLEEP THROUGH ANY MORE OF HIS LIFE!
HE BECAME A HARD WORKER AND A GOOD GRANDFATHER! - The End!"
POP-POP! WILL YOU SHOW ME HOW TO THROW A CURVE BALL?!
SURE! BUT FIRST-- DID I EVER TELL YOU ABOUT MY ADVENTURE WITH HENRY HUDSON'S CREW?
ONLY TWELVE TIMES TODAY!

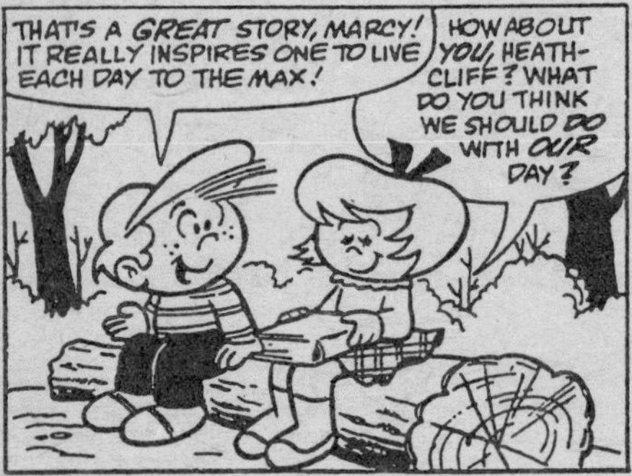
THAT'S A GREAT STORY, MARCY! IT REALLY INSPIRES ONE TO LIVE EACH DAY TO THE MAX!
HOW ABOUT YOU, HEATH-CLIFF? WHAT DO YOU THINK WE SHOULD DO WITH OUR DAY?

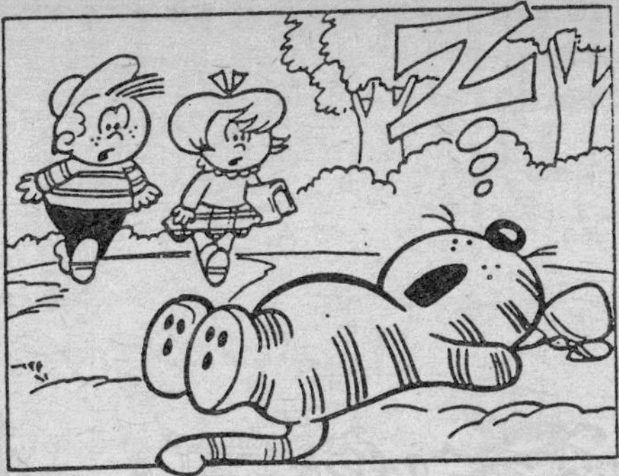
Z

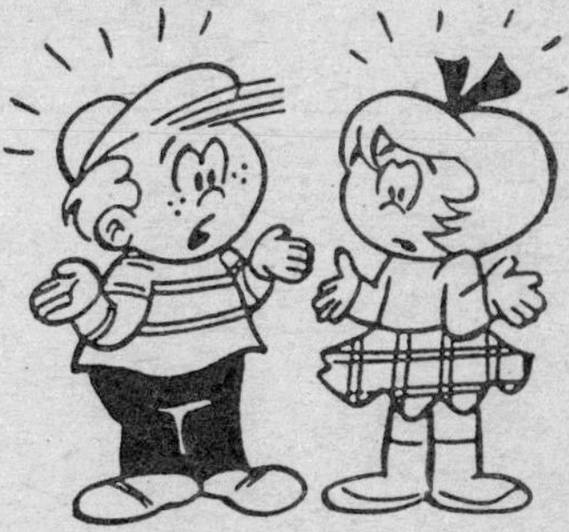

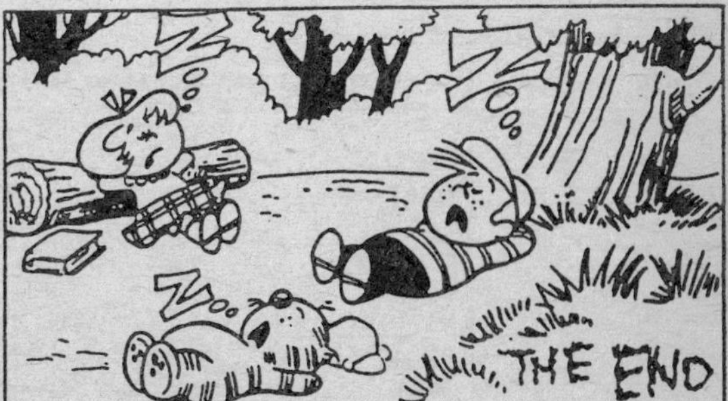
Z
Z
Z
THE END

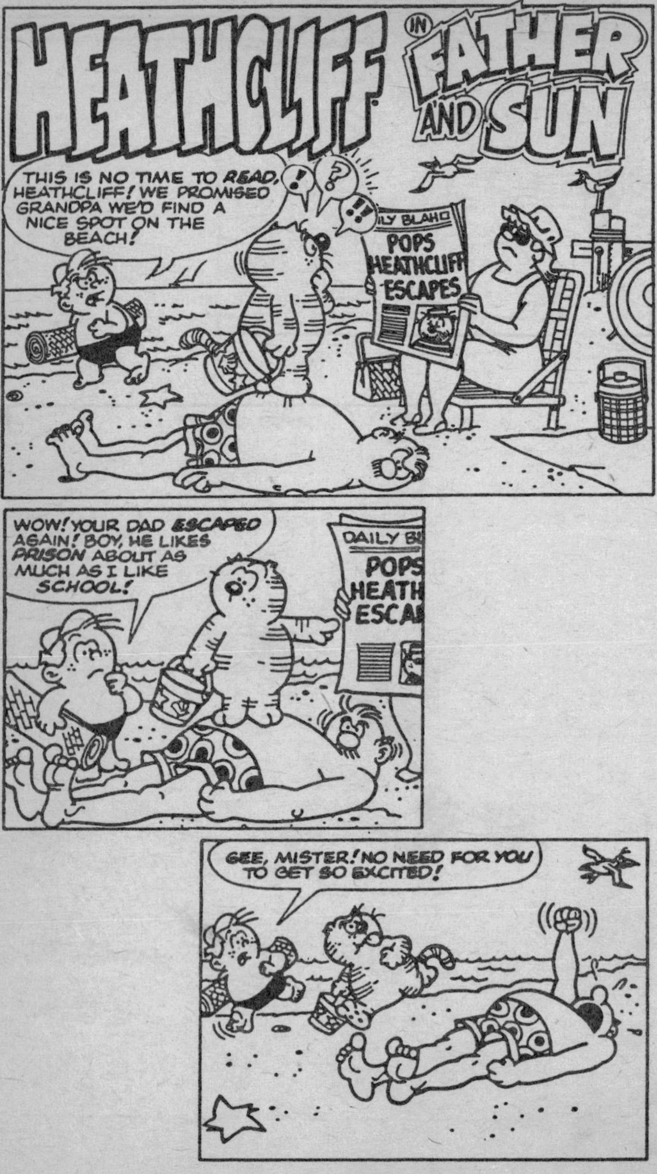
HEATHCLIFF IN FATHER AND SUN
THIS IS NO TIME TO READ, HEATHCLIFF! WE PROMISED GRANDPA WE'D FIND A NICE SPOT ON THE BEACH!
!
?
!!
POPS HEATHCLIFF ESCAPES
WOW! YOUR DAD ESCAPED AGAIN! BOY, HE LIKES PRISON ABOUT AS MUCH AS I LIKE SCHOOL!
GEE, MISTER! NO NEED FOR YOU TO GET SO EXCITED!

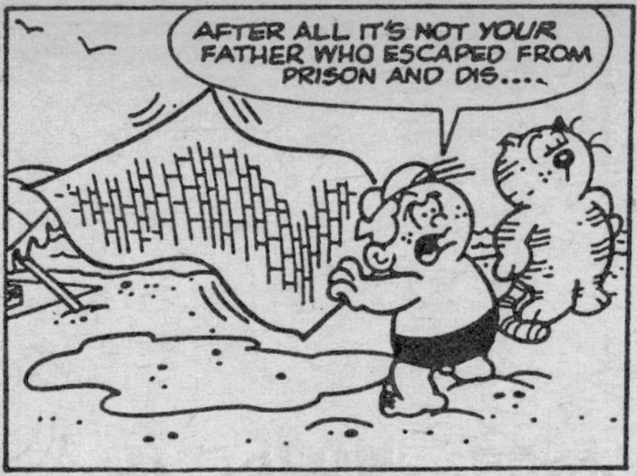
AFTER ALL IT'S NOT YOUR FATHER WHO ESCAPED FROM PRISON AND DIS....

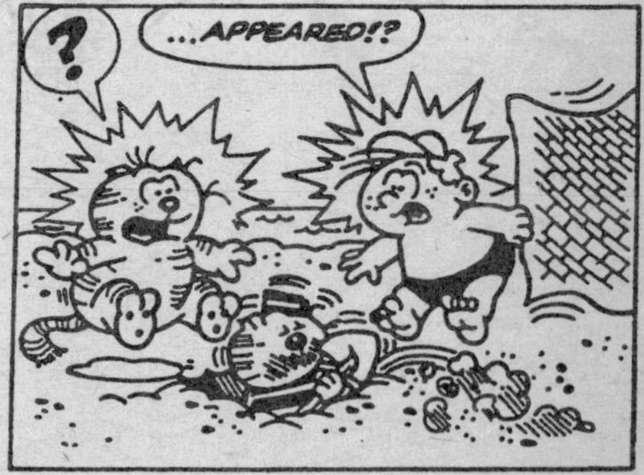
?
...APPEARED!?

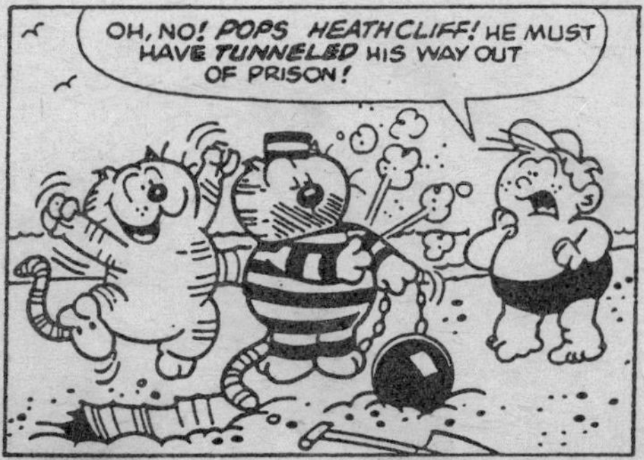
OH, NO! POPS HEATHCLIFF! HE MUST HAVE TUNNELED HIS WAY OUT OF PRISON!

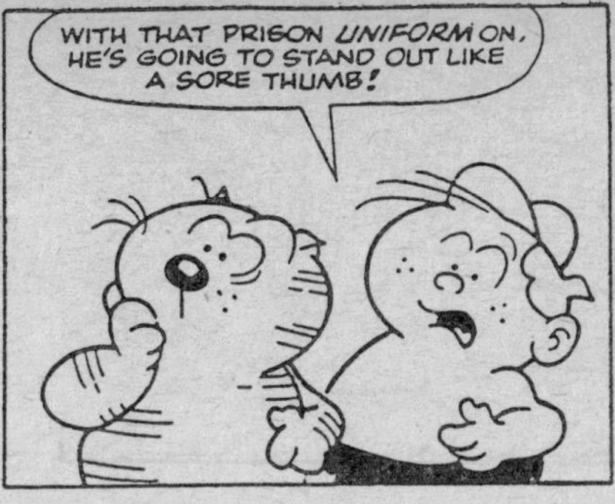
WITH THAT PRISON UNIFORM ON, HE'S GOING TO STAND OUT LIKE A SORE THUMB!

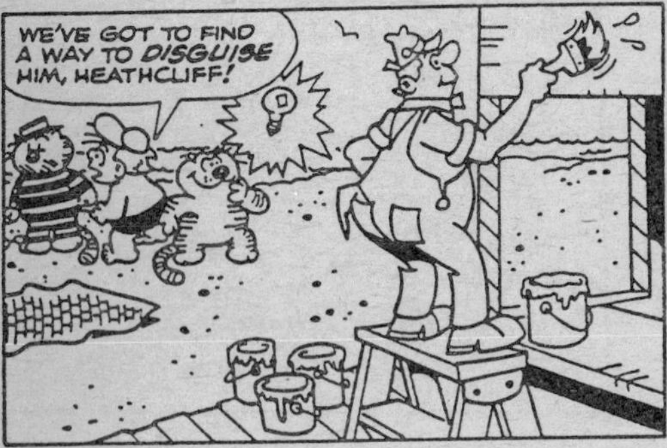
WE'VE GOT TO FIND A WAY TO DISGUISE HIM, HEATHCLIFF!

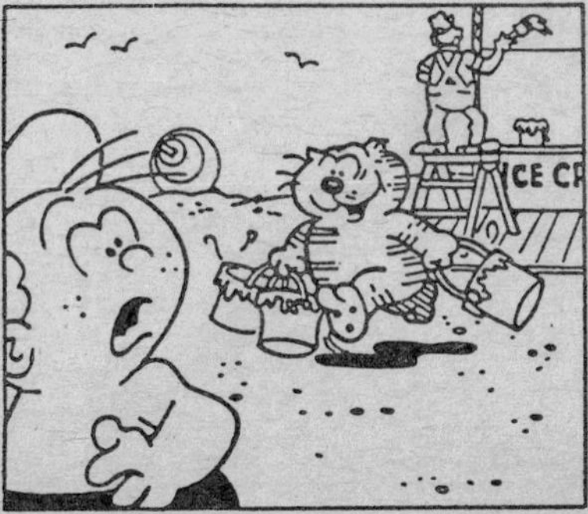

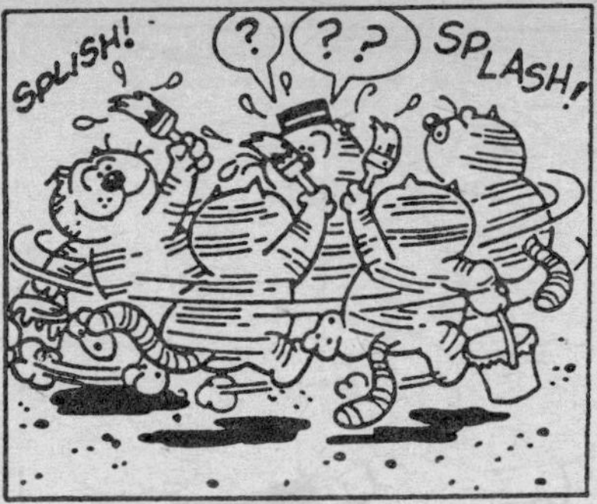
SPLISH!
?
? ?
SPLASH!

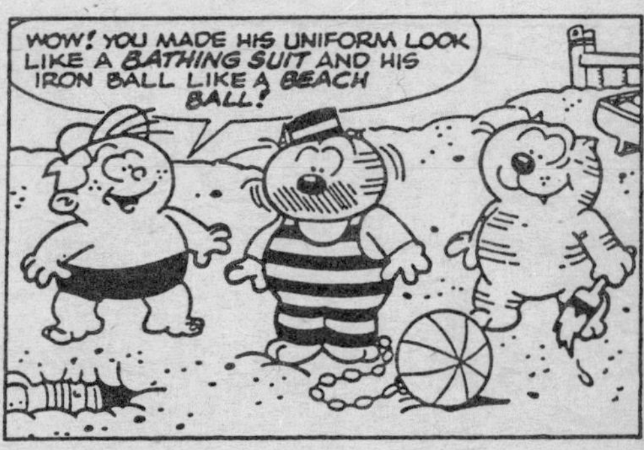
WOW! YOU MADE HIS UNIFORM LOOK LIKE A *BATHING SUIT* AND HIS IRON BALL LIKE A *BEACH BALL!*

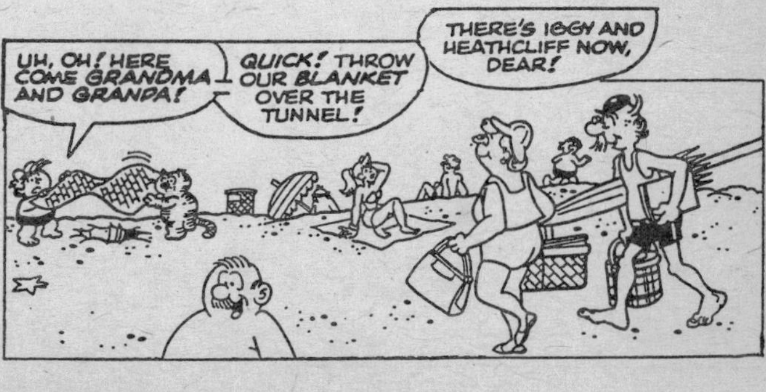
UH, OH! HERE COME *GRANDMA* AND *GRANPA!*
QUICK! THROW OUR *BLANKET* OVER THE TUNNEL!
THERE'S IGGY AND HEATHCLIFF NOW, DEAR!

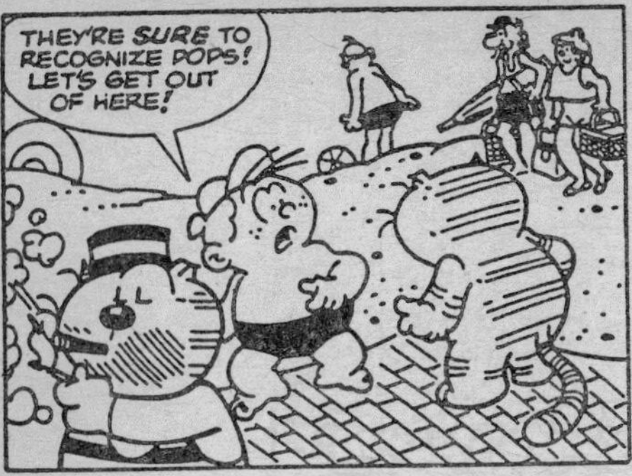
THEY'RE SURE TO RECOGNIZE POPS! LET'S GET OUT OF HERE!

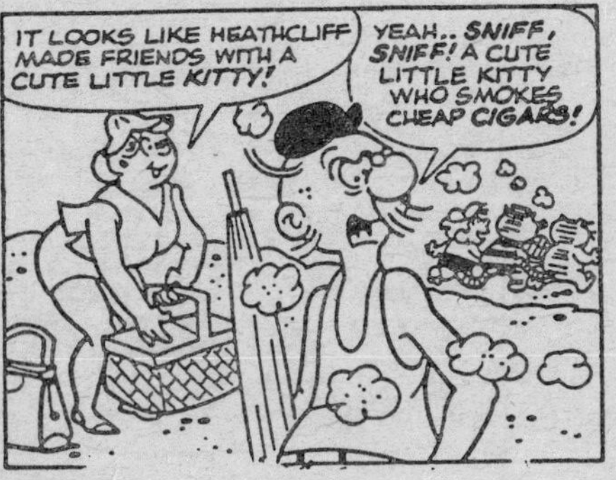
IT LOOKS LIKE HEATHCLIFF MADE FRIENDS WITH A CUTE LITTLE KITTY!
YEAH.. SNIFF, SNIFF! A CUTE LITTLE KITTY WHO SMOKES CHEAP CIGARS!

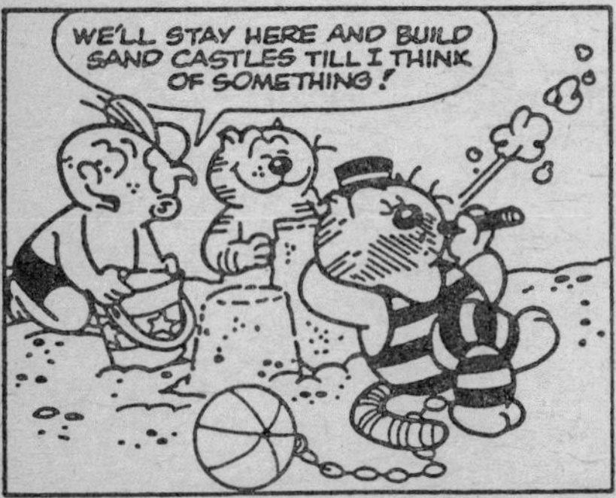
WE'LL STAY HERE AND BUILD SAND CASTLES TILL I THINK OF SOMETHING!

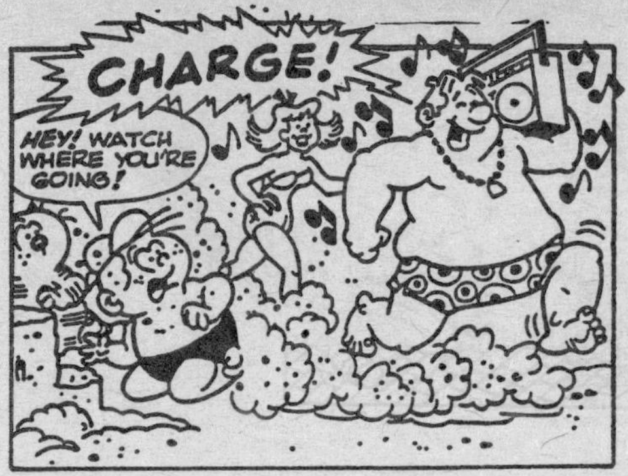
CHARGE!
HEY! WATCH WHERE YOU'RE GOING!

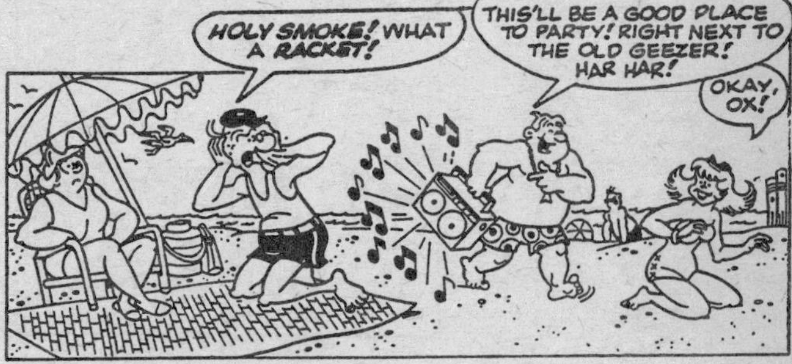
HOLY SMOKE! WHAT A RACKET!
THIS'LL BE A GOOD PLACE TO PARTY! RIGHT NEXT TO THE OLD GEEZER! HAR HAR!
OKAY, OX!

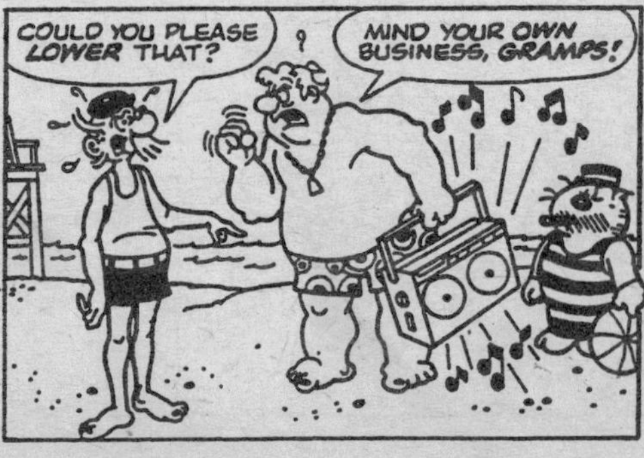
COULD YOU PLEASE LOWER THAT?
MIND YOUR OWN BUSINESS, GRAMPS!

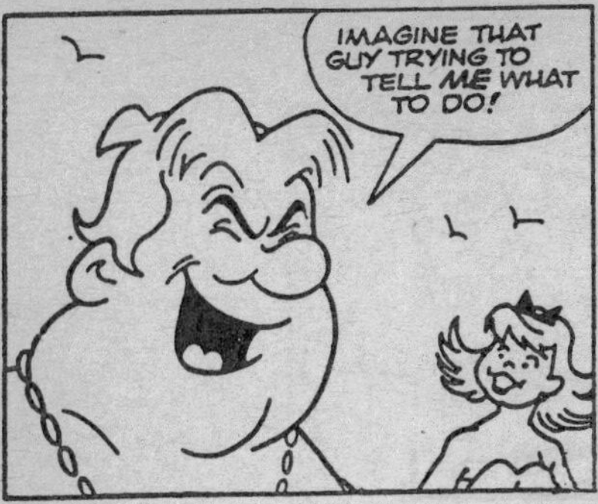
IMAGINE THAT GUY TRYING TO TELL ME WHAT TO DO!

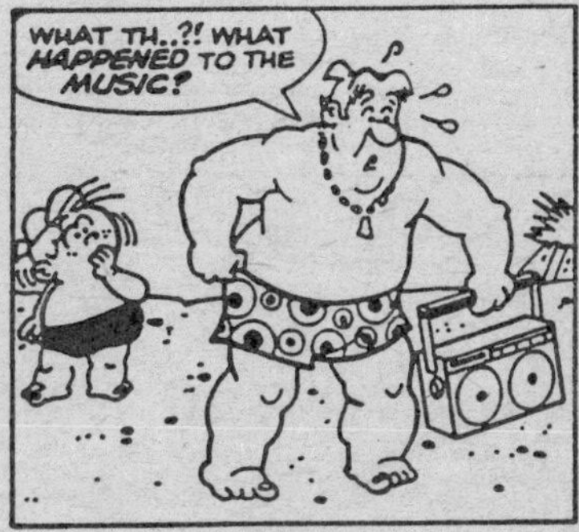
WHAT TH..?! WHAT HAPPENED TO THE MUSIC?

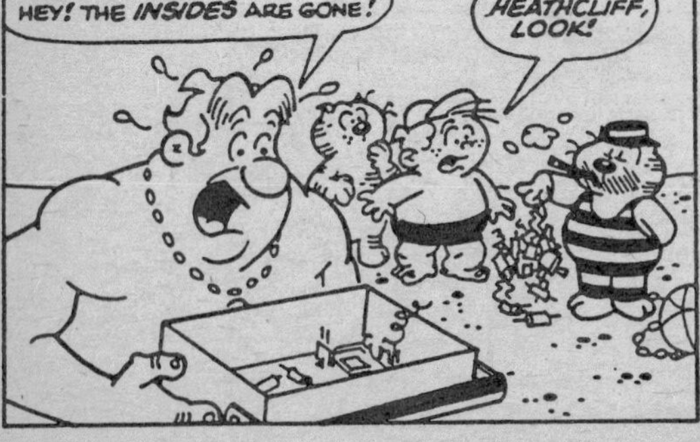
HEY! THE INSIDES ARE GONE!
HEATHCLIFF, LOOK!

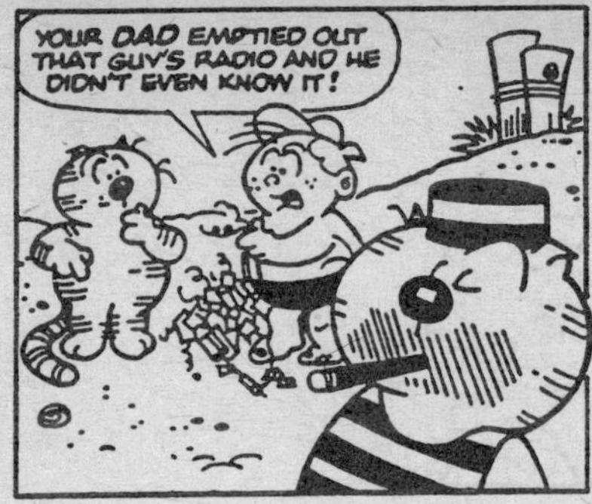
YOUR DAD EMPTIED OUT THAT GUY'S RADIO AND HE DIDN'T EVEN KNOW IT!

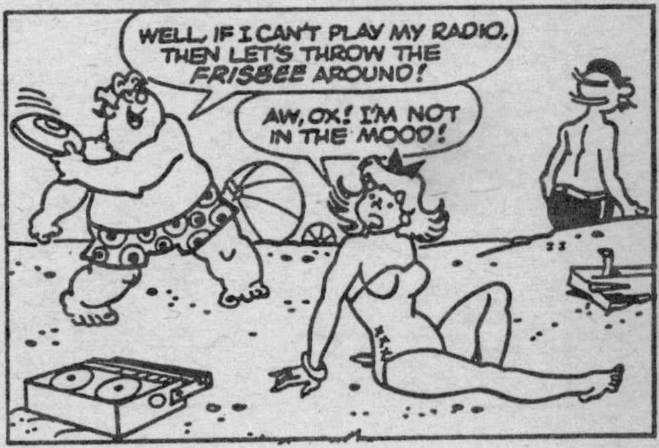
WELL, IF I CAN'T PLAY MY RADIO, THEN LET'S THROW THE FRISBEE AROUND!
AW, OX! I'M NOT IN THE MOOD!

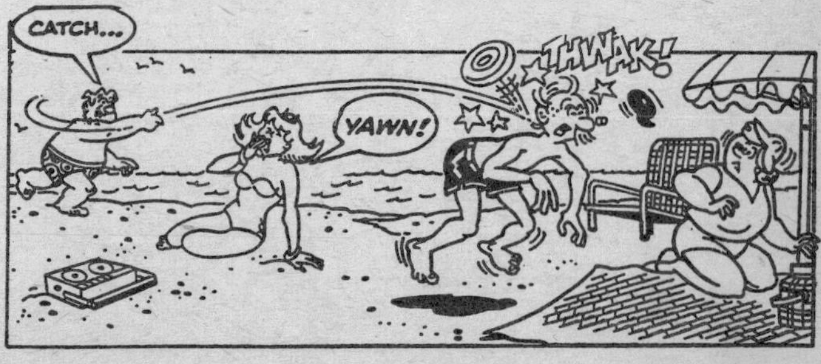
CATCH...
YAWN!
THWAK!

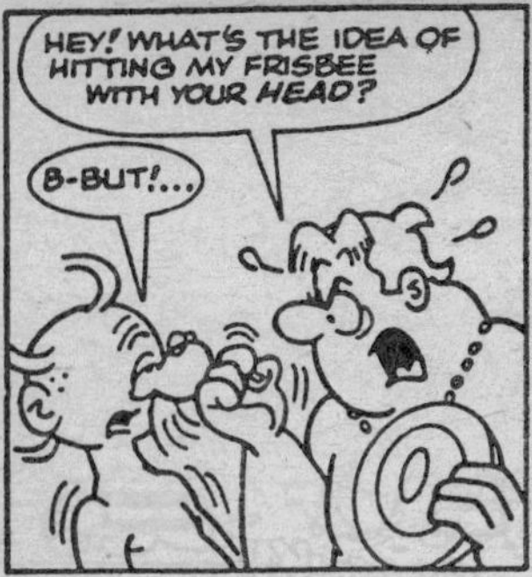
HEY! WHAT'S THE IDEA OF HITTING MY FRISBEE WITH YOUR HEAD?
B-BUT!...

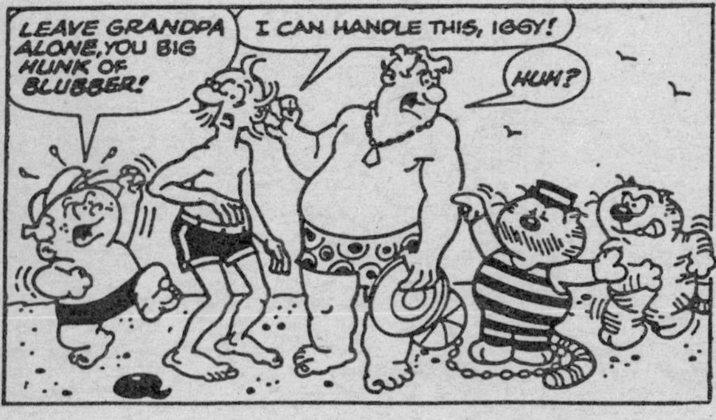
LEAVE GRANDPA ALONE, YOU BIG HUNK OF BLUBBER!
I CAN HANDLE THIS, IGGY!
HUH?

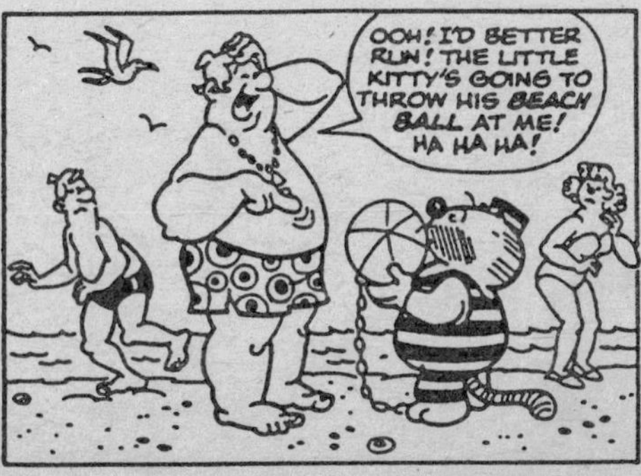
OOH! I'D BETTER RUN! THE LITTLE KITTY'S GOING TO THROW HIS BEACH BALL AT ME! HA HA HA!

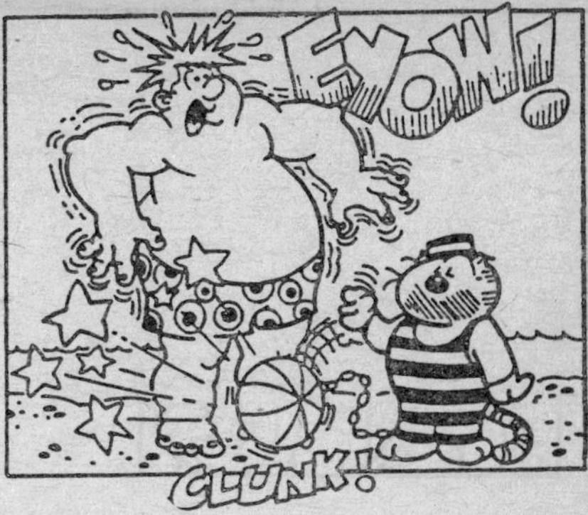
EYOW!
CLUNK!

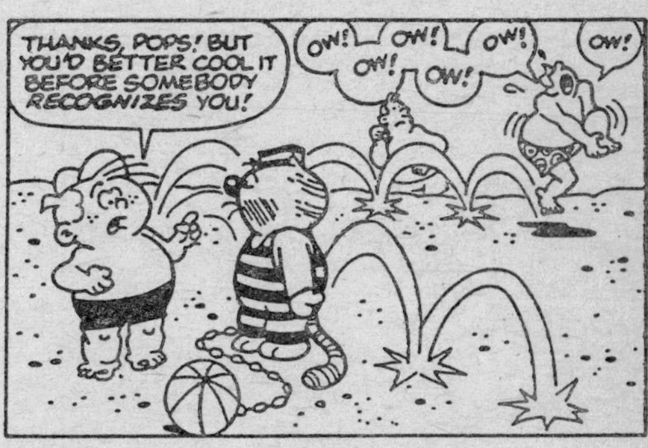
THANKS, POPS! BUT YOU'D BETTER COOL IT BEFORE SOMEBODY *RECOGNIZES* YOU!
OW!
OW!
OW!
OW!
OW!
OW!

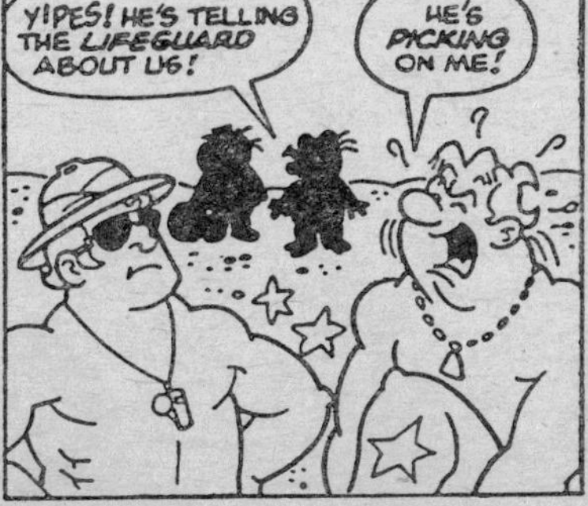
YIPES! HE'S TELLING THE *LIFEGUARD* ABOUT US!
HE'S *PICKING* ON ME!

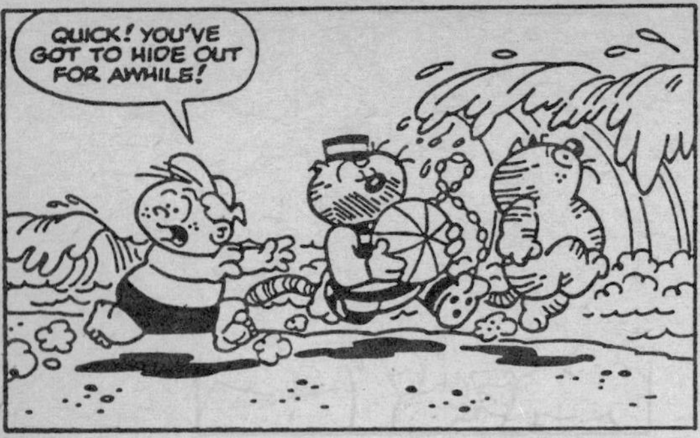
QUICK! YOU'VE GOT TO HIDE OUT FOR AWHILE!

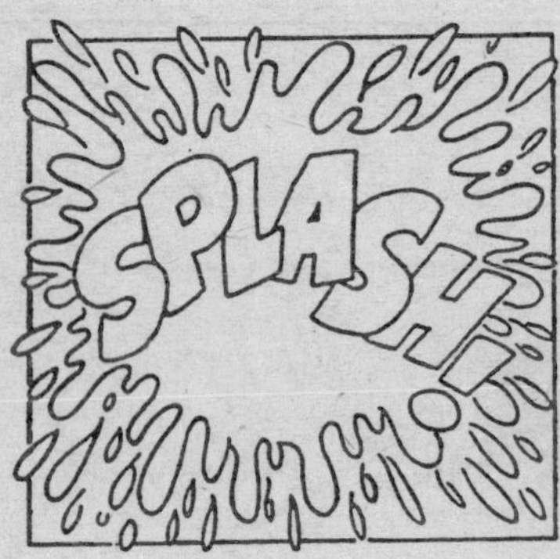
SPLASH!

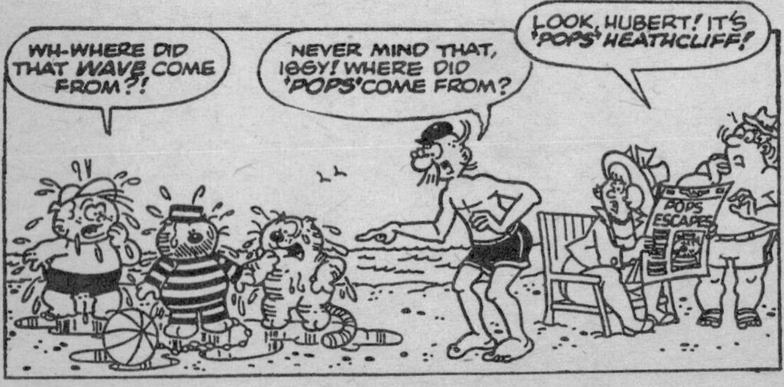
WH-WHERE DID THAT *WAVE* COME FROM?!
NEVER MIND THAT, IGGY! WHERE DID *'POPS'* COME FROM?
LOOK, HUBERT! IT'S *'POPS'* HEATHCLIFF!
POPS ESCAPES

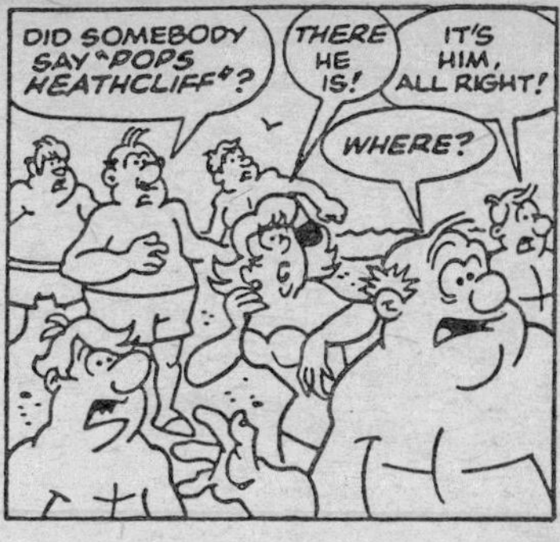
DID SOMEBODY SAY "POPS HEATHCLIFF"?
THERE HE IS!
IT'S HIM, ALL RIGHT!
WHERE?

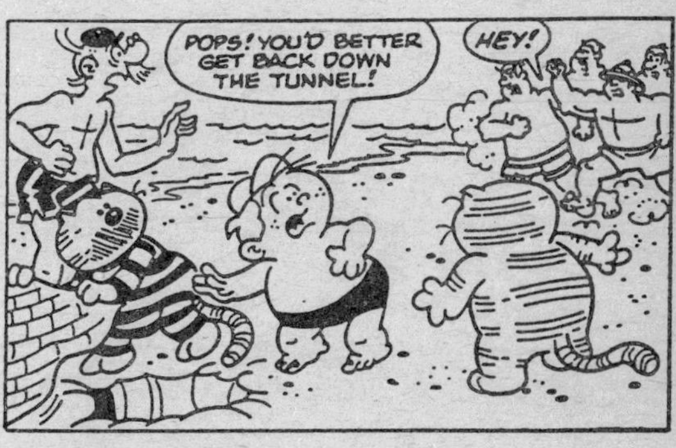
POPS! YOU'D BETTER GET BACK DOWN THE TUNNEL!
HEY!

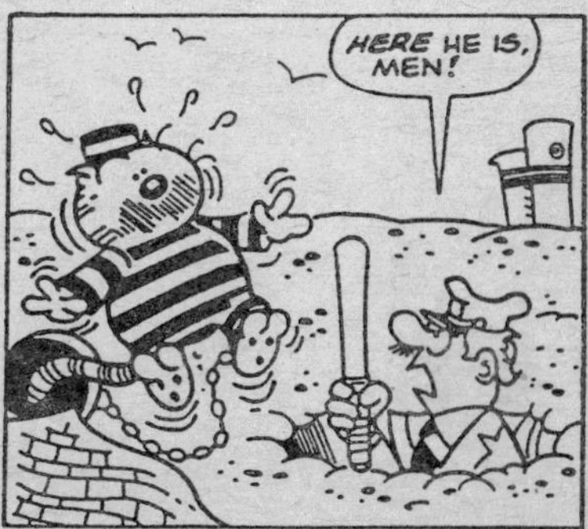
HERE HE IS, MEN!

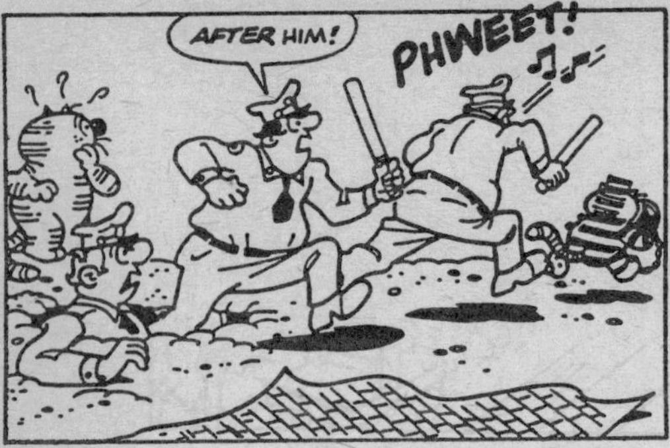
AFTER HIM!
PHWEET!

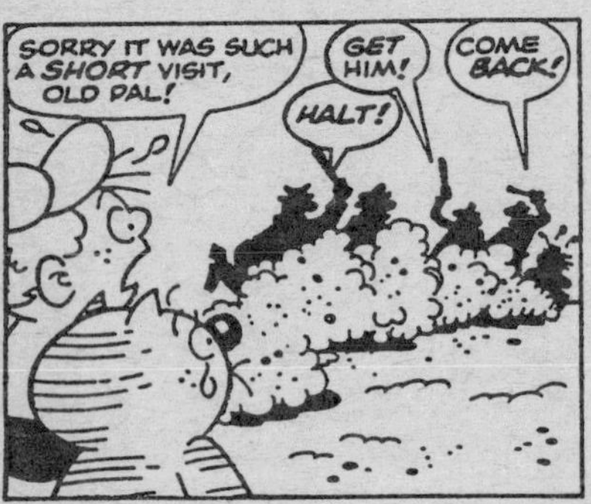
SORRY IT WAS SUCH A SHORT VISIT, OLD PAL!
GET HIM!
COME BACK!
HALT!

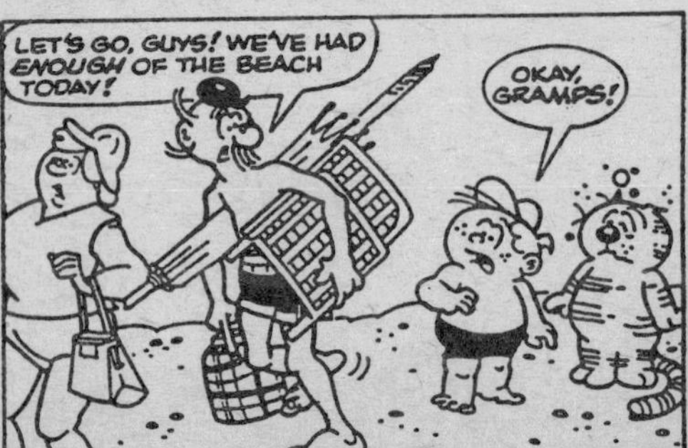
LET'S GO, GUYS! WE'VE HAD ENOUGH OF THE BEACH TODAY!
OKAY, GRAMPS!

CHEER UP, HEATHCLIFF! I'M SURE "POPS" WILL VISIT YOU AGAIN SOME DAY...
...REAL SOON!
THE END

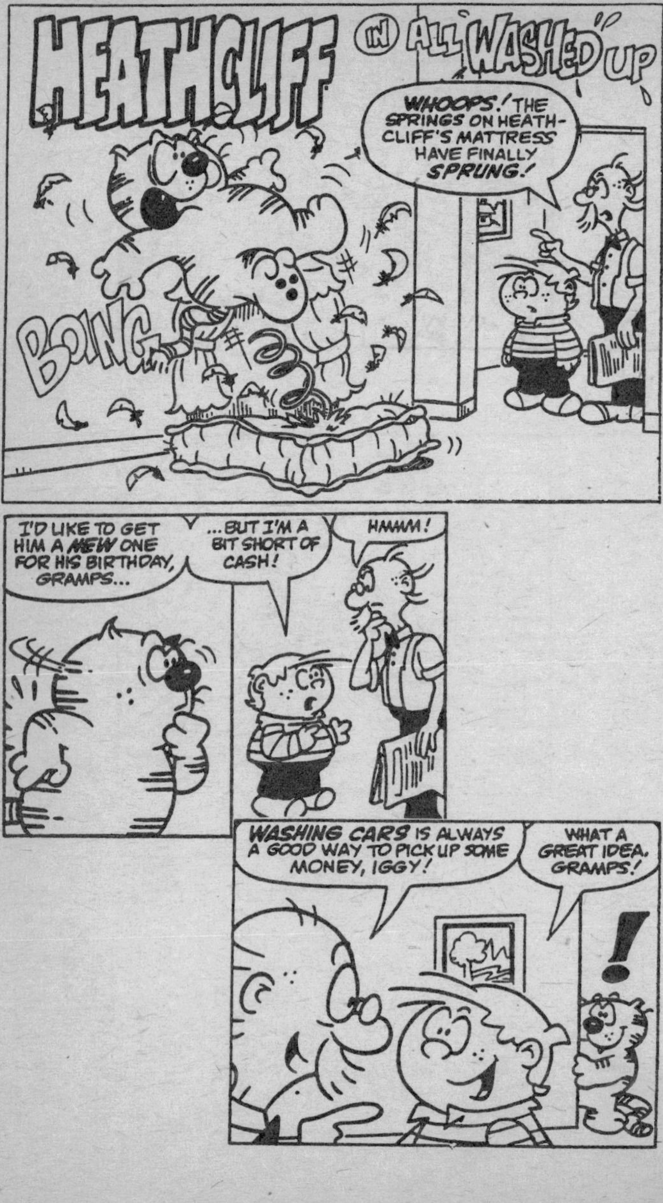
HEATHCLIFF
IN ALL WASHED UP
WHOOPS! THE SPRINGS ON HEATH-CLIFF'S MATTRESS HAVE FINALLY SPRUNG!
BOING
I'D LIKE TO GET HIM A NEW ONE FOR HIS BIRTHDAY, GRAMPS...
...BUT I'M A BIT SHORT OF CASH!
HMMM!
WASHING CARS IS ALWAYS A GOOD WAY TO PICK UP SOME MONEY, IGGY!
WHAT A GREAT IDEA. GRAMPS!
!

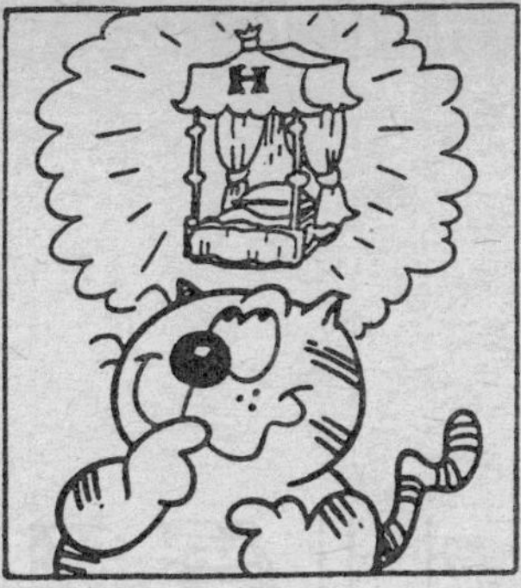

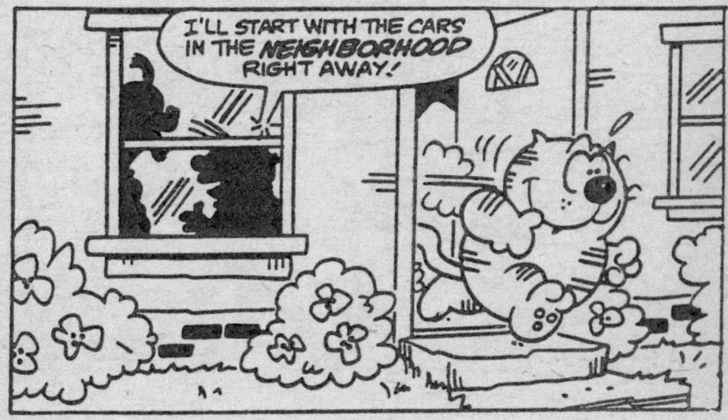
I'LL START WITH THE CARS IN THE NEIGHBORHOOD RIGHT AWAY!

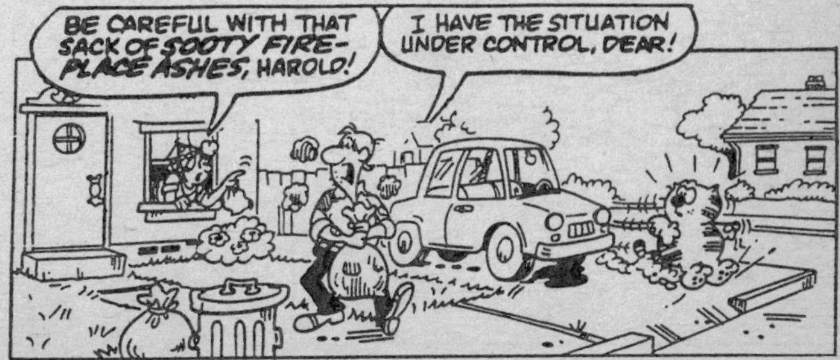
BE CAREFUL WITH THAT SACK OF SOOTY FIRE-PLACE ASHES, HAROLD!
I HAVE THE SITUATION UNDER CONTROL, DEAR!

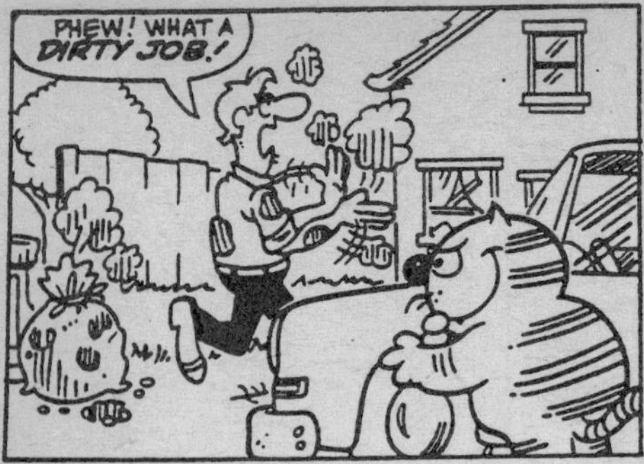
PHEW! WHAT A DIRTY JOB.!

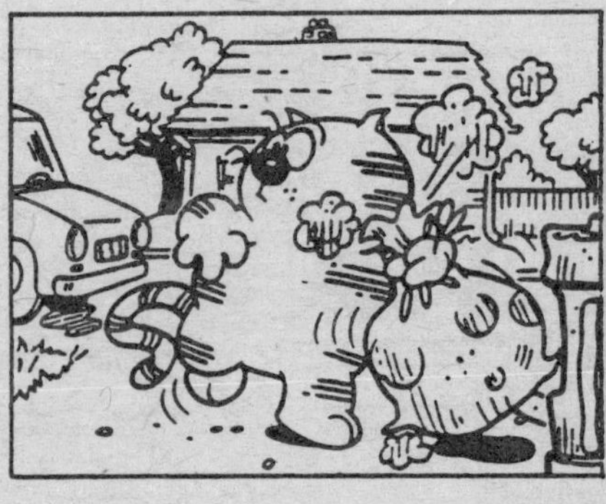

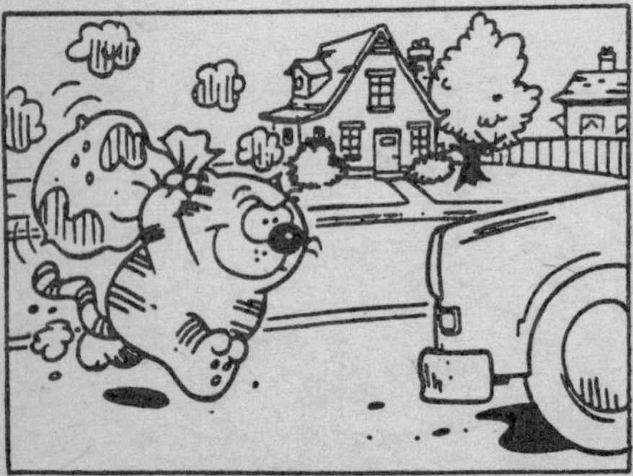

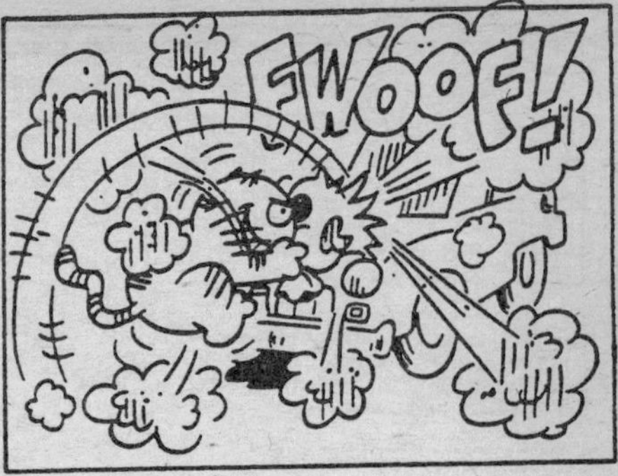
FWOOF!

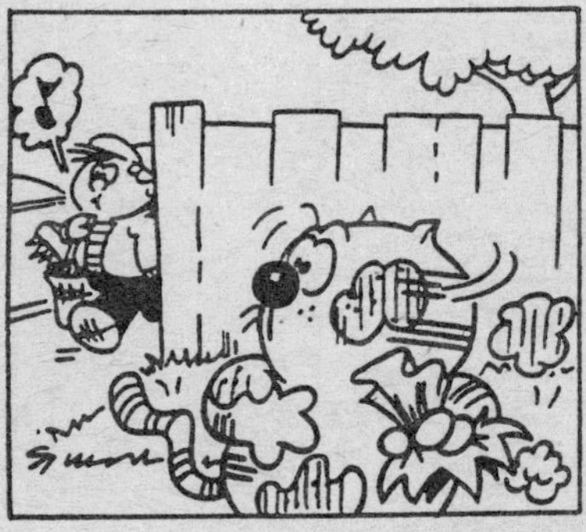

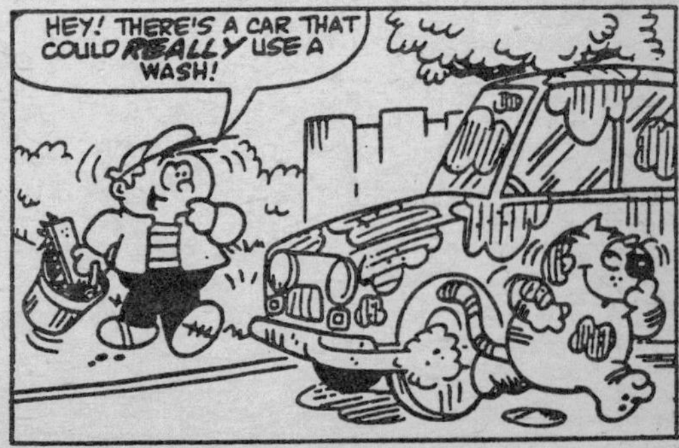
HEY! THERE'S A CAR THAT COULD REALLY USE A WASH!

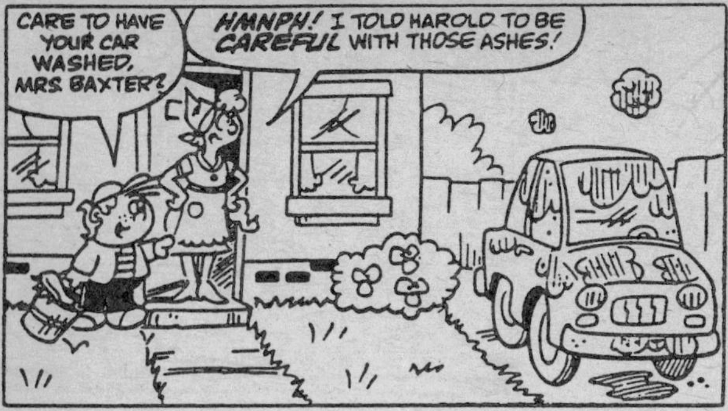
CARE TO HAVE YOUR CAR WASHED, MRS. BAXTER?
HMNPH! I TOLD HAROLD TO BE CAREFUL WITH THOSE ASHES!

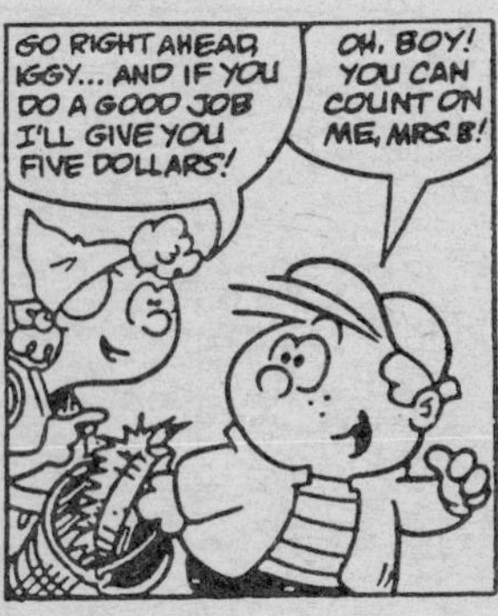
GO RIGHT AHEAD, IGGY... AND IF YOU DO A GOOD JOB I'LL GIVE YOU FIVE DOLLARS!
OH, BOY! YOU CAN COUNT ON ME, MRS. B!

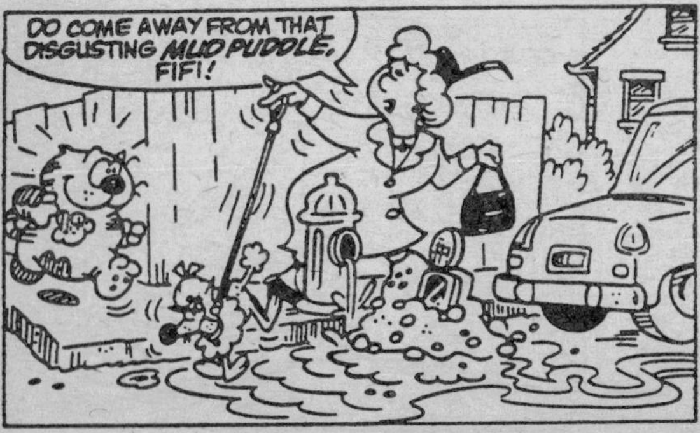
DO COME AWAY FROM THAT DISGUSTING MUD PUDDLE, FIFI!

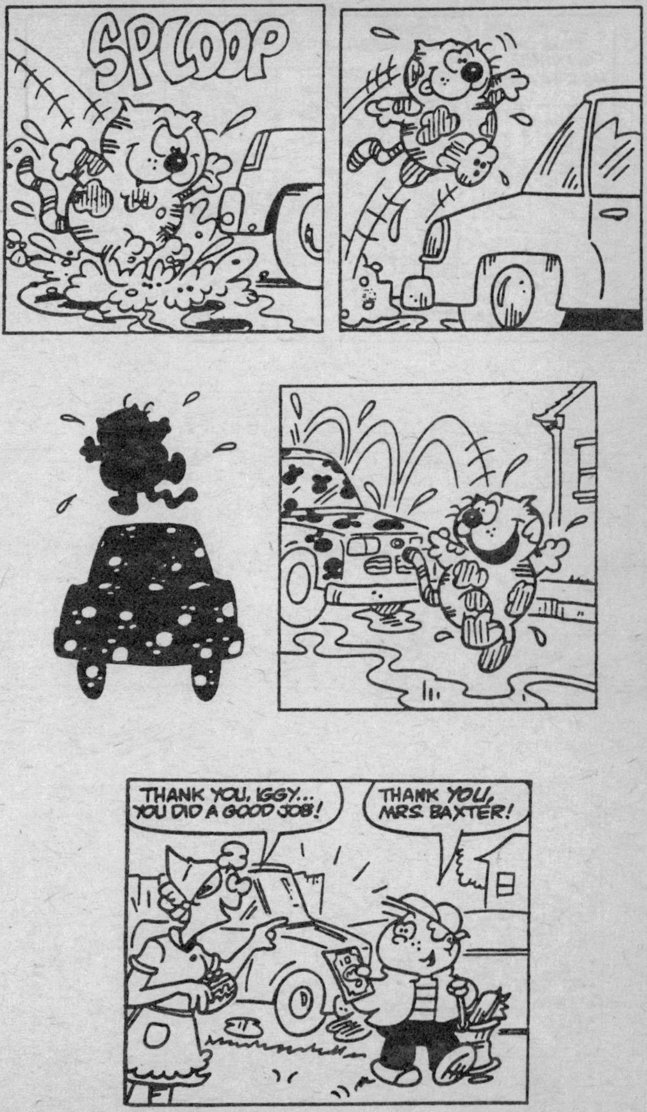
SPLOOP
THANK YOU, IGGY... YOU DID A GOOD JOB!
THANK YOU, MRS. BAXTER!

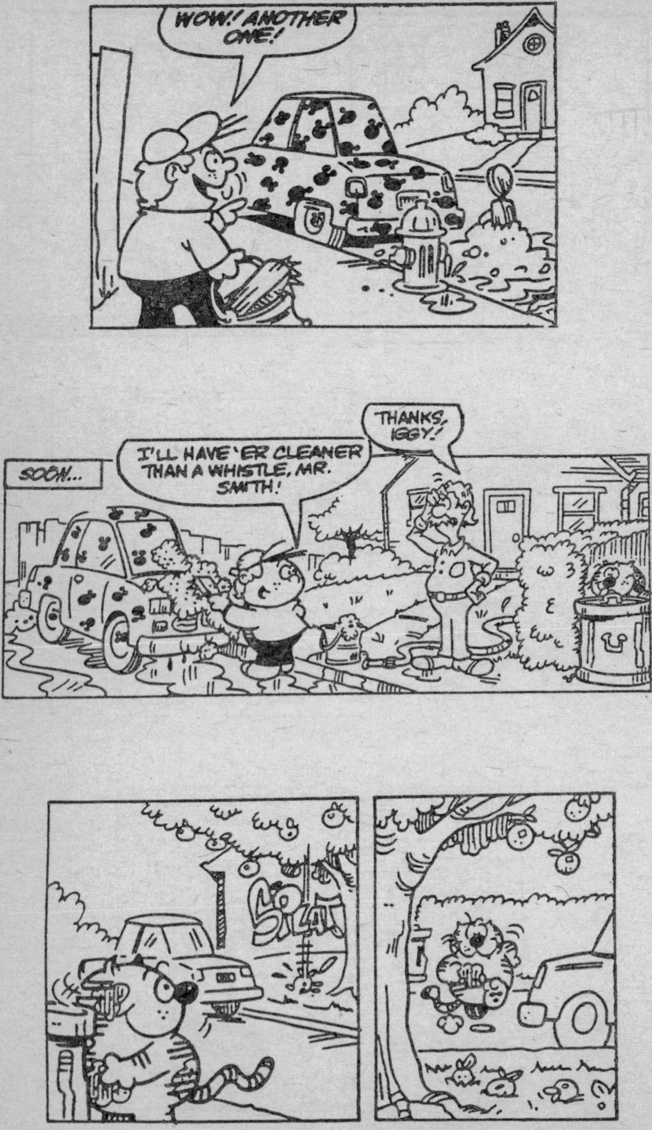
WOW! ANOTHER ONE!
SOON...
I'LL HAVE 'ER CLEANER THAN A WHISTLE, MR. SMITH!
THANKS, IGGY!
SPLAT

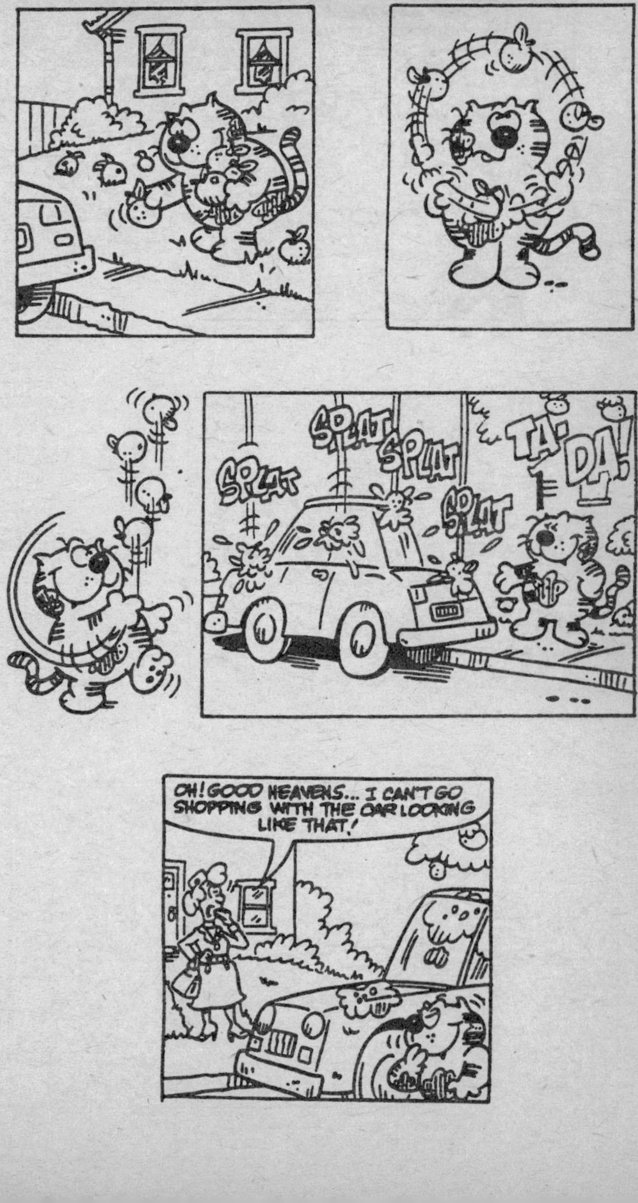
SPLAT
SPLAT
SPLAT
SPLAT
TA-DA!
OH! GOOD HEAVENS... I CAN'T GO SHOPPING WITH THE CAR LOOKING LIKE THAT!

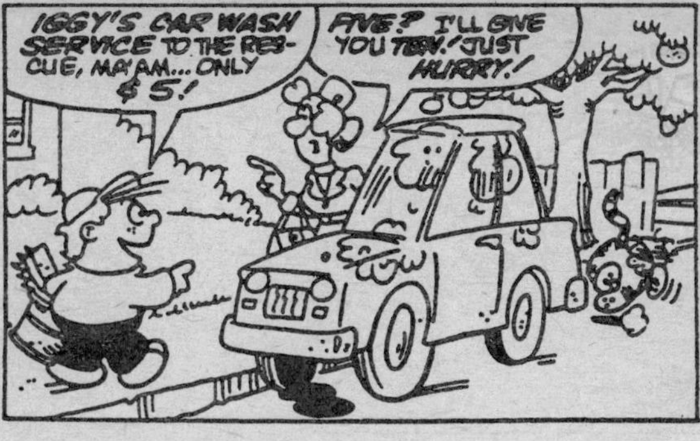
IGGY'S CAR WASH SERVICE TO THE RES-CUE, MA'AM... ONLY $5!
FIVE? I'LL GIVE YOU TEN! JUST HURRY!

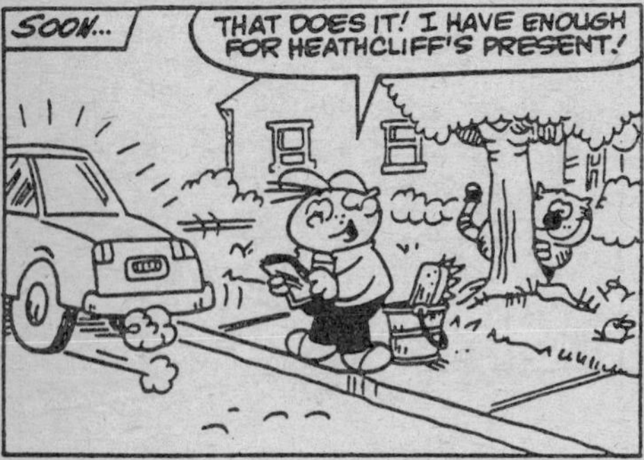
SOON...
THAT DOES IT! I HAVE ENOUGH FOR HEATHCLIFF'S PRESENT!

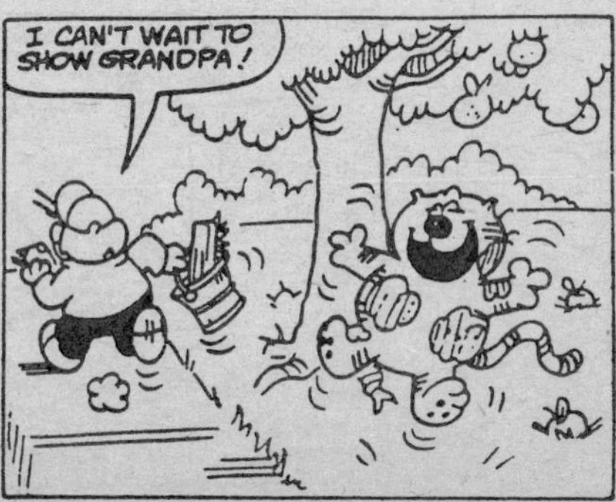
I CAN'T WAIT TO SHOW GRANDPA!

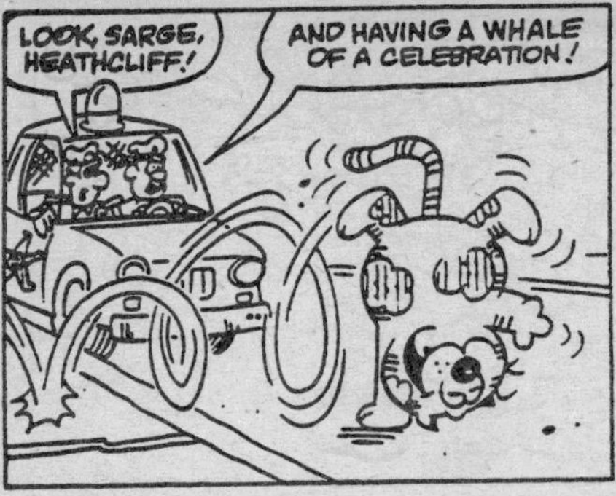
LOOK, SARGE, HEATHCLIFF!
AND HAVING A WHALE OF A CELEBRATION!

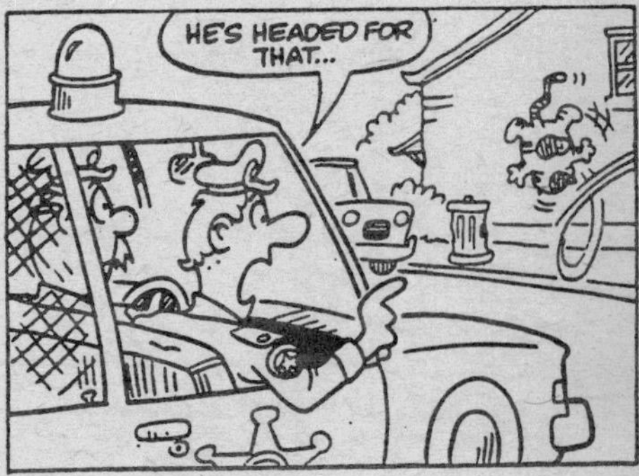
HE'S HEADED FOR THAT...

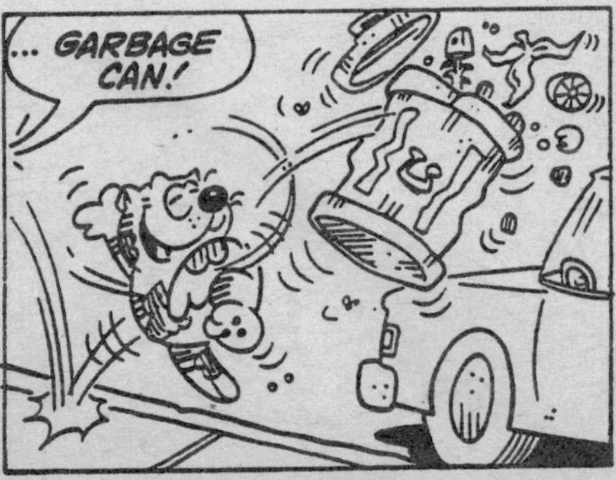
... GARBAGE CAN!

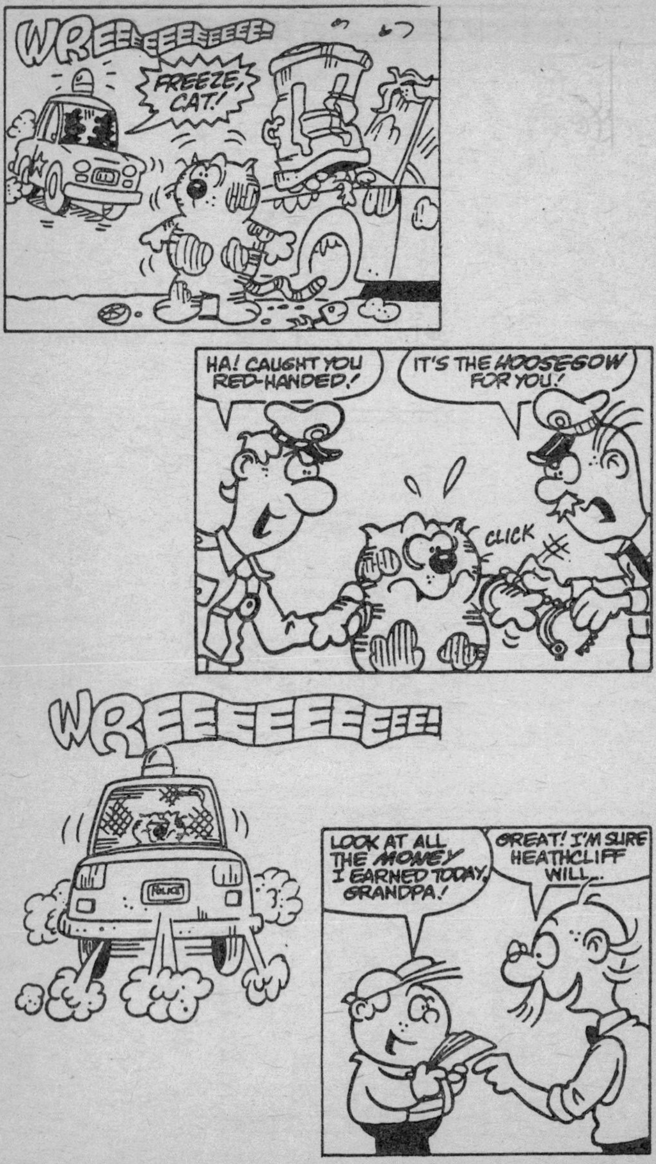
WREEEEEEEEEE!
FREEZE, CAT!
HA! CAUGHT YOU RED-HANDED!
IT'S THE HOOSEGOW FOR YOU!
CLICK
WREEEEEEEEEE!
LOOK AT ALL THE MONEY I EARNED TODAY, GRANDPA!
GREAT! I'M SURE HEATHCLIFF WILL...

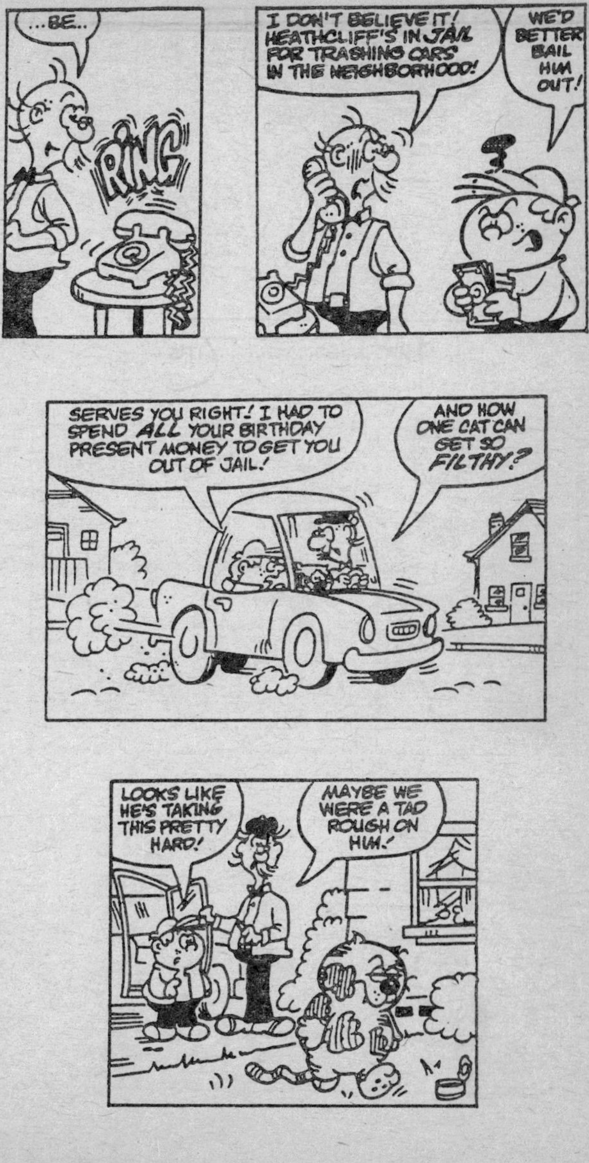
...BE...
RING
I DON'T BELIEVE IT! HEATHCLIFF'S IN JAIL FOR TRASHING CARS IN THE NEIGHBORHOOD!
WE'D BETTER BAIL HIM OUT!
SERVES YOU RIGHT! I HAD TO SPEND ALL YOUR BIRTHDAY PRESENT MONEY TO GET YOU OUT OF JAIL!
AND HOW ONE CAT CAN GET SO FILTHY?
LOOKS LIKE HE'S TAKING THIS PRETTY HARD!
MAYBE WE WERE A TAD ROUGH ON HIM!

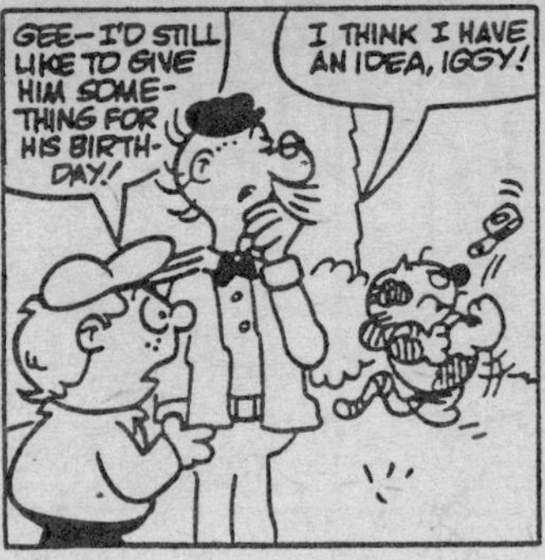
GEE—I'D STILL LIKE TO GIVE HIM SOME-THING FOR HIS BIRTH-DAY!
I THINK I HAVE AN IDEA, IGGY!

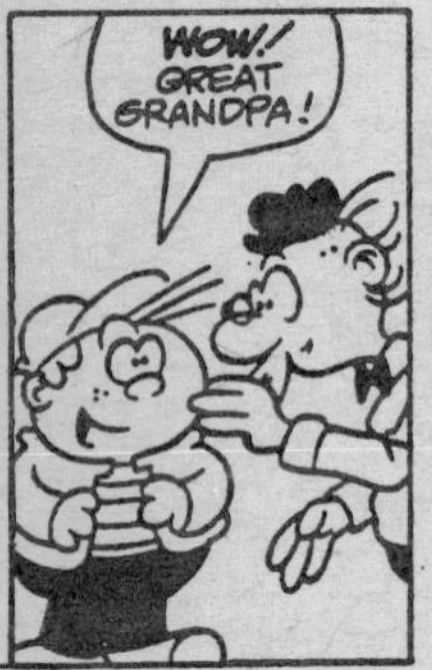
WOW! GREAT GRANDPA!

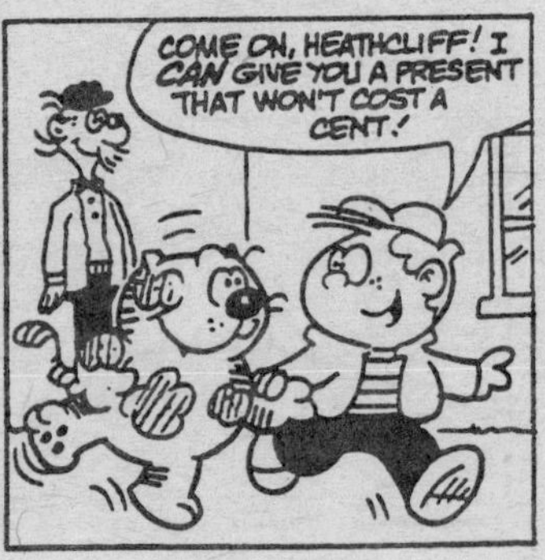
COME ON, HEATHCLIFF! I CAN GIVE YOU A PRESENT THAT WON'T COST A CENT!

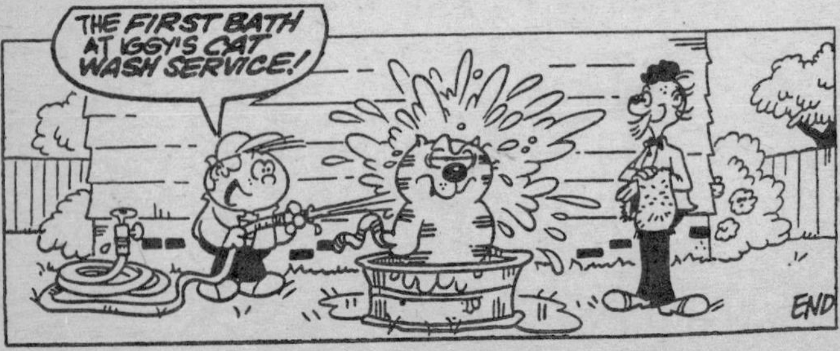
THE FIRST BATH AT IGGY'S CAT WASH SERVICE!
END

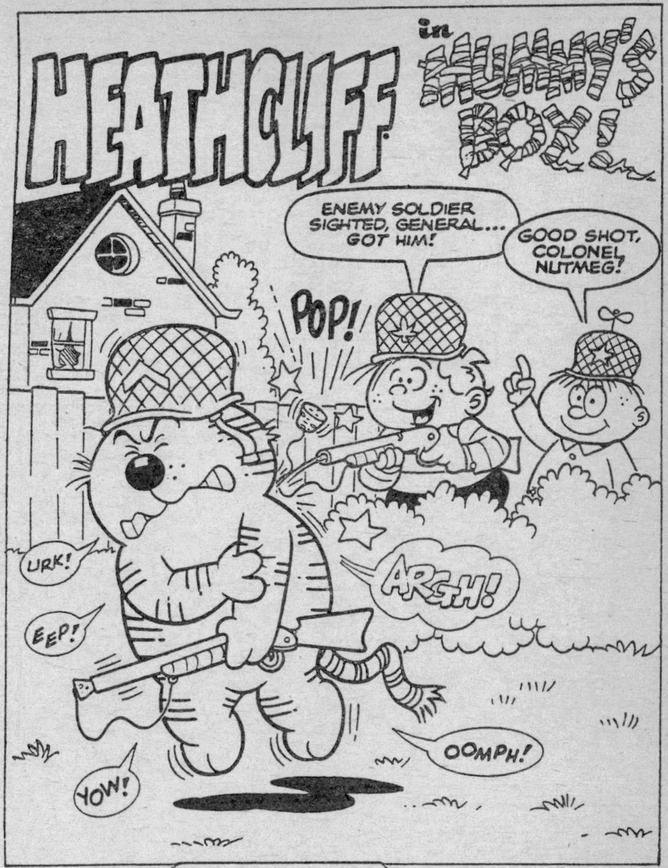
HEATHCLIFF
in
MUMMY'S BOY!
ENEMY SOLDIER SIGHTED, GENERAL... GOT HIM!
GOOD SHOT, COLONEL NUTMEG!
POP!
URK!
ARGH!
EEP!
OOMPH!
YOW!

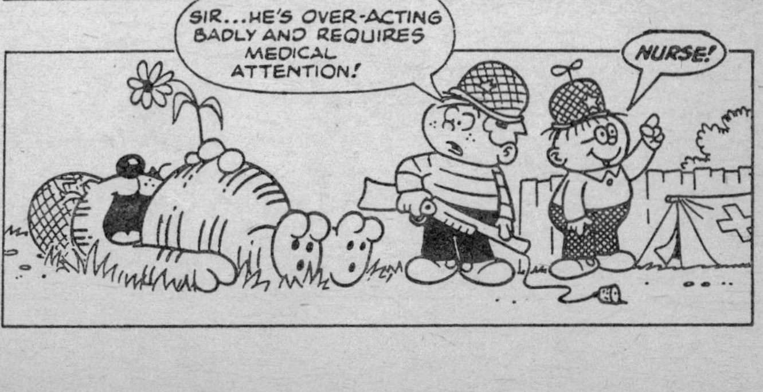
SIR...HE'S OVER-ACTING BADLY AND REQUIRES MEDICAL ATTENTION!
NURSE!

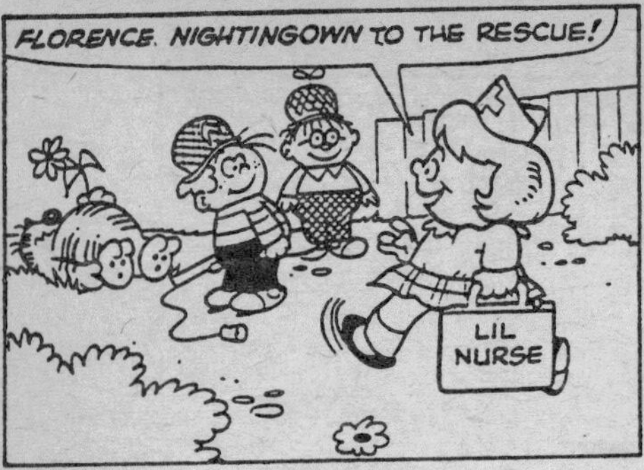
FLORENCE NIGHTINGOWN TO THE RESCUE!
LIL NURSE

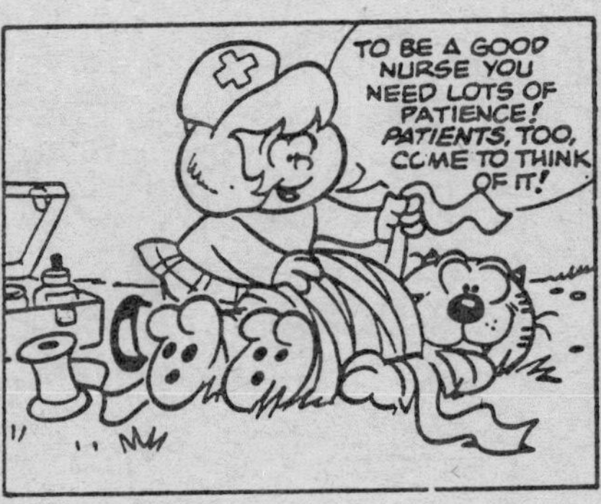
TO BE A GOOD NURSE YOU NEED LOTS OF PATIENCE! PATIENTS, TOO, COME TO THINK OF IT!

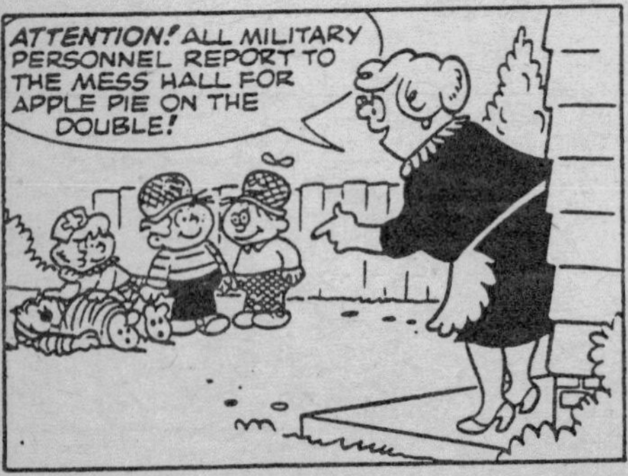
ATTENTION! ALL MILITARY PERSONNEL REPORT TO THE MESS HALL FOR APPLE PIE ON THE DOUBLE!

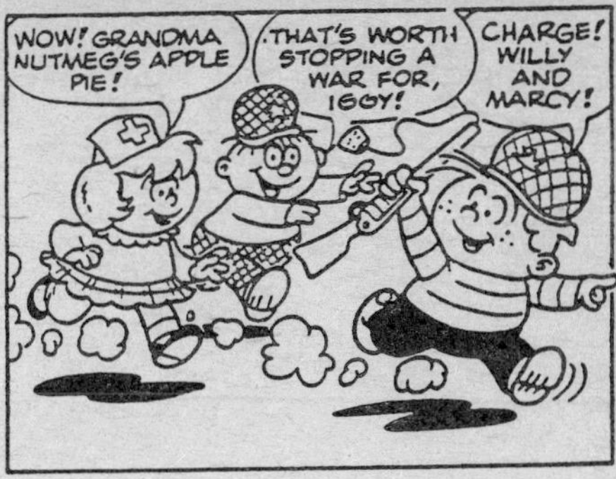
WOW! GRANDMA NUTMEG'S APPLE PIE!
.THAT'S WORTH STOPPING A WAR FOR, IGGY!
CHARGE! WILLY AND MARCY!

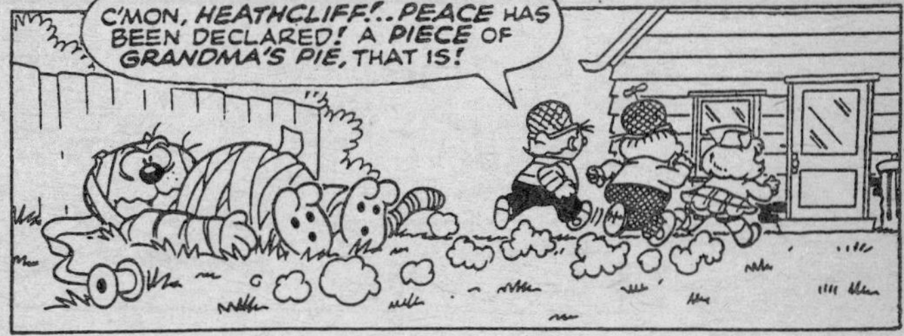
C'MON, HEATHCLIFF!..PEACE HAS BEEN DECLARED! A PIECE OF GRANDMA'S PIE, THAT IS!

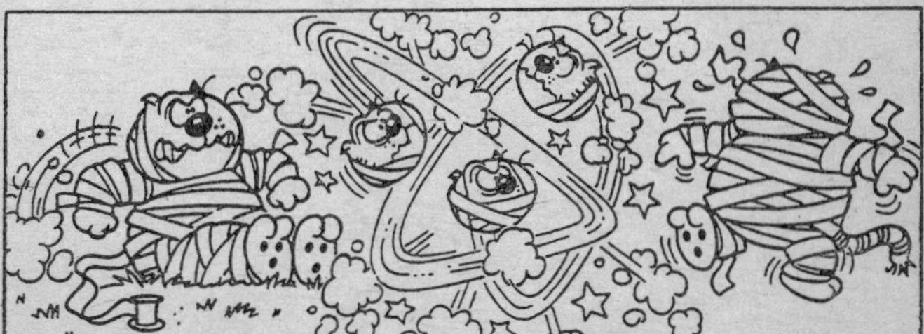

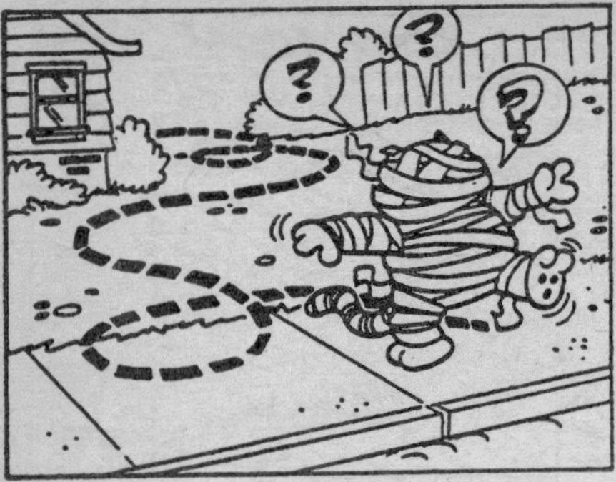
?
?
?

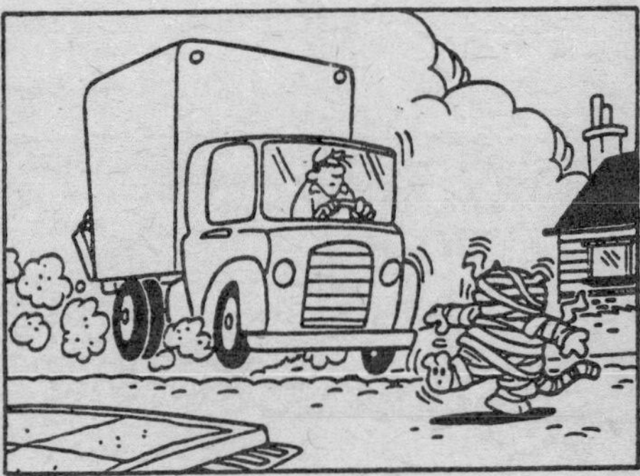

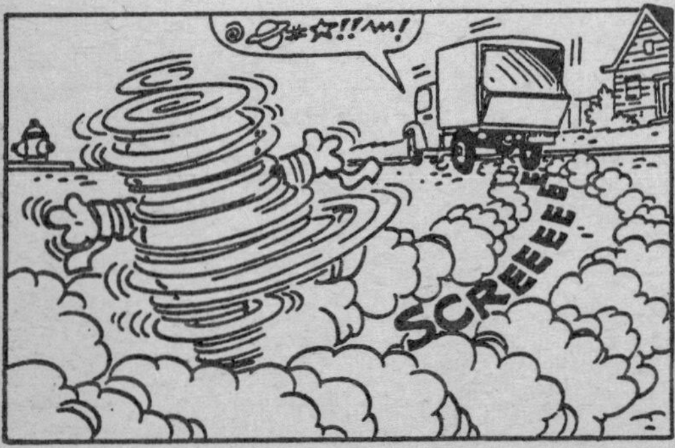
SCREEEEE

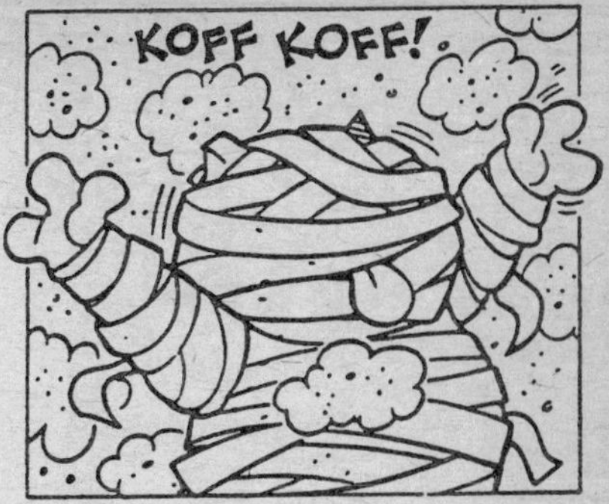
KOFF KOFF!

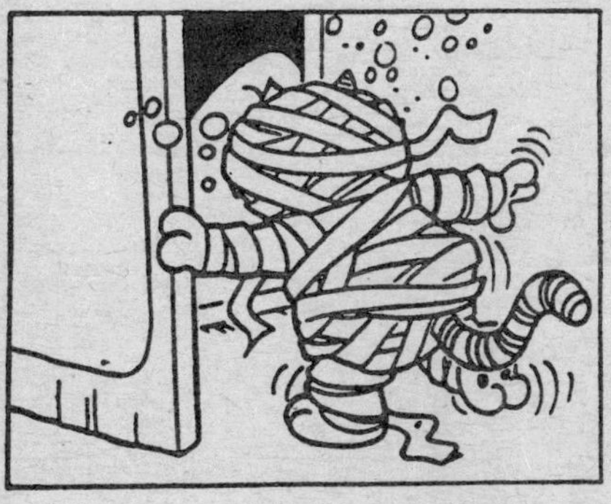

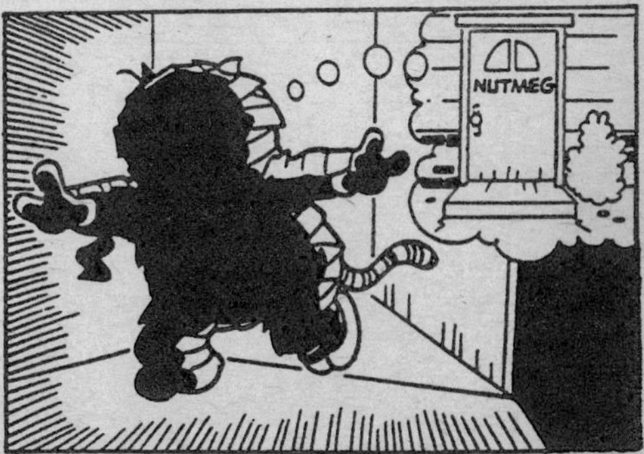
NUTMEG

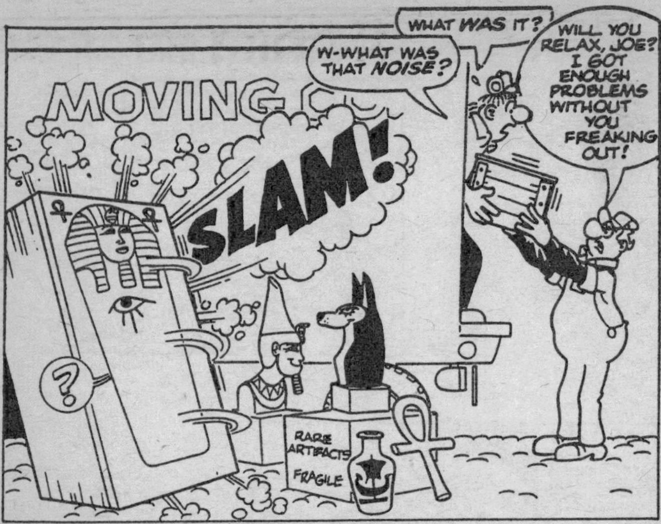
WHAT WAS IT?
W-WHAT WAS THAT NOISE?
WILL YOU RELAX, JOE? I GOT ENOUGH PROBLEMS WITHOUT YOU FREAKING OUT!
MOVING
SLAM!
RARE ARTIFACTS
FRAGILE

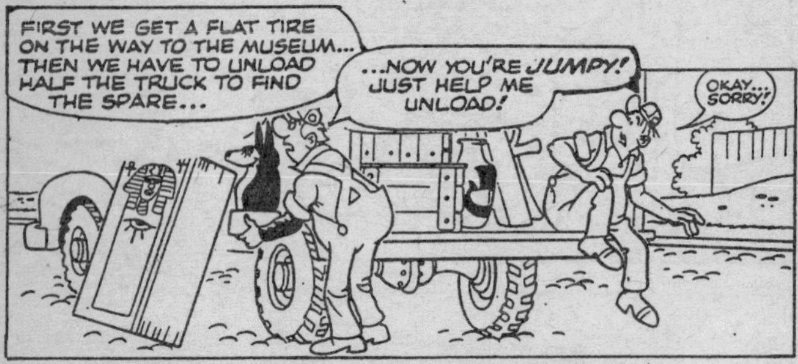
FIRST WE GET A FLAT TIRE ON THE WAY TO THE MUSEUM... THEN WE HAVE TO UNLOAD HALF THE TRUCK TO FIND THE SPARE...
...NOW YOU'RE JUMPY! JUST HELP ME UNLOAD!
OKAY... SORRY!

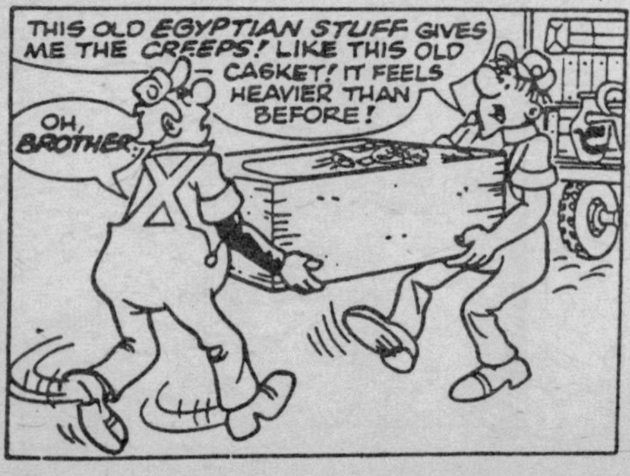
THIS OLD EGYPTIAN STUFF GIVES ME THE CREEPS! LIKE THIS OLD CASKET! IT FEELS HEAVIER THAN BEFORE!
OH, BROTHER

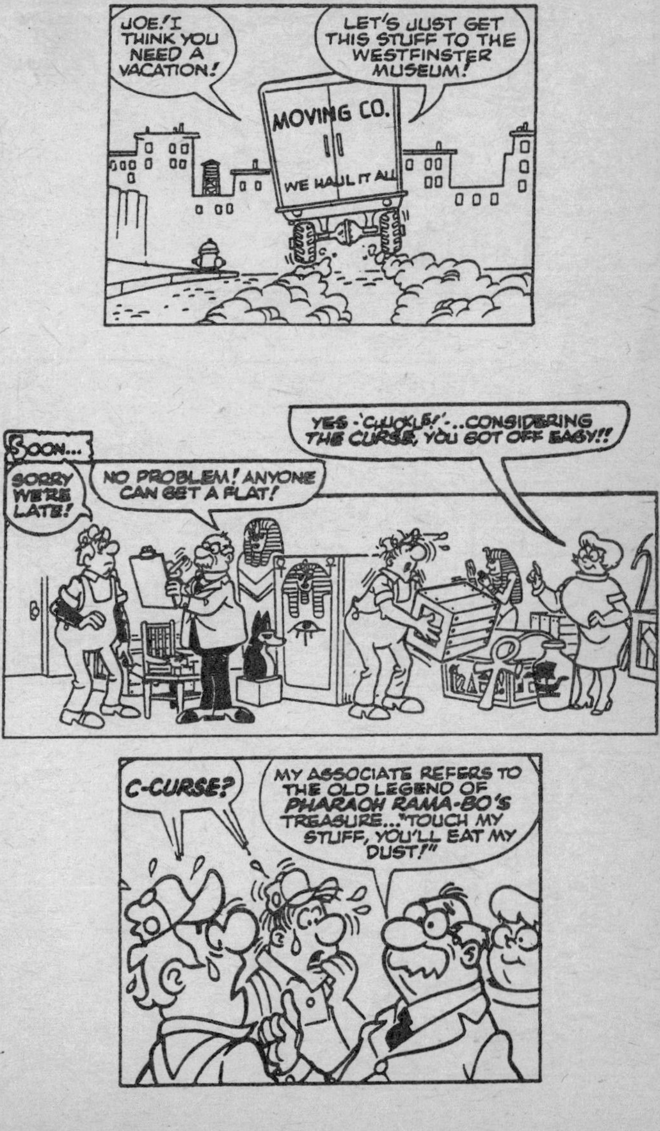
JOE! I THINK YOU NEED A VACATION!
LET'S JUST GET THIS STUFF TO THE WESTFINSTER MUSEUM!
MOVING CO.
WE HAUL IT ALL
SOON...
SORRY WE'RE LATE!
NO PROBLEM! ANYONE CAN GET A FLAT!
YES -'CHUCKLE!'-...CONSIDERING THE CURSE, YOU GOT OFF EASY!!
C-CURSE?
MY ASSOCIATE REFERS TO THE OLD LEGEND OF PHARAOH RAMA-BO'S TREASURE..."TOUCH MY STUFF, YOU'LL EAT MY DUST!"

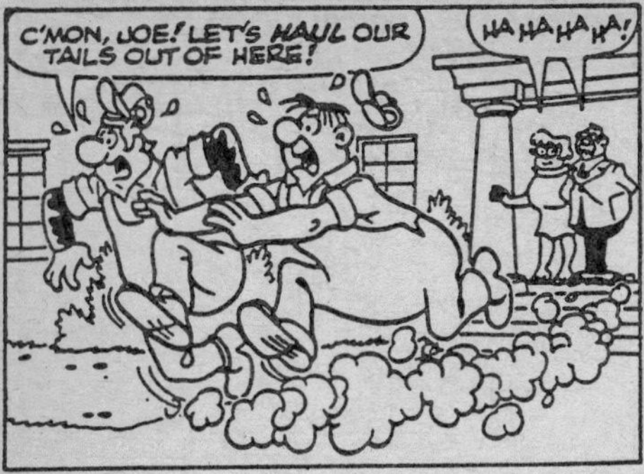
C'MON, JOE! LET'S HAUL OUR TAILS OUT OF HERE!
HA HA HA HA HA!

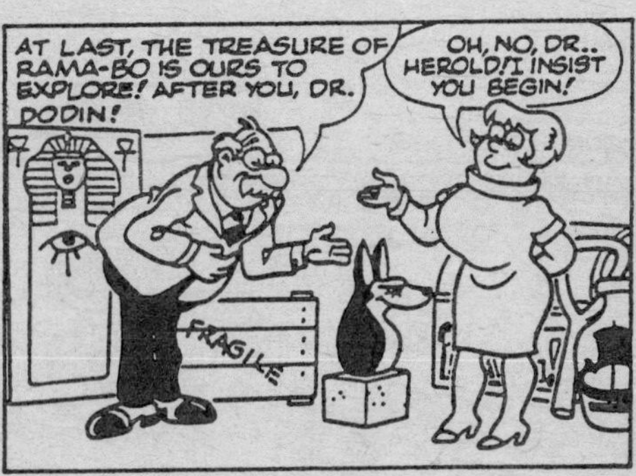
AT LAST, THE TREASURE OF RAMA-BO IS OURS TO EXPLORE! AFTER YOU, DR. DODIN!
OH, NO, DR.. HEROLD! I INSIST YOU BEGIN!
FRAGILE

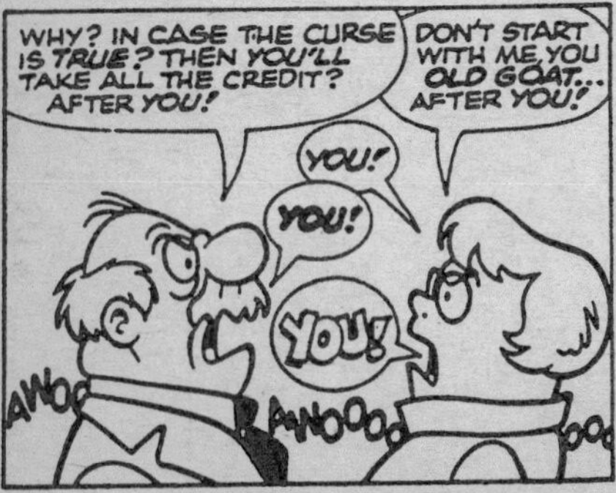
WHY? IN CASE THE CURSE IS TRUE? THEN YOU'LL TAKE ALL THE CREDIT? AFTER YOU!
DON'T START WITH ME, YOU OLD GOAT... AFTER YOU!
YOU!
YOU!
YOU!
AWOO
AWOOOOOOOO

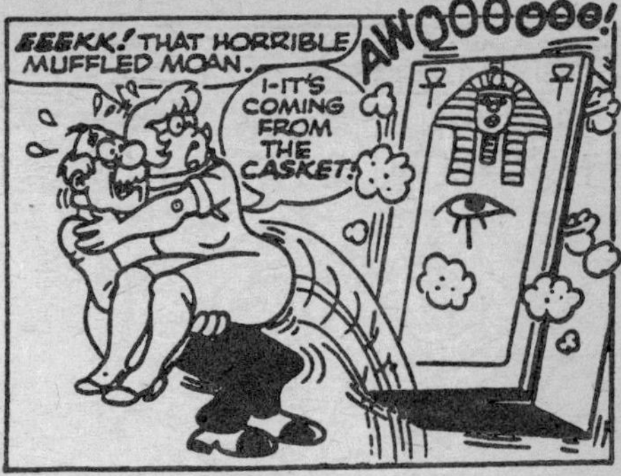
EEEKK! THAT HORRIBLE MUFFLED MOAN.
I-IT'S COMING FROM THE CASKET!
AWOOOOOOO!

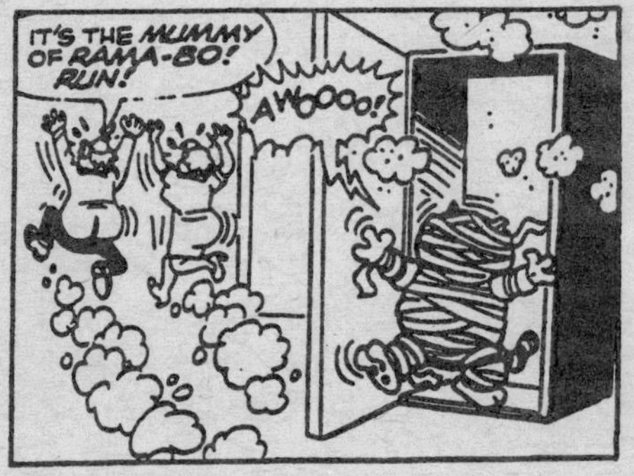
IT'S THE MUMMY OF RAMA-BO! RUN!
AWOOOOO!

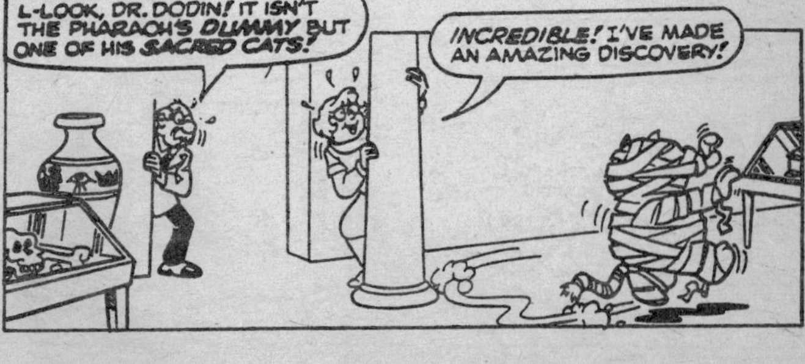
L-LOOK, DR. DODIN! IT ISN'T THE PHARAOH'S DUMMY BUT ONE OF HIS SACRED CATS!
INCREDIBLE! I'VE MADE AN AMAZING DISCOVERY!

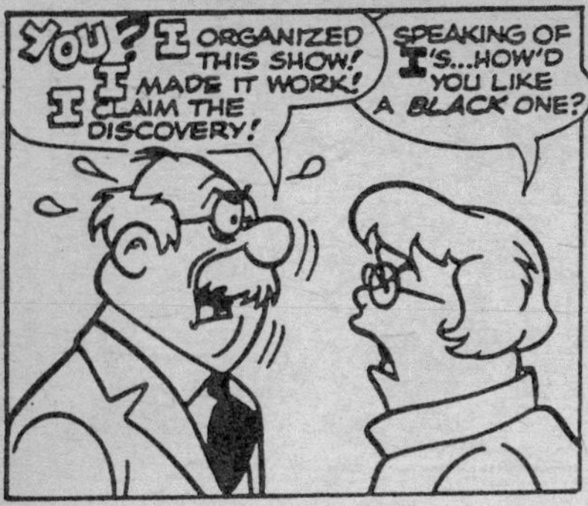
YOU? I ORGANIZED THIS SHOW! I MADE IT WORK! I CLAIM THE DISCOVERY!
SPEAKING OF I'S...HOW'D YOU LIKE A BLACK ONE?

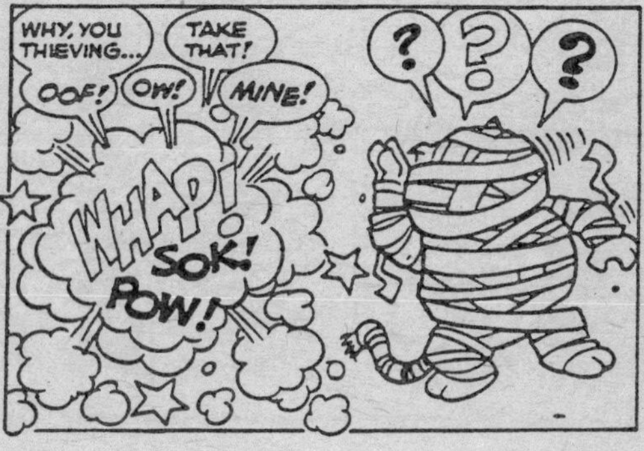
WHY, YOU THIEVING...
TAKE THAT!
OOF!
OW!
MINE!
?
?
?
WHAP!
SOK!
POW!

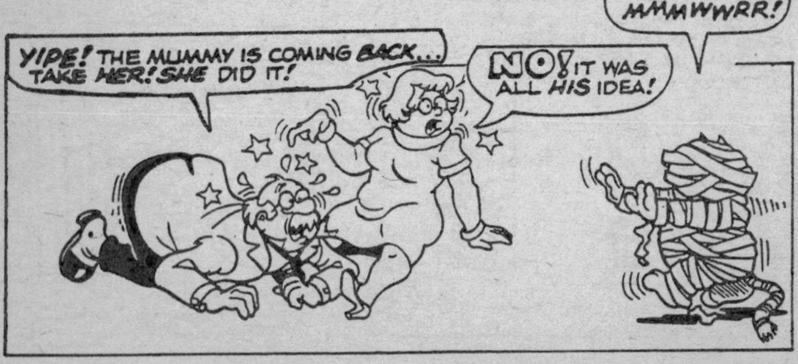
MMMWWRR!
YIPE! THE MUMMY IS COMING BACK... TAKE HER! SHE DID IT!
NO! IT WAS ALL HIS IDEA!

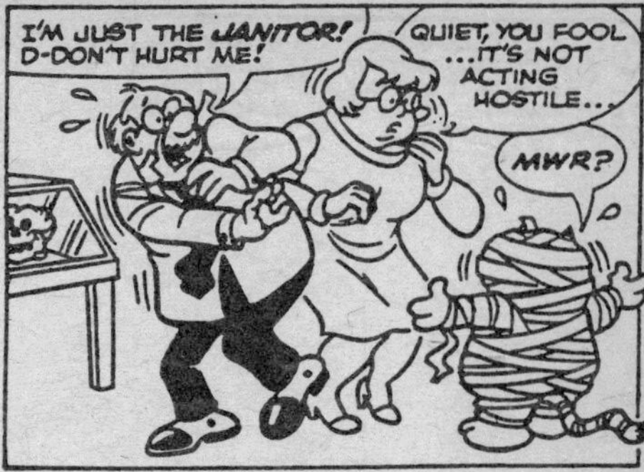
I'M JUST THE JANITOR! D-DON'T HURT ME!
QUIET, YOU FOOL ...IT'S NOT ACTING HOSTILE...
MWR?

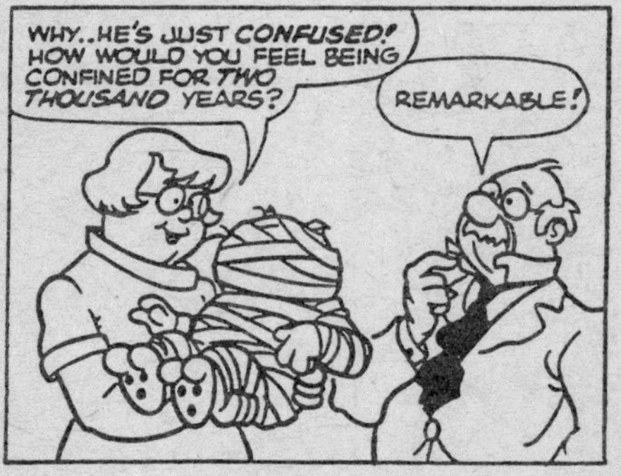
WHY..HE'S JUST CONFUSED! HOW WOULD YOU FEEL BEING CONFINED FOR TWO THOUSAND YEARS?
REMARKABLE!

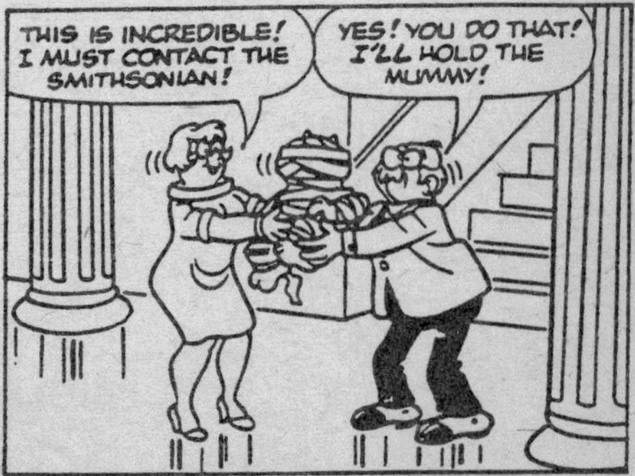
THIS IS INCREDIBLE! I MUST CONTACT THE SMITHSONIAN!
YES! YOU DO THAT! I'LL HOLD THE MUMMY!

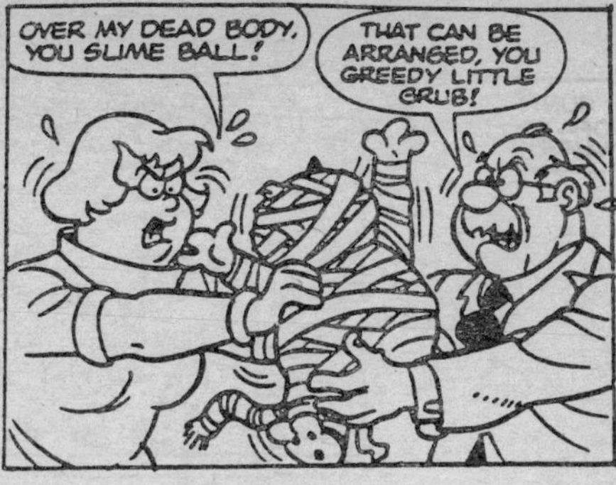
OVER MY DEAD BODY, YOU SLIME BALL!
THAT CAN BE ARRANGED, YOU GREEDY LITTLE GRUB!

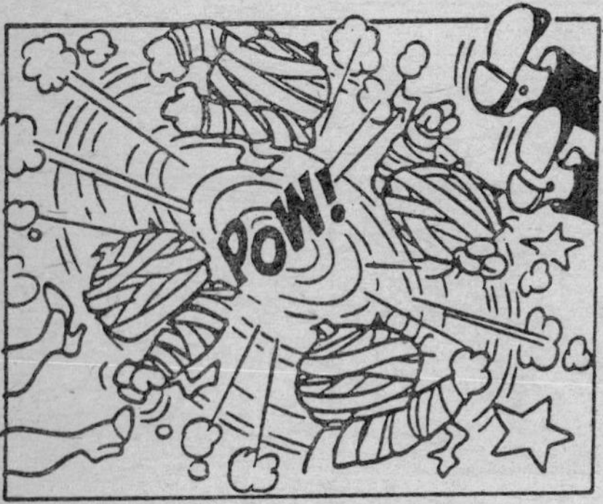
POW!

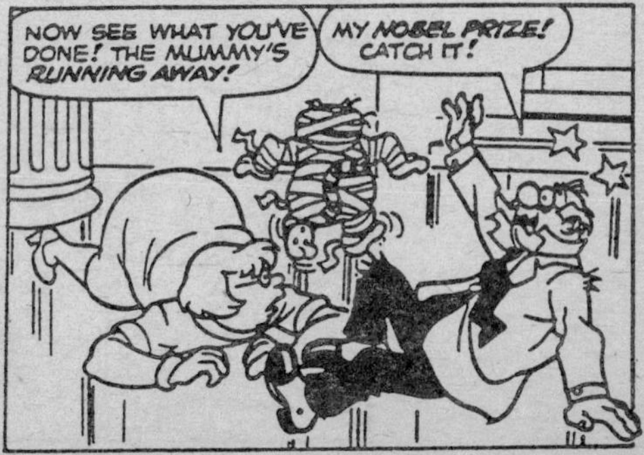
NOW SEE WHAT YOU'VE DONE! THE MUMMY'S *RUNNING AWAY!*
MY *NOBEL PRIZE!* CATCH IT!

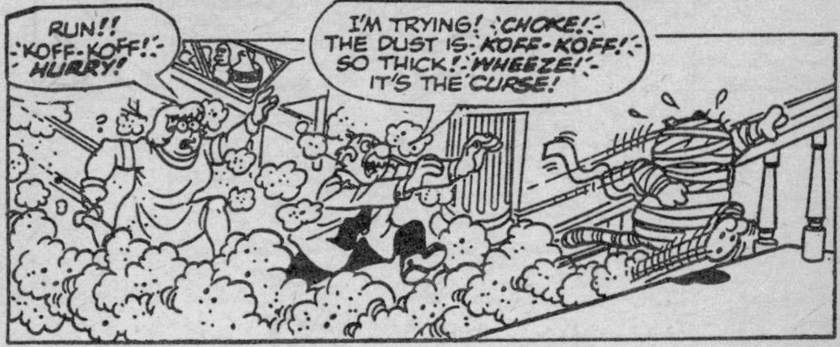
RUN!! -KOFF-KOFF!- HURRY!
I'M TRYING! -CHOKE!- THE DUST IS -KOFF-KOFF!- SO THICK! -WHEEZE!- IT'S THE CURSE!

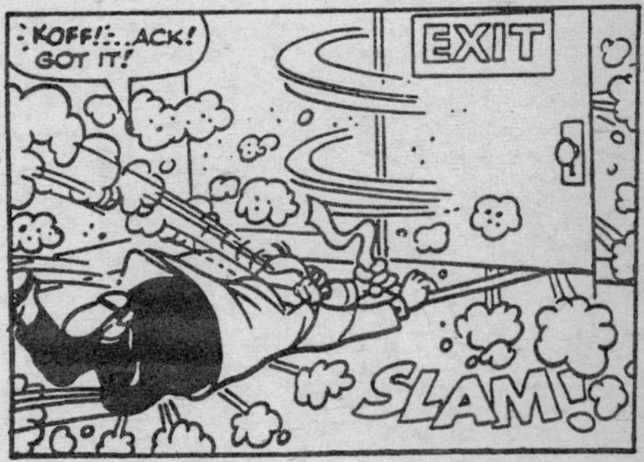
-KOFF!- ...ACK! GOT IT!
EXIT
SLAM!

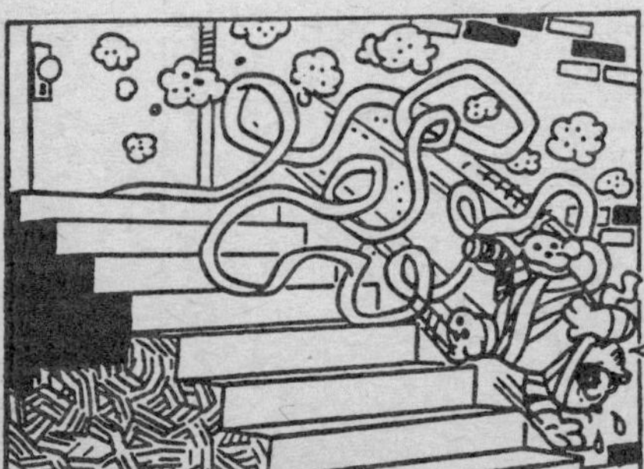

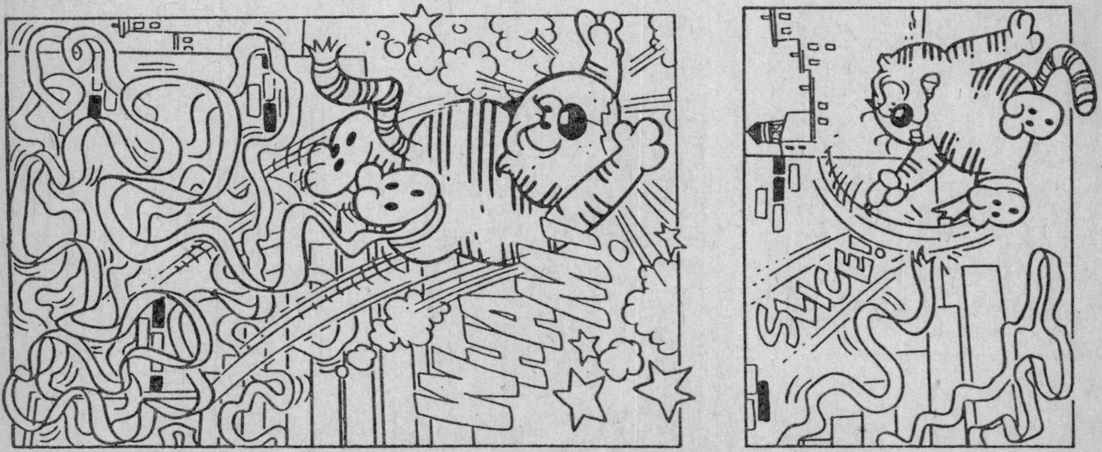
WHAM!
SLICE!

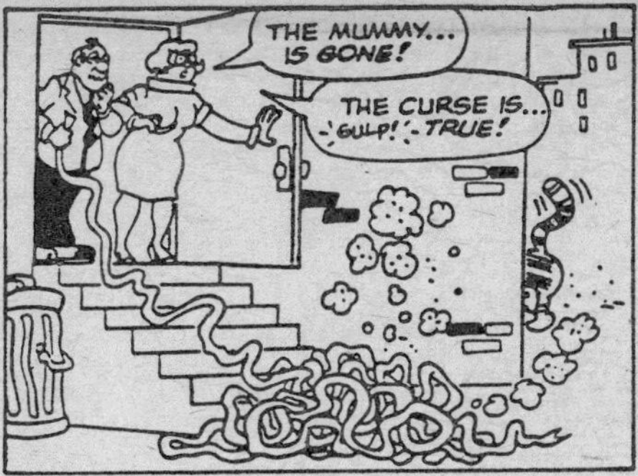
THE MUMMY... IS GONE!
THE CURSE IS... -GULP!- TRUE!

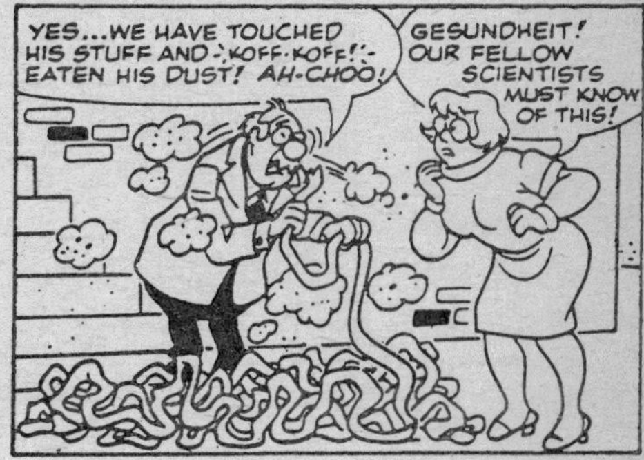
YES...WE HAVE TOUCHED HIS STUFF AND -KOFF-KOFF!- EATEN HIS DUST! AH-CHOO!
GESUNDHEIT! OUR FELLOW SCIENTISTS MUST KNOW OF THIS!

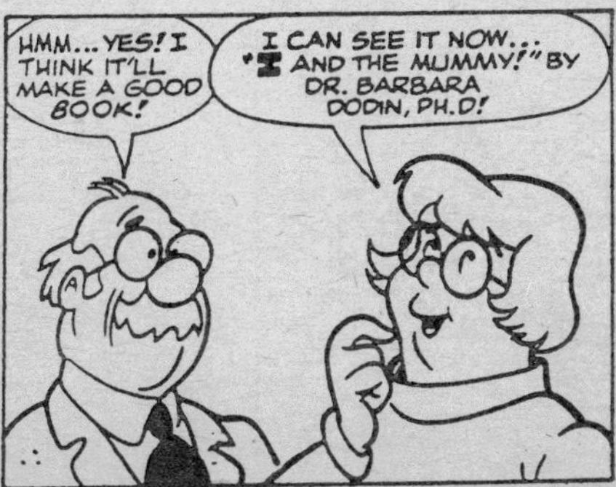
HMM...YES! I THINK IT'LL MAKE A GOOD BOOK!
I CAN SEE IT NOW... "I AND THE MUMMY!" BY DR. BARBARA DODIN, PH.D!

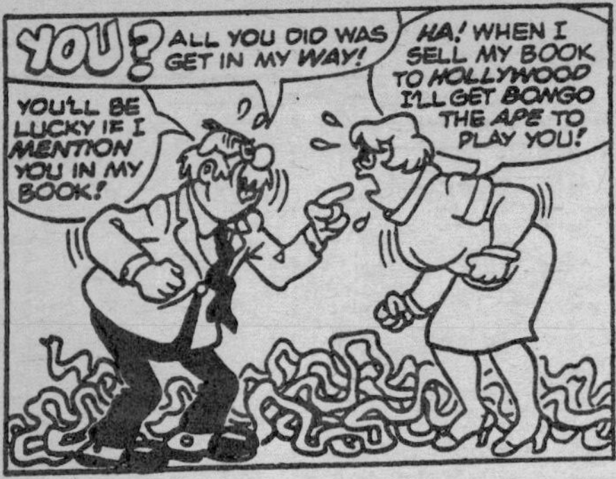
YOU? ALL YOU DID WAS GET IN MY WAY!
YOU'LL BE LUCKY IF I MENTION YOU IN MY BOOK!
HA! WHEN I SELL MY BOOK TO HOLLYWOOD I'LL GET BONGO THE APE TO PLAY YOU!

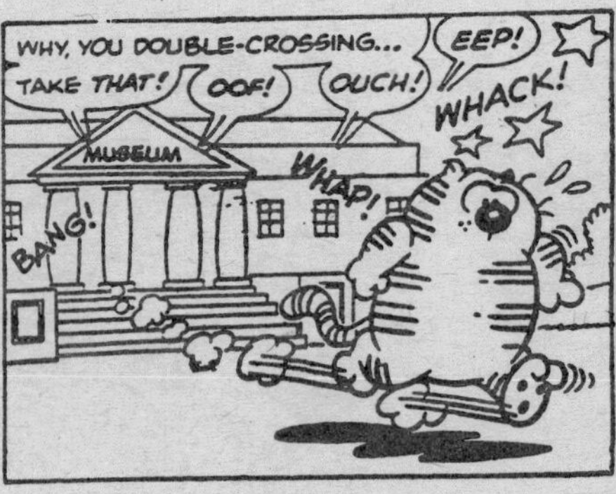
WHY, YOU DOUBLE-CROSSING...
TAKE THAT!
OOF!
OUCH!
EEP!
WHACK!
MUSEUM
WHAP!
BANG!

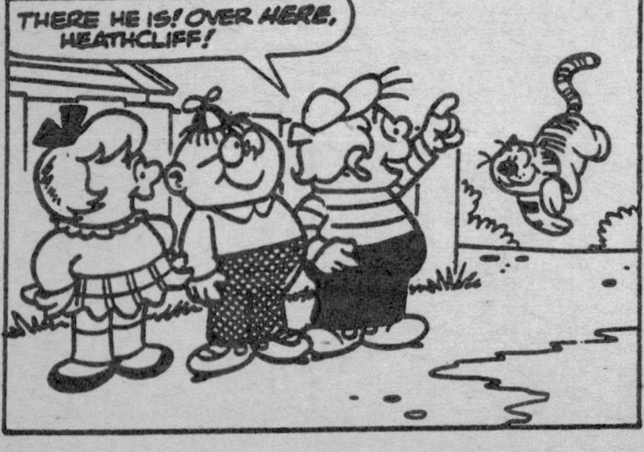
THERE HE IS! OVER HERE, HEATHCLIFF!

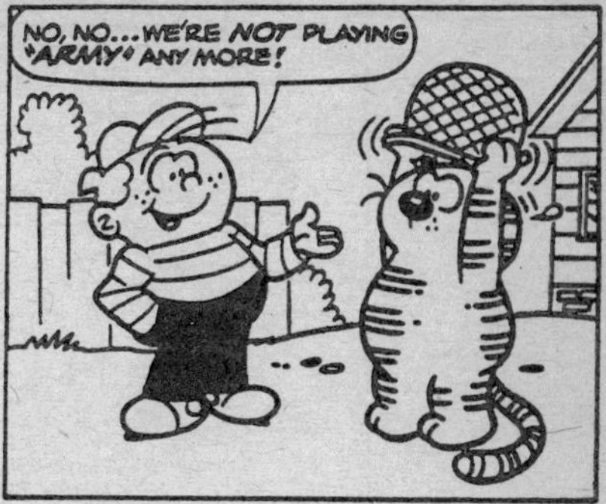
NO, NO...WE'RE NOT PLAYING "ARMY" ANY MORE!

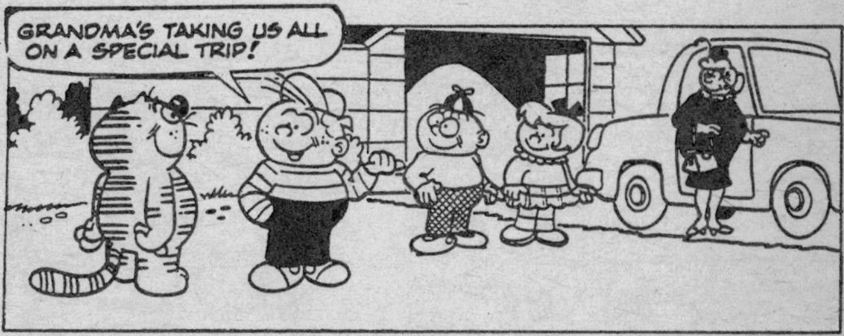
GRANDMA'S TAKING US ALL ON A SPECIAL TRIP!

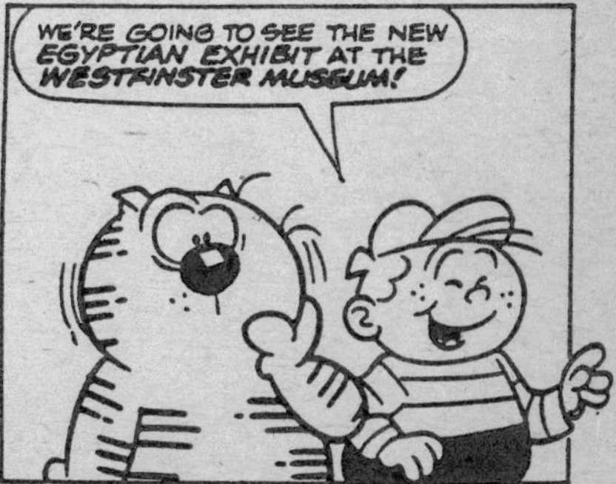
WE'RE GOING TO SEE THE NEW EGYPTIAN EXHIBIT AT THE WESTFINSTER MUSEUM!

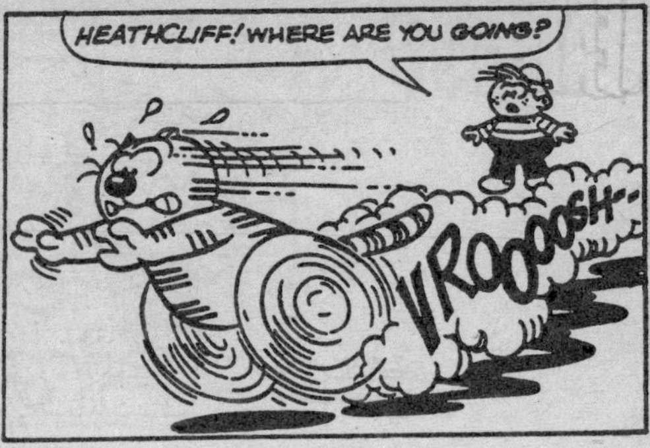
HEATHCLIFF! WHERE ARE YOU GOING?
VROOOOSH--

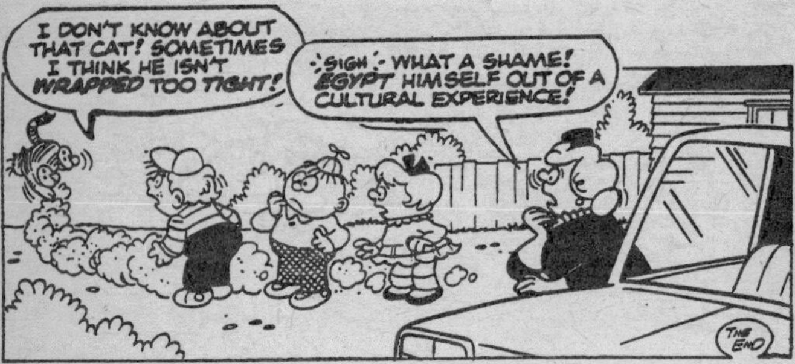
I DON'T KNOW ABOUT THAT CAT! SOMETIMES I THINK HE ISN'T WRAPPED TOO TIGHT!
SIGH - WHAT A SHAME! EGYPT HIMSELF OUT OF A CULTURAL EXPERIENCE!
THE END

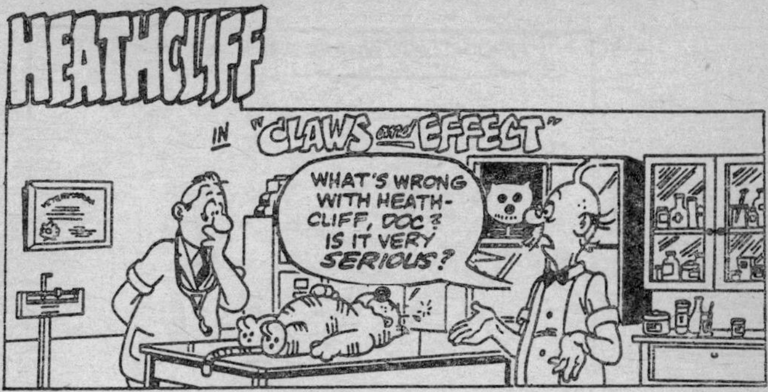
HEATHCLIFF
IN "CLAWS and EFFECT"
WHAT'S WRONG WITH HEATH-CLIFF, DOC? IS IT VERY SERIOUS?

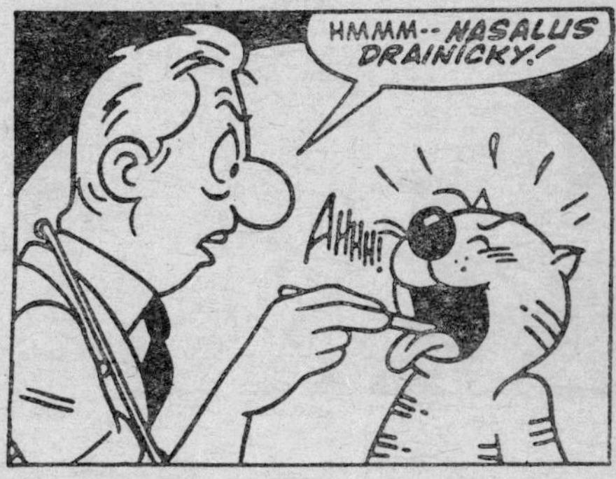
HMMM-- NASALUS DRAINICKY!
AHHH!

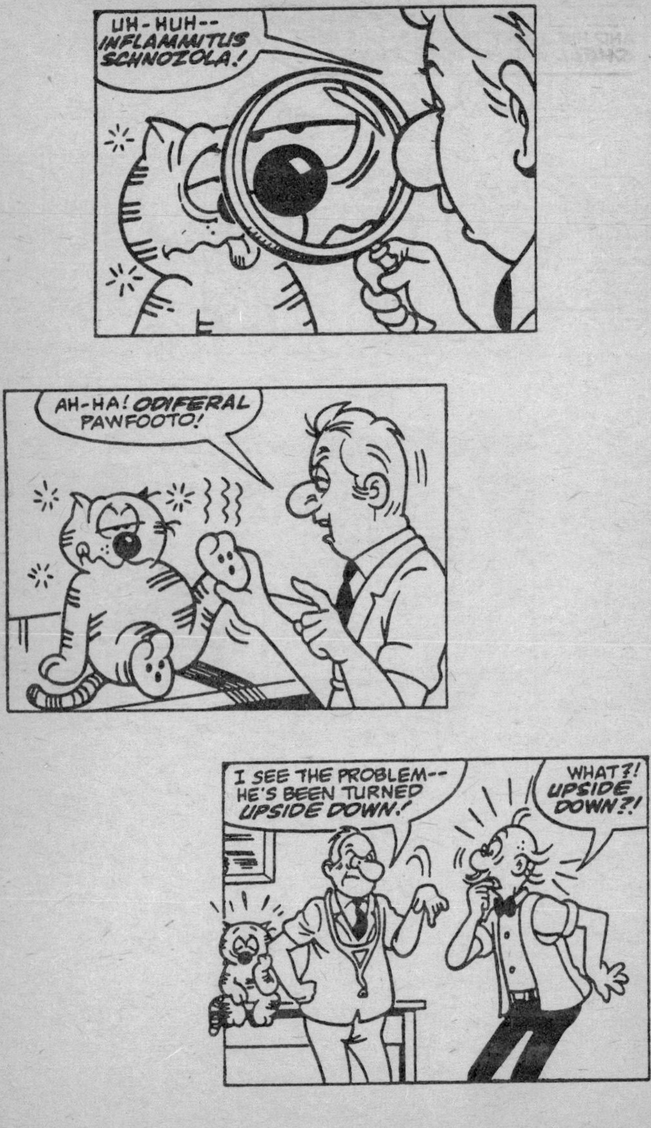
UH-HUH-- INFLAMMITUS SCHNOZOLA!
AH-HA! ODIFERAL PAWFOOTO!
I SEE THE PROBLEM-- HE'S BEEN TURNED UPSIDE DOWN!
WHAT?! UPSIDE DOWN?!

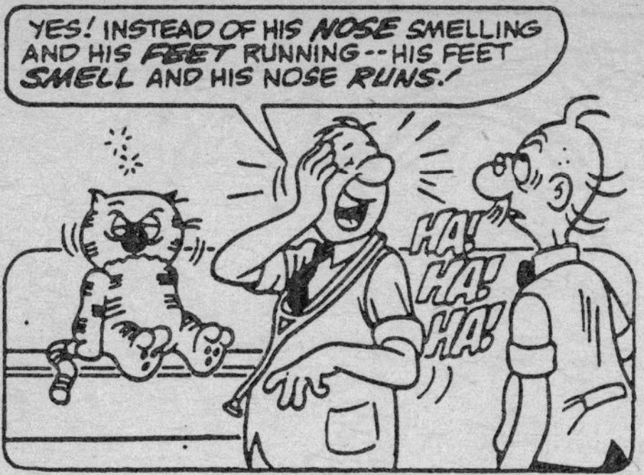
YES! INSTEAD OF HIS NOSE SMELLING AND HIS FEET RUNNING--HIS FEET SMELL AND HIS NOSE RUNS!
HA! HA! HA!

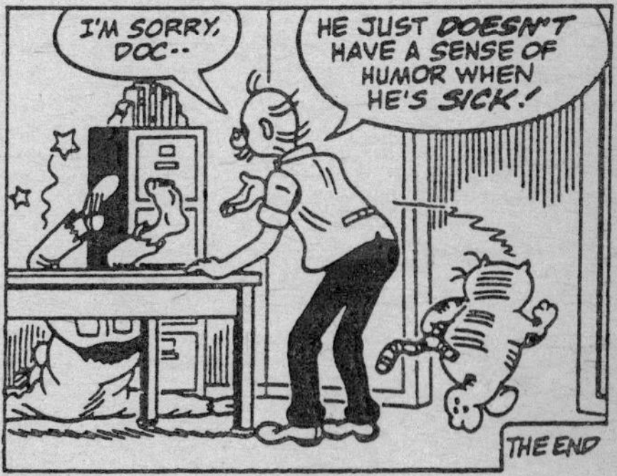
I'M SORRY, DOC--
HE JUST DOESN'T HAVE A SENSE OF HUMOR WHEN HE'S SICK!
THE END